SHELL-LIKE EAR

Coral looked up at me, and I knew she wasn't intentionally turning on the heat, but those hot brown eyes lit my fuse anyway. This gal didn't have to turn it on; she just couldn't turn it off. Man, she was more exciting than a game of strip poker with three blondes.

"Come," I said. "Join me on my white charger in a mad race over the desert sands to my secret tent. I have dates and camel milk and Zaffir wine."

She smiled. Hotly. She couldn't help it. She always smiled hotly. "All right," she whispered in what I sometimes call my Shell-like ear. "But what's Zaffir wine?"

"Why, it's bee-stung honey fermented with lotus blossoms. It puts moonbeams on a woman's lips and night winds in her eyes. Whatever that means."

"I'll have a pint of it."

My heart was pounding as if it were the wrong size. "A pint?" I said. "This is madness."

"Good. I feel like some madness . . . with you. I'll come to your tent tonight, darling."

SLAB
HAPPY

by Richard S. Prather

An Original Gold Medal Book

GOLD MEDAL BOOKS

FAWCETT PUBLICATIONS, INC., GREENWICH, CONN.

MEMBER OF AMERICAN BOOK PUBLISHERS COUNCIL, INC.

Chapter One

He LAY THERE in the silk-lined casket looking very waxy, but it was eight to five that he looked no more waxy than I.

His waxiness was due to the fact that he had been shot three times, including once in the head, and then embalmed—which would have been enough all by itself. Mine was due to the enormous possibility that—at any moment now—I might join him.

Well, since this was McGannon's Funeral Parlor in Los Angeles, this was the place for it.

The dead man had been one of the two biggest and most successful mobsters in this, the city of the "angles." And behind me here in the chapel were about four dozen of his "boys," forty-eight—give or take a slob—of the toughest, roughest, ugliest, most bloodthirsty hoodlums and stick-up men and gangsters and thieves and trigger-happy gunmen in California for sure, and maybe in the world and beyond.

All of them were anxious as could be to kill the man who had killed the guy in the casket. All of them were just waiting until the services were over and they could find Shell Scott, and get their hands on him, and murder him in several different ways. All of them were practically eaten up with the desire to corner Shell Scott and mangle him, to open his veins and let his blood run hot—and then cold; to beat him and shoot him and jump up and down on him. It looked like a bad year, a bad day, even a bad moment for Shell Scott.

You guessed it: That's me. I'm Shell Scott.

The organ was playing something soft and tremulous and depressing, but it should have been *I'll Be Glad When You're Dead, You Rascal, You!*—and I was the rascal. The blood those bloodthirsty hoods were thirsty for was *mine*. The arms and legs they wanted to break were *my* arms and legs. The head they wanted to shoot bullets into was *my* fat head.

If you think I was nuts to be present at the funeral of the egg in the casket when all around me were muggs dying to kill me for the job, then you are at least partly right. But it really was necessary for me to be here—though of course I hadn't planned it quite like this—and I was disguised. Well, sort of disguised.

That is to say I didn't look much like Shell Scott, private detective. Not on first glance, anyway. But at any moment one of these gunmen might do a double take which would mean a double funeral. Consequently I couldn't afford to make any unusual movements or do anything which would draw special attention to me, so I kept on walking toward the casket.

We were at the moment participating in the barbaric rite commonly known as "viewing the remains." This masochistic procedure might have made some sense in the case of the dead man's family and close friends—but he had no family, and only one close friend, at most. There was no heartache here, no sadness, no sobbing or tears. Nobody mourned this mugg, this mobster, thug and murderer. Nevertheless, everybody was filing past the coffin and looking at the dead man's body, and now it was my turn.

I moved down the center aisle in complete silence except for the organ music, and I felt about as conspicuous as I had ever felt in my thirty years. Normally I am a six-foot-two, two-hundred-and-six-pound chap who looks like an ex-Marine, which I am. Normally I have inch-long white hair that sticks up into the atmosphere like a magnetized crew cut, goofily slanting white eyebrows over gray eyes, a "slightly broken" nose, and clothing combining most of the visible spectrum.

But today was not a normal day and I didn't look like that at all. I didn't even look like an ex-Marine. My hair and eyebrows were darkened, and in my cheeks were rolls of cotton which made my face puffy, as if I'd been beaten up. Besides which, I *had* been beaten up. Twice. I was a mess.

I took another step toward the coffin, oozing perspiration, and more of the dead man came into view. I could see his white hands folded across his thick middle. I still hadn't seen what I'd come here to see, and I wasn't even sure that I would be able to see it when I stood right next to the coffin. But if it was there, I had to get it somehow. At least, I had to try.

I couldn't afford to stop as I walked by the casket. But I

stepped close to it and slowed enough so that I could look carefully into it while pretending to gaze at the dead man's face. And I saw what I'd come here to see.

On this side of the casket, shoved down between the dead man and the white silk were the edges of some white papers. If I hadn't been looking for them I wouldn't have seen them against the silk, but there they were; so there was still hope. In this case, where there was death there was hope. I let out my breath with a sigh that must have been heard in the back row of the chapel, and then I walked on by. It was like leaving my teeth to leave those papers there, but it couldn't be helped.

I walked from the chapel into the adjoining room, stopped and glanced around. Several men had preceded me here, but only two of them were in sight, the others having apparently gone on out front. I racked my brain, trying to think of some way I could get my hands on those papers before the funeral procession started. The two men stared at me curiously, it seemed. I swallowed, bent my head and, fumbling for a cigarette, lit it. The men went out the front door.

That left me alone in here, and I made up my mind, heading for the rear of the funeral home. I walked down a dim hall, past a long narrow table in the center of which was a large vase of fleshy white calla lilies, on to the back door. The organ music was fainter here, throbbing on the air like a soft pulse, and the air seemed wonderfully clear and fresh as I stepped into the shaded rear yard of McGannon's.

An enormous pepper tree shaded the green grass, and a few of the small narrow leaves dotted the white driveway bisecting the lawn. A gray cement walk led from the back door to the wide white driveway ten feet away, and on that drive, its rear toward me and the twin doors already opened wide, waited the hearse.

It was a gleaming black Cadillac, as clean and shiny as a general's boots. In a few minutes the coffin and its burden would be placed in it for the ten-minute drive to Woodstream Cemetery, a small and expensive graveyard "laved by the breath of orange blossoms"—according to the local radio and TV commercials—from the extensive Dimondsen groves which bordered it on three sides. My throat was dry. It had been dry for half an hour or more now, thirty minutes that seemed to have been fashioned from a longer time, the kind you knew as a kid when a day lasted half of forever.

The driver of the hearse leaned against the front fender of the Cadillac, smoking a cigar. Two other men, both large and very unpleasant to look upon, stood several yards to my right, where the driveway entered Forest Street. That was where the hearse would go, to Forest and then left to the cemetery. Nobody else was in sight; most of the men would be already in their cars out front, waiting for the procession to start.

The hearse driver was staring at me. I ducked my head down as I dragged on my cigarette, watching the man from under my artificially darkened eyebrows. He looked familiar, and in a second I placed him—Zipper Gray, so called because of the way he zipped around dirt tracks in stock car races and through traffic driving getaway cars for members of the mob. He had probably been recruited specially for today's five-mile trek; nothing was too good for the boss.

Zipper was frowning a little, his mouth half open as he eyeballed me. There was no question about it; that look on his chops was the look of a man saying, "Who's that ape? I know I seen that ape before." No doubt words to that effect were passing through Zipper's little brain. At least they would be moving slowly; Zipper's IQ was about equal to the average daily temperature—in Siberia.

Zipper raised a hand and pointed a finger at me, his mouth dropping even farther open. My heart gave a great thud and squirted blood everywhere through me. I dropped my cigarette and started to reach for the .38 Colt Special under my coat. Zipper began to say something—and then there was a noise behind me. I swung around, and stopped the motion toward my gun in time. Six men were carrying out the casket.

I looked back toward Zipper, but his attention was focused on the activity now. My knees were starting to feel like toasted marshmallows. The men slid the coffin into the hearse, shut the two doors in the Cad's rear, then went back into the building. That made the odds a little better. If the two large guys near the street would only leave now, I could handle Zipper— maybe even manage to do it without fuss and actually take off with what I'd come after.

A minute passed. All of a sudden I thought: I'm going to get away with it. I'm really going to make it. In that dizzy moment I even imagined myself reaching into the coffin, grabbing those papers, and dancing away with them to the Police Building.

And then Zipper yelled, *"Hey!"*

The two big guys jerked their heads around toward us. Zipper had that finger pointing at me again, waving it up and down a bit now. His face reflected wild astonishment. *"Hey!"* he yelled again, higher and louder. "It's—"

By that time I was going toward him. In a hurry.

Zipper's brain struggled with the problem. "It's—whatchama-callit! Whosit! Oh, murder, it's—"

I'd reached him, fist cocked, and that murder he was yelling about was in my heart. Zipper never did think of my name. But he squawked, *"He blasted the boss!"* just as I launched my fist at him.

At the same moment he leaped toward me like a bird. His sudden movement spoiled my aim enough so I missed his chin. My fist banged against his ear and then he landed on me—and at the same moment I heard one of those guys near the street shout in a booming voice that sounded at least as audible as nine cannons: *"Shell Scott!"*

Well, maybe Zipper hadn't managed it all by himself, but he had sure been a contributing factor, like the man who may not pull the switch but wires the chair. I'd had it. The fathead was really in the fire now.

Zipper was all over me, like a guy with five arms and several legs, not doing any damage but getting much in my way. I could hear feet slapping on the drive, and I knew they would be big feet. I swore under my breath, got my right hand and arm free, pulled it back and threw my fist forward like a hammer, driving Zipper's nose into his face like a tack. He flew away from me, and I jerked my head toward the two burly boys.

They were almost on me. One of them had a gun in his hand, but he didn't use it. I leaped forward, out of their path a little, and took two long strides toward the black Cadillac, digging under my coat for the .38. At the car door I turned my head and flipped up the Colt, squeezing off a shot that missed both men but sent them diving to the ground. One man hit the white cement and let out a yell, but the other landed rolling on the lawn. I tossed two more shots into the grass to keep them rolling, then climbed into the Cad and got behind the wheel, looking frantically for the keys. If they were in Zipper's pocket . . . but they were in the ignition.

As the engine caught, a dozen simultaneous yells tore the air in front of the Funeral Home, and McGannon's back door slammed. I hit the gas. The next sixty seconds were a blur, a jarring screeching kaleidoscope of color and movement laced with wild shouts, confusion and bedlam like a circus exploding; but at least it was movement, and *away* from McGannon's. I kept the gas pedal down as I roared out of the drive and hit Forest Street, yanking the wheel left and sliding around in a turn that raked rubber off all four tires. Then the car straightened, and I tried to push my foot through the floorboards. Slowly the big buggy gained speed, and with the surge of power under its hood I got a new surge of hope in me.

I still couldn't quite believe it, but I had actually walked in among those more than forty thieves like a modern Ali Booby and gotten out again. What was more, I'd gotten out with what I had come after. I glanced at the casket in the middle of the hearse, behind me—and my eyes fell on the dead man's white, heavy face. I had gotten out with quite a lot more than I'd come after.

And then I discovered that I had brought from McGannon's even more than I'd thought. I had come away from McGannon's with—McGannon's. At least that is what it looked like. Behind me, as if it were a long metallic chain with which I was towing the building, was a line of cars stretching clear back to the funeral parlor.

It was a ragged line, strangely spaced and wobbling, but it was there. At least a dozen cars were already in the procession, and more were about to pull away from McGannon's to join the parade. They must all have dug out like boys in hot rods— after this cold rod; and it looked as if this might become the speediest funeral procession in history. Anyone watching would think the dead guy's friends and relatives just *hated* him and couldn't wait to get him buried.

But the fastest part of this procession wasn't the hearse. All those cars were gaining on me now—and my foot was jammed to the floorboards. This thing just wouldn't *go* any faster. And the popping sound I heard wasn't an exhaust, it was guns. The men in the nearest car were shooting at me.

Up ahead I could see the rolling green hills of Woodstream, the chosen cemetery, and it looked as if I were going to enter it appropriately, as a corpse. I could imagine all those hoods behind me dropping me into an open grave and then taking turns tossing in shovelfuls of dirt, like civic-minded cats planting a tree. I groaned aloud, and grabbed the .38 in my left hand, steering with my right.

That nearest car was almost up with me now, and as I leaned out and looked back the man next to the driver fired at me, and I heard the hearse's windshield crack and sliver as the slug tore through it. I fired twice, trying to aim while steering with my other hand, fired once more, and then the hammer fell on an empty cartridge case. That was all for me.

The car behind me wavered in the road and fell back several yards, but immediately it started gaining on me again. Another gunshot cracked out and the slug slapped the Cad's roof over my head. In the rear-view mirror I could see not only that car so close behind me, but also the long string of other hood-filled cars in hot pursuit. I pulled my eyes away from the mirror, stared ahead through the hearse's shattered windshield and waited. Just waited, my mind sharp and clear, thoughts racing through it.

Well, I thought, at least I was going out in style. I was going to die as I had lived: wildly.

For just a moment the vision of bright eyes and smiling lips, lush curves that almost asked for it, sweet soft voices like summer air, and all the color and excitement of the last few days rose up before my eyes. The Hollywood dolls and hoods and musclemen, the beauties and the uglies, the living that was really living and the living that was more like death. It had been a time, it had been quite a time.

As that nearest car began pulling up on my left again, and the green of the cemetery loomed on my right, I wondered if it had been worth it, wondered if I would do it over again, if I had the chance.

And in what appeared to be the last moments left to me, I decided I would. Yeah, I would do it over again. I don't think I'd have wanted to miss it. Not even the bad spots—some of them anyway—if they went with the good spots.

Uh-huh, I was sure. I'd do it over. . . .

Chapter Two

IF I WERE going to do it over again, it would start with me driving my own new convertible Cadillac coupé, which is pale blue with white leather upholstery and not at all like a hearse—there have been no dead bodies in *this* one—up to the gates of one of the big-three movie production companies in Hollywood: Magna Studios.

Magna covers something less than 300 acres off San Vicente Boulevard at the edge of Hollywood, a sprawling chunk of extremely valuable ground on which Paul Revere galloped to Lexington; Salome tossed off six of those veils; Atlantis trembled, crumbled and slid beneath the Pacific; and David slew Goliath—to mention only the Academy-Award-Winning movies of Magna's last fifteen years. On this land, too, had been cowboys and Indians and pioneers and Pilgrims, and even one lovable Gronk from Jupiter. These acres had been involved in much of the best and worst that Hollywood had produced, and the hand at the Magna helm had been then—and was now—Harry Feldspen, for whom I'd done a couple of jobs in the past, and whom I was here to see today.

This day was one made by gods for men and not yet spoiled by men. The obscenity of smog was temporarily absent—or at least invisible—and the sun was friendly and bright in a clear blue sky. It was early in a new year, cool enough for coats and ties to be comfortable, so I was wearing a pearl gray silk-gabardine suit with a very pale blue shirt and a bright blue tie. I felt magnificent, whether I looked it or not, and life had never seemed livelier.

I stopped at the last gate, which is the tricky one to get past unless you've got an appointment or a pass. A tall, rangy, sharp-faced man stepped from the small trailer-sized gatehouse and said, "Yeah?" He wasn't the guard who'd been here on my last visit to Magna.

"Shell Scott," I said. "To see Feldspen."

"Shell Scott, huh?" The top was down on the Cad and he looked at my white hair, slightly bent nose, the ear from which a thin slice had been shot, at the car, back at my face again and said, "Yeah. Ain't that the nuts."

I had a hunch that this boy wasn't going to last. His appearance was somewhat familiar, but I couldn't place him. He said, "What you want?"

"I told you. I'm here to see Feldspen. He phoned me."

"What about?"

I stared at him, and after a few seconds he shrugged. "O.K., O.K.," he mumbled, went into the gatehouse and returned with a white pass, filled out and stamped with the time. He pointed. "You can park the heap down there, past the Writer's Building."

I took the pass, drove to an area with white parking lines painted on the black-asphalt street, parked and got out. The guard was leaning back against the wall of his little wooden building, looking at me. I went into Building Three, the Administration Building and down a cool highly polished hallway toward the office of *H.J. Feldspen, President.* I'd been here to see Feldspen several times before, though not for several months now, and I had enjoyed visiting the lot. For one thing, I liked Harry Feldspen himself. For another, I invariably lamped a number of the choicest examples of Hollywood's super femininity—the most opposite of the opposite sex—during my wanderings. It was interesting, too, to be briefly part of the varied activities on the sprawling lot, with the chance of running into anything from Captain Kidd in costume or a bewigged George Washington to busty, butty Mavis Travis in shorts at the helm of the *Santa Maria* in Hollywood's version of Mrs. Columbus discovering America.

I was about to go in through the door marked H.J. Feldspen when it opened suddenly, and a girl stepped into the hall right in front of me. For just a moment we stood face to face looking at each other. Both of us were surprised at the suddenness of our meeting, but I was more than surprised by this one. I was stunned. This one had it. This one had it all.

Not quite a redhead, not quite what I used to call a strawberry blonde, her hair was a beautiful fiery glow that swirled around her head like a net for men's eyes. She was just tall enough to reach me, and reach me she did. She reached way in and warmed my insides, including my heart, and she made that heart kick up several extra beats a minute in the time it takes for a double-take. She had pornographic eyes and wise warm lips and a body that would make a burlap bathrobe look like an Arabian nightgown.

Over come-hither breasts and slim waist and sensual hips, she wore a sleek white nylon jersey dress which looked indecent, but wasn't—it wasn't that the dress was revealing, though, but just that she had such a revealing body. This one was unique; this one was special. She was saying something in a soft low voice, but I didn't make out the words, just the music.

I said, "I beg your pardon," and stepped back.

She said smiling, "It's lucky we didn't run right into each other."

I grinned. "Lucky for you, maybe."

"Oh-ho. One of those fresh ones." She was still smiling.

"No. Not really. Just—yeasty."

"Oh," she said with mock solemnity. "Yeasty's all right."

Then she smiled sweetly, with her lips closed and slanting upward from the middle like smooth red wings, and blinked her big brown eyes at me, then walked on down the hall. It is proof that I was still in a state of pleasant shock, that she got away. Ordinarily, too, I am not a guy who goes ga-ga on lamping a babe, even though, like this one, she may make it appear that other gals run on gas and she's an all-electric model. Usually I am reasonably swift on the uptake and recovery, and in anything like my usual state of alertness I would have found some logical reason for detaining the lovely.

But I just watched her go. She walked all the way down the hall without looking back. She went to the double doors and pushed them open. She stepped outside. And *then* she looked back. She looked back at the office and smiled when she saw me still standing there. Then she shut the door and was gone.

Gone, but not for good, I told myself.

That one, I'd find; that one, I would for sure see again.

Then I went into Feldspen's outer office. His secretary, Marie, was a very nice, curvy blonde seated at a desk on my right, but after the visual wallop of the last few seconds, she was just another blonde. We said hello, she spoke into an intercom, then she waved me with long red fingernails toward the door of Feldspen's private office. I went in.

Two men were already in the large room, and one of them was Harry Feldspen. I don't know quite why it was, but you always noticed Feldspen first, even when he was in a small crowd. There wasn't any single thing to make him stand out, but it somehow all added up to an impressive package.

He wasn't a big man, maybe five-nine and slim. About sixty,

with tightly waved cotton-white hair and a ruddy sun-lamp tan, delicate, graceful hands and a friendly white smile. He wore expensive clothing with casual grace and always looked very neat and clean. Feldspen wasn't like a number of the studio heads and individualistic producers who are seldom found in offices without their "props," the props which scream—it is hoped—*This man is an eccentric genius.* He had no polo mallet or riding crop or sawed-off tennis racket, nor did he wear a riding habit, didie, or kilt. All he had was a fourteen-foot-wide desk. He sat behind that extraordinarily wide and tall desk on an especially high easy chair, with one light fixed in the ceiling above him dropping a flattering glow on him as if on an old master in a museum. When you walked into Feldspen's office you felt only a little like a midget in a world designed for giants, and he looked only a bit like the lord high executioner prepared to sentence you to death by pinpricks.

Actually, he was a kindly man, and it may well have been that the stage setting was necessary in order to give him the appearance of unearthly authority needed when dealing with many of the highly emotional Magna emoters.

Harry Feldspen showed me that white friendly smile and even stood up behind his huge desk as I entered. The smile was just a bit strained today, though; Harry had things on his mind.

"Shell," he said in his soft voice, "You wasted no time. I appreciate it."

I had come in quite a hurry. But when he'd phoned me a few minutes ago, Harry Feldspen had sounded like a man who'd taken four ounces of castor oil and couldn't find the john; there had been a tightness in his voice I'd never heard there before. He hadn't told me what was wrong, just that there was trouble.

I said, "You sounded as if you were going up in a leaky balloon, Harry. What's up?"

Feldspen looked at the other man in the room with us. "Theodore, I should have warned you about this—" he waved a hand gracefully in my direction—"this rather blunt-speaking, and blunt-looking individual. Theodore, this is Sheldon Scott."

I looked at the man, a tall guy, as Feldspen said, "Shell, Theodore Valentine."

"Ted," he said to me and grinned, and I said, "Shell here," and we shook hands.

When he smiled the man was handsome, with a most engaging assortment of features including dark blonde hair, pale blue eyes, a small neat mustache and a Cary Grant cleft in his square chin. But when he stopped smiling and glanced back at Feldspen,

his face got a pinched look. There were furrows corrugated between his brows and in his forehead, and his eyes looked tired.
When he glanced back at me, his face solemn again, those eyes
held an expression that you might see in the eyes of a fox
hunted by red-tongued hounds and red-coated beasts. He looked
hunted and harried himself, tired and drawn, somehow pinched
all over, as if his skin didn't fit.

Feldspen seated behind his big desk again, said suddenly,
"I'm being blackmailed. It's monstrous."

"What's the man got on you?" I asked. "Is it a man?"

"It was a man who phoned me. And, actually, it's not anything I've done. In fact, it's Magna that's being blackmailed."

"Magna? That sounds like a neat trick. Like blackmailing
General Motors, or the British Empire."

He indicated a heavy leather chair with short silver legs and
flat silver buttons set in the arms. "Sit down, Shell." I sat and
he made a steeple of his hands, glanced at Valentine and then
back at me. "I've already told Theodore—who, incidentally, is
my right-hand man. He is appalled."

On my last two or three visits to Magna I'd seen only Feldspen himself, but though I hadn't met Valentine before, I'd heard
the name a time or two. If I remembered correctly, he'd been in
this spot a year or more.

Harry went on, "Here is all I know. Two hours ago a man
phoned here and asked for me. I don't know who it was, but the
voice was a man's. He said that I should listen carefully, that he
would say his piece just once."

I interrupted. "Say his piece—was that his phrase?"

"Yes. I believe his exact words were, 'I'll say the piece just
once, H.J.'" An expression of distaste flickered briefly over
H.J. Feldspen's red-tanned features, then he went on. "He said
that he, or rather the individual he represented—he was just a
go-between—was at this very moment actually receiving payment, payoffs, from *three* Magna people, stars in soon-to-be-re-
leased films. He said that he would prefer one large purchase
to several little installments—again his words as near as I can
recall—and that for a million dollars he would cease all his
activities and turn over to us the materials which supported
those activities. He didn't actually use the word blackmail, but
he might as well have."

"Wait a minute." I stopped him again, but this time because
I was slightly incredulous. "Did you say a *million* dollars?"

"I did. There was no chance of an error on that point—he repeated it two or three times."

I whistled softly. I have been a private investigator in and around Hollywood and Los Angeles for a long time, and I have become involved in some fairly high-powered cases including almost the gamut of extortion, but I had never become involved in a case with a million-buck bite. The only case I'd even heard about with a bite near that size was one involving another private investigator, a guy named Chet Drum. But he was a Washington D. C. man. As far as I knew, this was a record even for Hollywood.

I lit a cigarette and said to Feldspen, "That sounds to me like the biggest extortion this side of the Federal Income Tax. Are you sure the guy was serious?"

"He seemed *quite* serious. He stated that he would give me—me personally—one week in which to get the money. Money—cash. Nothing larger than a hundred-dollar bill—why, it's preposterous. Except . . ."

He paused and I prompted him. "Except what?"

"Except that he did seem to know exactly what he was talking about, and if so it would be worth a million dollars to avoid all the eventualities of which he spoke. He said that the million dollars 'insurance' would among other things spare Magna Studios enormous financial damage, loss of the services of three of our top stars, decreased revenues from their unreleased pictures, and unbelievably nasty publicity in all communications media."

Feldspen paused, ran a hand lightly over the tight waves in his white hair. "At the end of a week he is to phone me here again and tell me how to handle payment of the money. Why, it's . . . it's like a kidnaping."

I said, "Do you think he's really got something on three of Magna's stars?"

Feldspen shrugged. "I don't know. That's one of the things I hope you can find out. But *if* he does, it could be disastrous. The man mentioned also that a million would be cheap in view of the fact that we've got thirteen million invested in unreleased films featuring them."

"How did he know that?"

"I don't know. I don't know anything except what I've told you."

Valentine, who had been silent until now, spoke to me. "Except his alternative. If we don't pay he'll release whatever information he has to the press, all the wire services, radio and TV—the works, everything he can hit, including the slime magazines. That would, of course, end his blackmail, the

..nents' he mentioned, but at the same time it would ...ps ruin those three lives—certainly the three careers. ...ention Magna's financial loss."

I s.. ., "Did you talk to the man?"

"No." He gestured jerkily toward Feldspen. "Harry filled me in just before you arrived." He nibbled on his upper lip.

"Any idea who the three are?"

He shook his head. "No. It's difficult to say. And we're still . . . rather unstrung by the suddenness of this."

Feldspen spoke again, "I don't want the police in this, either, not now at least. If there's anything to what the man told me, it's possible one or more of his victims is, well, breaking the law. Involved in criminal activity. That means the police, if they found out about it, would probably put the individual concerned in jail." He shuddered. "We can't have that, either."

It was quiet for several seconds. I smoked my cigarette. Feldspen said to me, "I know it isn't a great deal to go on, but do you think you can help?"

"I can try, and I will. I can start by talking to some of your people here on the lot. People being blackmailed sometimes get sicker than dogs when you ask them if they're being blackmailed. So I'll ask a few."

Feldspen slid a red-bordered card across his desk. "This pass authorizes you to visit any place on the lot."

I grinned. "Another dream come true," I said, but Feldspen wasn't listening. He looked up and said, "It's rather a dilemma. To pay would probably only lead to more paying."

"You can make book on that."

"Not to pay, though, seems horrid, considering what it might possibly do to those three people—assuming all this is true." He paused, shaking his head. "All this comes at an especially bad time, too."

"How do you mean?"

"Financially speaking. Profits are way down—not just at Magna, but all through the industry. Television has hurt us badly, no question of it. We'll profit in the long run, immensely, I'm sure. But it's difficult right now."

Valentine said gloomily, "All the new movies sold to television have cut box office even more. I don't see how we're going to combat that." He chewed on his lip and scraped at one finger with his thumbnail.

A thought crept into my skull. I pushed it around, and it kept looking better, so I tried it out. "Harry, you say the guy mentioned thirteen million tied up in unreleased pictures?"

"That's right."

"And you also said you didn't know how he got the info. Well, if he *is* blackmailing three of your people, those people could—and would—tell him the budget or cost on each or all of their films. So that would explain how he might wind up with that exact figure, right?"

"Right. But . . ." Feldspen's face sagged. "Oh. You mean that makes it appear his information is authentic. True. That he is, in fact, already blackmailing them."

"Uh-huh—but more than that. If you have three or four films in the can, or nearly completed—involving three top stars —films on which production costs total thirteen million bucks, wouldn't that tell you who the three people are?"

There was silence for about five seconds, then Valentine snapped his fingers. "Of course. Harry—we should have thought of that ourselves." He paused, digging at his finger with his thumbnail, chewing on his lip, blinking rapidly, and in general giving the impression of a man with a mouse inside of him eating its way to freedom. This guy had nerves with individual breakdowns, or else his skin was creeping up on him. Something was obviously eating the life out of him, and if it was Hollywood or the movie business, it was time he began selling grass skirts to Polynesian tomatoes. He wouldn't last much longer in *this* business.

He snapped his fingers again, and said, "It would have to be three from among not more than six people. And James would have to be one, there's eight million right there." He glanced at Feldspen; "They'll finish retakes on *Howdy, Stranger* with Palomino this week—and there's three million dollars more in that one."

Palomino could only be Johnny Palomino, star of nearly all of Magna's big-budget westerns. He was a big name for sure, a well-established star; I didn't know who the "James" was.

Valentine seemed to be under considerable stress. He chewed on his lip some more, pulled pad and pen from his pocket and scribbled something, scribbled some more and lined something out. After two or three minutes he said, "That—does it." He looked at me. "I'm indebted to you for the insight, Mr. Scott."

"Shell, remember."

He grinned again, and was handsome, almost placid again. An extremely pleasant-appearing egg when he wasn't in the process of going to pieces. "Yes—Shell," he said. "But you were right. Three stars, four pictures—thirteen million." He looked toward Feldspen. "With the two James' films, it comes out *Howdy, Stranger* and the Suez. Only way it adds up."

Feldspen slowly nodded.

I said, "What would that mean to me, Ted?"

He turned, blinking. "We've got three million in *Howdy, Stranger,* starring Johnny Palomino. The big item is two films both starring Coral James, each of them in at about four million. A period picture called *Sins of Pompadour,* which we've held up until now, and one set in ancient Rome called *Sins of Messalina.* We've just completed *Night Wind* with Suez, a beautiful young girl starring for the first time." He held up his open hand and counted them off on his fingers, "Coral James, Johnny Palomino, Suez. Thirteen million."

"O.K.," I said. "I know Palomino when I see him. I'll shake him up a little and see what falls out of him. What about this Suez and Carol James? And it's Suez what?"

"Just Suez," Harry Feldspen said wearily. "We're identifying her with the single name, hoping it will attract more attention to her. She's probably on Sound Stage One right now." He paused, sighed, then went on, "As for Coral James, you must have seen her."

"Seen her? What do you mean?" I knew what was coming, and I didn't want him to say it.

He said it anyway. "You couldn't have missed her. She left the office just before you came in."

Chapter Three

HARRY NOTICED the expression on my face and said quickly, "What's the matter?"

"It's just . . . you startled me with that one. You mean, Coral James is that luscious, sort of reddish-haired gal who waltzed out of here . . ."

"Moments before you came in. Do you know her?"

"Only from now on. She registered on my retina like a sock in the eye, I'll admit."

"Yes, she does that to everyone." Feldspen grimaced suddenly. "Oh, dear. *She's* one of them. One of the three. I . . . hate to think that."

Valentine broke in. "Well, I could be wrong. I don't really think I am, but . . ."

"I'll check it," I said.

The conversation limped a bit after that. Valentine and Feldspen got into a discussion of money and money troubles, which was of little interest to me. I let my thoughts turn again to Coral James. But in a minute I heard something which pushed thoughts even of that lovely out of my mind. It jarred me, pulled me to my feet.

I almost sprang out of my chair. Looking from Feldspen to Valentine, I asked them, "What did you say? Who?"

They had been droning on about financing, television the bug-eyed monster, new money being welcome practically all through the industry now, the bankers who actually financed operations at the studio, and unless I had heard it completely wrong, one of them had said or intimated that a "Mr. Rio" had become one of the Magna backers.

Apparently it had been Feldspen. He blinked at me in surprise and said, "I was discussing with Theodore the fortunate investment, by Mr. Louis Rio, of a sizable sum of money in Magna."

"I thought I heard something crazy like that. Nobody else has called Lou Rio *Mr.* for years."

"Why . . . do you know him?"

"Know him? Not so long ago I did my best to send him to San Quentin. He's one of the two biggest racketeers on the West Coast. Between him and Nick Colossus, they might steal California."

The two hoods I had mentioned in the same breath, like garlic with halitosis, were quite often mentioned in the same breath by others familiar with the local crime picture, because they were certainly the two biggest mobsters in Southern California, at least, and perhaps in the entire state. It seemed especially natural for me to speak of them at the same time because both of them would cheerfully have sawed open my throat with old hacksaw blades.

Feldspen and Valentine were speaking almost simultaneously, Valentine saying, "You can't be serious," and Harry ejaculating, "Preposterous!"

"I'm serious. You've never even heard of the crumb?"

"Not in any—derogatory way," Feldspen said. "What did you mean, you tried to send him to prison?"

I gave them some of the background, and telling them brought it all vividly back to me. Vividly and uncomfortably. To have one of those guys unhappy with you was bad enough, but to wind up with both of them snarling at you was tantamount to suicide. I had earned the snarls of both several months ago when I had appeared before a California State Senate Committee investigating crime in Los Angeles. During that appearance I had named Lou Rio and Nick Colossus as the dangerous hoodlums I truly felt them to be, and had gone into as great and specific detail about them as I could, including my opinion that, since it was well and widely known that they hated each other, it would be the best thing for California since the Gold Rush if they would simply kill either themselves or each other. Naturally neither of them had felt any warmer toward me after that, and they'd been quite cool before then.

It was true enough, though, that these two biggest of local mobsters hated each other, and this hate of the bosses extended down as if by osmosis to their followers, their lieutenants and strong-arm boys. Consequently L.A. was always on the verge of an old-time gang war, like the Chicago days in the early twenties, but the war had never really been declared, or even gone much beyond sniping. But the potential was there.

I finished my explanation to Feldspen and Valentine by saying, "Nothing much came of my appearance before the committee. At least nothing happened to Rio. One result of my testimony was that, after some good police work and a trial, a couple of Rio's boys were sent to Folsom."

Feldspen said, "It must not be the same Rio. It must be a different—"

I interrupted him. "Lou Rio is five-ten, stocky, big head on him, thin brown hair, forty-five years old but the way he lives has taken ten years off his life and put them on his face. Ugly as sin but eyes like a saint's—"

This time Feldspen interrupted me. "Yes. Yes." He sighed, looking shocked. "With that description there's no doubt it's the same man." He paused. "Then—he's a criminal."

"And *how* he's a criminal."

I filled them in on part of Rio's record; all of it would have taken half the day. And none of it pleasant. Lou Rio was, despite his commanding position in the local rackets, among the lowest of those low forms of life. He had come out here from the east about twelve years ago, been smitten by the climate and sights—especially the Hollywood lovelies, because he could not resist a well turned ankle or fanny—and opportunities for fast bucks—and stayed. An ex-pug with one mangled eyebrow, he'd come up in the rackets the hard way, battling for every inch he got, and he was still belligerent, angry, stupid, always ready and even anxious to take a poke at somebody, anybody. It was as if he generated inside himself the poison which kept him continually irritated and angry and sick, like a snake that insists on biting itself.

Not likeable, not jolly, he was a do-badder with cirrhosis of the conscience, and his heart was in the wrong place. Always for the overdog, that was Lou Rio, and now he was the overdog. In two words, he was a slob's slob.

"I'm shocked," Feldspen said. "He seemed, well, rather unpolished. But not criminal. We had lunch in the Velvet Room only yesterday."

The Velvet Room was the Studio Commissary, a fine place to eat if you wanted to eyeball movie stars and lovely lasses. The food was lousy. I said to Feldspen, "You mean he was here? On the lot?"

He nodded. "Yes. He's here a good deal. Likes the atmosphere, he says."

"I'll bet. I know what Lou Rio likes, and it's not the Velvet Room's soggy egg sandwiches. . . ." I stopped. "Harry," I said, "doesn't it now strike you as more than passing strange that a bigtime hoodlum buys into Magna and then, of a sudden, some anonymous hoodlum attempts to blackmail Magna?"

"I hadn't thought of it. Not previously knowing about Mr. Rio. But it does seem odd."

"It doesn't have to mean anything," I said. "You were talking about the movie business needing money. Well, the successful crooks need investments, legitimate spots into which they can sink their illegitimate bucks. So a place like Magna, with the movie business in a bit of trouble and welcoming outside money, is made to order for ready-money slobs like Rio. Probably that's all it is. But with Rio and blackmail so close, it sure smells."

Valentine said wonderingly, "Wouldn't it be the most unique situation if the blackmailer were investing his blackmail profits *in* the studio?"

"Yeah, but extremely good business—from Rio's point of view. And pretty neat, at that. Getting the illegitimate money from the legitimate business in which he then invests the illegitimate money has a kind of criminal poetry to it. But it seems *too* neat for a simple mugg like Rio." I thought a minute, then asked, "How much loot did he drop into the kitty?"

Valentine said, "I don't know. Quite a lot, I understand."

Feldspen said, "Several million. I don't know the exact amount myself." He paused. "The bankers really own the place, you know, Shell. I'm head of the studio, but I'm still just a salaried employee." I wondered what he was getting at. He hesitated and went on with a wry smile. "It would be difficult, for example, for me to order Mr. Rio off the lot, or discharge him. He is one of my employers."

That made it nice, I thought. Get a couple more crooks into Magna and it would start turning out nothing but films glorifying Billy the Kid, Dillinger, Al Capone—and Mr. Louis Rio.

Valentine had been thinking about something. Now he looked toward Feldspen, digging at his index finger with that busy thumbnail. I noticed he had actually drawn blood at one spot. He said, "Harry, I wonder if Mr. Rio's interest in Suez' career has any added significance now."

Feldspen shook his head silently, but I asked Ted, "What do you mean by that?"

"Ever since Mr. Rio became associated with the studio, he has pressed us to give Suez bigger and better parts. He tried to have us give the Messalina part to her instead of Miss James, for example. I think he . . . ah, has a personal interest in her. She's an extremely beautiful girl."

"You mean he's hot for this Suez?"

"That's—about as good a way to put it as any." He smiled that handsome smile again and added, "None of the heat is radiated upon him in turn, however. At least I feel reasonably sure of that."

I hadn't met Suez, but even without meeting her I was pleased that she seemed not to like Lou Rio. Anybody who didn't like Rio was that much over on my side. We jawed for another ten minutes and then, because it was already four in the afternoon and I wanted to talk with all of the stars in question, I told them I'd get to work and see them later in the day. Not until then did we settle my fee. Harry simply named a figure which even under the circumstances was a fabulous amount, and I told him O.K. and left.

Valentine had told me that *Howdy, Stranger* retakes were being wrapped up on Sound Stage Three, and that's where I headed.

Only there was a delay. My walk took me back near where I'd parked and thus fairly close to the gate where I'd talked with the thin-faced, big-mouthed guard. I glanced that way and saw a shiny black Rolls Royce parked there. The only guy I know who drives around in a Rolls is Lou Rio.

Feldspen had told me Rio spent a lot of time here, so I squinted toward the car, making sure. Yeah, it was Rio. He didn't drive himself but sat up front with the driver. I changed my course and walked toward the gate as the driver got out and started chinning with the guard.

I honestly didn't go over there to shoot Rio, or sock him, or engage in any kind of violent activity except maybe some pointed conversation. All I wanted to do was talk to the man, sound him out, try to satisfy myself about whether or not he might have had anything to do with the blackmail pitch. I thought that, even though we heartily disliked each other, we could trade a few words like normal uncivilized adults. I thought he'd be able to control himself. But, of course, muggs in the rackets have never learned to control themselves—which is one reason why they are muggs in the rackets.

When he spotted me walking toward the Rolls, Rio leaned over and spoke to his driver. Then the glare of sun on windshield blocked my view of him for a moment. The next time I got a look at him he was climbing out of the car. All three men went into the gatehouse and disappeared from my sight. When I reached the little wooden house and stepped through the door myself, Rio was waiting for me, arms folded across his thick chest.

It wasn't just his chest that was thick; he was pretty thick all over. Or rather he was thick, and there was nothing pretty about it. Rio was just thick, thick, thick. He was going to fat a bit now, at forty-five, but the fighter's muscles were still there under the flabby layer, though probably a bit too elastic this year.

I stopped in front of him and he grinned. "Well, what about this? Scott, the righteous fink. Rio's glad to see your ugly face."

"Let's keep it impersonal, shall we, Rio?"

He kept grinning. It was a wide face, and he grinned with his jaws clamped together, flesh bunching around his mouth and in a rubbery fold beneath his chin. The nostrils in his scythe-like nose flared widely. And above that compelling, eyecatching nose were his big, gentle eyes.

Those big, soft eyes didn't look as if they could be the eyes of a brutal man. You would expect the owner of those eyes to feed stray dogs and cats and buy Girl Scout Cookies. Those eyes would belong to keepers of canaries, to writers of odes and sonnets, not to Louis Rio. But belong to him they did. Maybe they were what Lou might have been, the evidence of good once in him. No matter, all they did for him now was to make the rest of him look harder, more brutal, more ugly.

He said finally, "You know you're gonna pay plenty for blabbing against Rio, don't you? A man like Rio's got to keep up his prestige, keep up his rep." He liked to speak of himself in the third person; that way he could say more wonderful things about himself without seeming too immodest.

I said, "That's not why I came over here."

"Don't make no difference why you come over, Scott. Glad you did. Several things Rio's been wanting to tell you."

"I can guess. There's something I want to tell you, too. There's a rumble, Rio, that an operator's putting the squeeze on a few of the Magna family. I'm now part of the family."

"What squeeze?"

I went on without answering him, but kept watching his face for any unusual reaction. "Naturally I'm now nearly as interested as those getting the bite put on them. So, as my first official act—"

He interrupted me. "What in hell are you running off at the mouth about? You talking about somebody on the shake here in the *studio*?"

He acted as if that were a blow to his personal prestige. Naturally he would feel that way, now that he had his own money in Magna—if he weren't just acting, period. Rio was still thinking—or pretending to think—about my previous remarks. He looked to his left, at the driver of his Rolls, and said, "You know anything about any shakedown, Ganny?"

I followed his gaze. I had been interested solely in Rio, and as a result had paid no attention to the driver. But I paid some attention to him now. It was hard to do otherwise.

Hoodlums, mobsters, men on the turf, men of the so-called "underworld," are remarkably imaginative in at least one way. That's in their choice of nicknames or "monickers" for themselves and their buddies. The number of a hood's police-blotter aliases may reach twenty, thirty or more, but usually the monicker sticks. And almost invariably the monicker is bestowed because it neatly sums up some facet of the individual's personality or appearance, character or history. The full monicker of the man Rio had called Ganny was Gangrene. And it just about summed the man up.

I had seen him several times before, and always with a shudder. No more gangrenous-appearing individual had ever stalked down the pike. Today he was wearing a black suit that looked as if he'd won it on a punchboard, a pink tie over a dark blue shirt, pointed black shoes and dark glasses, and he looked the way Death might have looked when young. Even in Hollywood this guy was unbelievable, but he was true. He was overdone, an almost comic exaggeration, a burlesque—but there was nothing funny about him, not a thing. Unless you think death rattles are funny, just a different kind of laughter.

No, this boy was about as bad as they come. He was mean, he was evil. Forget the clothes, the trappings, and take a look at the man, at the face.

There was a lot of hair, black and straight, matted with too much thick grease, parted on the side and combed straight back in two lopsided wings. The forehead was high and white and his eyes were like black ice cubes. The nose was thin, the nostrils pinched. The lips were thin and pale, pressed together. I didn't know if he had any teeth, because I'd never seen him smile. His lips seemed sewn together, like a corpse's. Tall, thin, bony, he looked ill. He looked abscessed. He looked mouldy.

I had thought before, after the first time I'd seen him, that if I had led a very mean, wasted, dissolute, evil and cruel life, and were dying of thirst in the middle of the Sahara Desert, just at the moment of death I might see something like him—reaching for me.

He said to Rio, barely parting his lips, and still not showing any teeth, or even gums, "News to me, boss."

Then Gangrene looked at me. The gate guard stood behind him, grinning slightly at me. It was the kind of grin which expresses no great amount of admiration, an insulting grin in fact. Gangrene said, "You lucky you still alive after what you done atta hearings."

His English wasn't quite Harvard or Oxford. It wasn't quite English. In his brain, Broca's convolution was not very convoluted but he made himself understood, one way or another.

"Yah," he said again, "you lucky you alive."

I ignored him and turned back to Rio.

He'd moved a little. I didn't know why, not then, but he'd stepped closer to the front of the gatehouse and I had to turn to my left in order to face him. He said, "What's this shake? Who's getting it?"

I shook my head. "That's all the news I've got today, Rio."

There was a slightly twisted, tight look on his face. He said, "I hear from Ham and Jake the Caddy." They were the two men I'd helped send to prison with my talk before the Committee. "They don't like it up there at college."

"That's because they graduated last time with F's. So they flunked in again. Fortunately for people." The college he referred to was Folsom, where they would spend their next several birthdays without cakes.

"Asked me to send their greetings," Rio went on.

I was going to make a fitting reply, but there wasn't time. It happened so suddenly that I was caught flat-footed. We were fairly well hidden inside the gatehouse here, but I just hadn't expected physical trouble from Rio today. Not here, anyway. I should have known better.

He just hauled off without warning and launched his left fist at my face. My reflexes are not only fast to begin with, but well trained, so even caught by surprise I managed to get out of the way of his fist. His thumb bounced along my cheek but didn't do any damage. I'd even started my own right fist driving forward automatically toward Rio's gut when I heard Gangrene grunt behind me.

I knew what that meant, knew far too late, and there was just too much for me to do. I tried to stop my fist and jerk my head aside at the same time, trying to turn, but I didn't even get a good start. My reflexes aren't nearly *that* good.

It must have been a sap, but it felt like a jagged half-ton rock when it landed. The blow wasn't solid, but it was solid enough.

If it had landed the way Gangrene must have meant it to, I'd have been out on my way down. As it was, the world just dimmed and didn't go black.

My knees stopped working, but I could still see everything near me through the sudden grayish fog, and I saw the wide grin in Rio's wide face as he slammed his fist at me again. This one got me on the way down. It landed on the side of my jaw and jarred me, but for just a moment it made the world brighter.

I landed hard but without pain. And then my arms were stretched out in front of me, hands pressing against the floor, but I couldn't feel them. I raised my head, straining, aching with the desire to get up, get to my feet before another blow fell. I pushed against the floor, pushed with all my strength, but somehow it got closer.

I did manage to pull my head up on my neck. And just in time. Just in time to see Lou Rio's big foot coming toward my face. It seemed to take quite a while, just as it seemed that I had been pushing against the floor for a long time, and I could still see quite clearly in that unnatural brightness.

The foot floated toward me as if legless, disembodied. I saw it all, the heavy sole, and intricate design of little holes on the cap, leather glossy and gleaming in the sunlight, the round leather laces, and above that the silk stocking and cuff of trousers. Just before the pointed toe crashed into me there was one thought swirling in my brain:

That big foot is going to land right on my chin and half kill me.

As usual, I was right.

Chapter Four

THE EARTH revolved around the sun like a green-blue-and-brown marble on a string of light, for billions of years, and the sun dimmed and went out. Then a brightness came swirling out of darkness, many-armed and pinwheeling, and slowly took form and was a sun and earth again. From wherever I was I floated in closer to the blue-green-brown marble and it swelled into an earth and swelled still more until . . .

It was a foot. It was that ugly, rock-hard foot again. No . . . it was a different foot. There were no little holes in the cap of the shoe, and it wasn't moving. That was good, because neither was I moving. I felt like not moving for about another billion years. But I tried anyway. And surprisingly enough I could still work.

The message went down from my brain to my hand and it flattened on the solidity below it, the arm tensed and extended. Good for you, Scott; you're moving. You've made an inch. You can do anything. I did it, too, an inch at a time.

I got up onto my hind end and just sat on it for a while, bathed in sweat. Finally I raised my head from those feet—I could see two of them now—and up the pants legs and over the coat to the face.

It was the insolently smiling guard I'd chatted briefly with at the gate. And he was insolently smiling. I was still in the gatehouse with him. I managed to look around. We were alone. I sat on the floor and considered the fact.

The guard said happily, "Wasn't nothing I could do to stop them, sir. It was over before I knew what was happening, sir." The sir had a very nice twist to it. He was pretty good.

I carry my gun in a clamshell holster at my left armpit. A little more rapidly now, because I was getting back to normal except for the skull-splitting throb somewhere inside my brain, I reached up and slid my hand inside my coat.

The Colt Special was there. I guess if they'd wanted to take the gun they would also have taken me—out into the low dry rolling hills. I pulled the .38 out, and it just happened to point at the tall thin guard.

He got taller and apparently thinner. He went sort of up on his toes and his mouth got a funny pucker to it and his eyes went wide. "What the hell?" he said. "They should of—"

"But they didn't. What's your name?"

"Goose!" It came out high and thready.

"O.K., Goose." I held the gun on his nose and thumbed back the hammer. A gun pointed at your nose is bad enough; but the same gun with the hammer laid back like a cobra's fanned-out hood is one of the most unpleasant sights in the world.

Goose said, "Sir. I didn't do nothing. I swear I didn't, sir."

It was a different sir this time. It was a far cry from the same word before, practically in a different language. But that figured; it was from a different man.

"Is that right?" I said. "You just watched."

"Yeah. That's all."

"You just watched while Gangrene sapped me and Rio slugged and kicked me."

"Yeah. I . . . well, there wasn't time to do nothing. If I could of, I'd of done something."

"Yeah. Like standing on my ear." I paused. "No lies this time, friend. You understand?"

He nodded, eyes never leaving the bore of the .38.

"You're Rio's boy, right?"

He nodded again.

"He put you on the gate. Why?"

"Just to keep an eye on who goes in and out—like you, for instance. What goes on. Just the usual thing for him. He got some money in the joint." Ah, he was respectful now. His words dripped sweetness like honey. Why, he wasn't a bad man; he was just an erring boy.

I was beginning to feel reasonably good physically. I got to my feet, during which operation Goose closed his eyes briefly. When he opened them they focused on the gun muzzle again. I went on, "Tell me what Rio's part is in the blackmail play here."

"There ain't none, not so far as I know." I wiggled the gun. He got paler, but said, "I swear. If Lou's working some kind of shake I don't know about it. He don't say nothing to me anyhow."

That was about all he could tell me, it seemed. There was little point after that in standing there with my gun on him so I eased

the hammer down and put the Colt back in its holster. Goose
looked very relieved. It seemed Lou was, among other things like
working off his perpetual anger and getting back at me in part
for my trial testimony, showing his contempt for me by leaving
me on the gatehouse floor.

"Goose," I said. "One last question. Where did Lou and Gangrene go?"

"To see Feldspen."

"You mean they're still *here?* On the lot?"

"Yeah. Lou wanted to see Feldspen, he said. He also told me
to tell you . . ."

"Spit it out."

"Tell you to get off the lot and stay off if you didn't want
more of the same lumps."

I turned and walked out of the gatehouse and into the lot
again. Marie, the blonde secretary in Feldspen's outer office
opened her mouth and started to smile when I stormed in, but I
barged on past, threw open the door and walked into Harry's big
office. The first thing I saw was Lou Rio's fat face.

He was at the left of Feldspen's long desk. I walked toward
him with the mark of his fist and shoe on my face, the lump
from Gangrene's sap on the back of my head, and the desire to
break his neck on my mind.

Movement on his left was Gangrene. There was quite a lot of
movement in the big office, it seemed, but my attention was focused on Rio's face—which looked at least unhappy and maybe
even a little scared—and I didn't even wonder what the movement was at first. Somebody yelled, "Shell!" but I kept on going.

That young-Death face moved closer, and Rio yelled something at me.

Some of the other movement got a little clearer in the next
half second as I continued to move forward. I was looking at
Rio, but from the corner of my eye I got glimpses of white hair
that I assumed was Feldspen's, and then the swirl of hair
that was long and black. Then I caught the not-red, not-pink
glow of hair I'd seen before, and the blur of a white face. There
was something else, too; the room seemed loaded with people.
But then I pushed all that from my mind and yanked my eyes
from Rio's face as Gangrene reached for me.

He didn't come at me with the sap this time. Maybe he was
just trying to keep me from the boss, reaching for me or swinging
a fist at me. I didn't know and I didn't care at all.

I was moving forward, so I just moved faster, pivoted as Gangrene's hand slapped the lapel of my coat. And then I got my left foot planted solidly again and leaned forward. I just leaned into him, left foot shoving and left fist driving, leaned way into him and pounded my fist into his belly.

He had teeth after all. His mouth came open so wide that I actually saw the yellow-stained, twisted things in his mouth, and the air burst out of his throat so fast it seemed odd that it didn't carry those frail-looking teeth along with it. Gangrene reeled backward, arms flapping, and I knew he would be taking no part in the action for quite a while. So I turned and headed for Rio again.

"Shell! Are you out of your mind?"

This time it got through the pink haze in my brain. The voice was Feldspen's. I looked at him, at his shocked face. An expression like revulsion mixed with a kind of fright was written on his features. This wasn't in a movie, after all. This was for real, and right here in his office. This was 3-D and real blood. Feldspen looked stricken. And that was what stopped me.

I stopped a yard from the left end of Feldspen's huge desk, four or five feet from Rio, who had gotten up out of a leather chair there. I looked at him and he stared back, not moving.

It was very quiet. I could hear a whispery, brushing sound. That would be Gangrene, moving painfully down there on the carpet. I didn't look at him.

The silence seemed to last forever. I managed to get a good grip on my anger, to throttle down the steam in me. Then I said softly, "Lou, you made a mistake out there. Up till now, it wasn't a personal thing between you and me. Now it's personal."

The voice that answered me was Feldspen's. "Shell," he said in a tight voice, "what's the meaning of this?"

I looked at him. As I turned my head I saw Valentine standing at the other end of the desk. He'd looked bad enough before, but he seemed on the way out now, a man with milk in his arteries and clabber in his veins. He reached up with a twitching hand and yanked unconsciously at his neat mustache as if he were trying to pluck it. That Cary Grant valley in his chin seemed even deeper, as if his face were starting to split apart there. How he managed to remain fairly good-looking I don't know, but he managed it.

I said to Feldspen, "The meaning is that this slob Rio and his punk gunman worked me over outside. So I came in to—well, to register a complaint."

As I spoke I was turning my head to the left side of the room

—and to the people against the wall beyond him. There were three of them. Most important was the fiery-haired one: Coral James. She looked straight at me from those pornographic brown eyes, and they still looked hotter and more exciting than strip poker with three brunettes, but there was no smile in those eyes now.

Seated next to her on a long low leather couch was the dark-haired woman I'd seen briefly. She appeared to be a little taller than Coral, a little heavier, her body a bit fleshier, more earthy and openly sensual if not quite as classically beautiful. This one was beautiful, too, but with dark lush beauty of Mexican and Spanish women—though I felt sure she wasn't Latin. She had the deep full breasts and smooth olive skin, the bright black eyes and long black hair of many Latin women, though. Those eyes were large and soft and dark, with a look of deep pain in them.

Gangrene was doubled up on the floor, both hands pressed to his middle. Farther to the left, a couple of yards from the couch the girls were on, a man was leaning against the wall. He was about six-four or maybe six-five, a good 250 well-distributed pounds, wearing faded blue jeans and a brown-corded white silk shirt. On his feet were intricately worked red, green and white cowboy boots. He had a face as open and rugged and honest as a split-rail fence. He was Johnny Palomino.

Then it clicked. Palomino and James—that meant the black-haired beauty would be Suez. All three of them here.

What was going on?

Feldspen said, crisply, "All right, Shell. Tell me once again, slowly and in more detail this time, what brought this about." He had regained not only his composure but his high seat behind that desk.

I decided against a long drawn-out explanation and said simply, "I met Rio and his human goofball outside. We—well, we've been saving up for a beef for a lot of months. Today we stopped saving up and had it." I looked at Rio. "Had the first one." Then I said to Feldspen, "Now tell me something, Harry. What's going on here?"

I was facing that wide desk and I had temporarily forgotten about Gangrene. But I heard a sort of scuttling sound—and then a shrill scream, louder than you would think a scream could get, a veritable masterpiece of a scream. I swung around just in time to see Gangrene coming up off the floor, a heavy .45 automatic already in his right hand.

I grabbed for my Colt, jumping to the side, but on Gangrene's left Palomino was already moving forward, one long leg swinging. That chased-leather cowboy boot caught Gangrene's hand and the gun flew clear across the room, smacking into the wall. Gangrene didn't even turn his head. His eyes were on me, his face was without expression except for the usual cold, corpselike fixity of his features.

My fingers touched gun metal, but as Gangrene's automatic flew through the air I let my hand drop again. Gangrene didn't even appear to realize the gun had been kicked from his grip. His eyes stayed on my face and their black-ice look was dulled now, more like black dry ice, and it looked like death. It was like seeing eyes in the skull holes of a corpse as he got to his feet, as if some elemental ugliness stared through those sockets at me. He got to his feet and took a step toward me. Oddly, nobody moved. They all seemed either caught by surprise, or held in a momentary paralysis, unable to say anything or stop him.

I said softly, "Hold it there, Gangrene. This time something's going to break." I didn't ball my hand into a fist but spread it open; if he came at me again I wasn't going to just knock him down, I was going to ruin him. He acted as if he hadn't heard me. A shiny smear of saliva glistened at the side of his mouth. He took a second step toward me, another. His hands came up easily in front of him. I got ready to swing at him.

Rio said suddenly, "Ganny! Cut it."

He moved away from the desk toward Gangrene, who didn't pay any attention to him. He was reaching for me when Rio slapped him on the cheek. It wasn't a hard blow, but only a light tap—as if he'd done it before.

Gangrene stopped and just looked at me for a moment, while his eyes seemed to undergo a change. This boy was like some kind of Frankenstein monster dug up and given ugly life and movement for a while, and now running down, running out of juice. His eyes seemed to change focus, and then he let out a faint sigh and licked his lips once.

"O.K., Lou." he said in a thin voice.

So I merely said to Rio, my voice tight, "Get him out of here."

He looked at Gangrene. "Come on, Ganny. Ain't no more we can do."

Gangrene said to me, hardly moving his thin lips, "You're all caught up, Scott. All used up."

I looked at Rio. "If you don't get this punk out of here I'm going to embalm him again myself."

He gave Gangrene a little shove, pushing him toward the

door. Gangrene didn't say anything else, but Rio looked past me to Feldspen. "I'll call you, H.J."

Feldspen didn't speak. The two men went out.

Somebody released breath in a puffing sigh. Valentine moved, pulling a chair up from behind him and dropping into it as if exhausted. He probably was. I know I was. After what seemed a minute of silence, I walked around behind Feldspen's big desk and got the .45 automatic off the floor, checked it, and dropped it into my pocket.

Then I looked at Palomino and said, "Thanks, friend."

He grinned slowly. "Ah must've been out of my haid."

"Wherever you were, I'm darned glad you were here. I owe you one."

He just grinned some more, relaxed as a cat.

I turned to Feldspen. "Well, Harry? Did I miss something?"

He gave it to me straight. "Mr. Rio came in and found Theodore; I was temporarily out of the office. He told Theodore that you had informed him of the blackmail threat. He demanded the story and Theodore gave it to him. All of it. At that point I returned. Mr. Rio then requested that we summon the three stars in question to my office and ask them about the, ah, suspicions. I did so." He paused and, undoubtedly noting the unhappy expression on my face, added, "If I had not done so, he undoubtedly would have hunted them up himself."

Which was no doubt true. I felt like swearing, but I said, "So what do we know now?"

Feldspen said, "Not a bit more than we did an hour ago."

Somehow I had expected that. Palomino spoke on my left, and I turned as he said, "Sure is a funny thing about how it added up like to us three. That figure you mentioned—" he looked at Valentine—"Coulda been grabbed right out of the air, you know. If it wasn't *all* made up to start with." He paused, then added—directly to me this time—"I already told 'em I sure don't know a thing about any blackmail." He grinned once more. "Not that I've got such a angel-like past, but nothing I'd pay good money to hide."

"I beg your pardon," Feldspen said suddenly. "In all the . . . excitement, I forgot you haven't met."

I grinned. "Not formally." I looked at Coral James, and her brown eyes were fixed on me. She wasn't smiling, though.

Feldspen performed introductions and explained why I was here, that I was a private detective. Coral managed a little smile when we said how-do-you-do's as if we'd never seen each other.

In repose like this, face flushed, she was even lovelier than when I'd almost run into her at Feldspen's door. She had it, all right; the magic was there.

The dark-haired girl was Suez, as I'd guessed. She was quite a dish herself, one who would have been monopolizing virtually all of my attention if Coral hadn't been in the room.

In Hollywood, "exotic" means anything farther away than San Francisco, but this one looked exotic in the authentic sense —beauty with a truly foreign flavor, and the flavor was delicious. She looked like a woman who might have lived in the Casbah, ridden camels past the Sphinx, danced naked around a tribal fire in Africa, strolled down the Champs Elysees in spring. She was warm and sensuous and lush, like the earth on a summer morning. To say the least, she was interesting; to say the most would be against the law.

As we were introduced, Suez gave me a soft smooth hand and said, "That was awful. That awful friend of Lou's. You're a bear, aren't you? A regular *grizzly* bear."

"Not really." I grinned down at her. "This little episode here was not typical of my days—or nights. I really loathe this sort of thing. See? I'm not at all grizzly."

She smiled, teeth startlingly white next to her velvety skin. "*I* know a grizzly bear when I see one."

"Well, have it your way."

Coral wasn't looking at us, and seemed not even to be listening, but she had a mildly annoyed look on her face, as if a tiny fly had lit in her ear. I finally let go of Suez' soft smooth hand and Coral said, "Do you want us any more, Mr. Feldspen?"

"I suppose not. Is there anything you want to ask, Shell?"

There were things I wanted to ask, but it was worse than useless to ask any one of them about blackmail in front of the other two, and in front of the three of us. So I said to Feldspen, "I guess you've covered the important questions. That's good enough for me."

"That's all, then," he said to them.

The girls got up and, after a few words, went out. I shook Palomino's hand and thanked him again.

He said, "It was just like runnin' through a take in *Howdy, Stranger*, Mr. Scott."

"Call me Shell. Everybody who keeps me from getting shot calls me Shell."

"Sure, Shell." He looked at Feldspen and Valentine. "So long, then." He went out.

It wasn't until the moment when he looked across the room at Feldspen and Valentine that I noticed his eyes. The pupils were very small, making the irises seem abnormally large. After I got one look at his eyes, he was out the door and gone. It didn't have to mean anything; perhaps it was even normal. And maybe he was used to bravely kicking guns out of outlaws' hands, too. But that is also the way a man's eyes look when he's popping with a narcotic drug. Like morphine.

I didn't mention it. Instead I said to Feldspen, "Well, this fouls everything up beautifully."

Valentine said dully. "It's my fault."

I spoke without thinking. "Telling Rio the three names wasn't the brightest play imaginable."

He winced. Maybe from the mouse eating its way out of him. Maybe—probably—because of my words. He looked hurt, and penitent. "I . . . I know it," he said. He fingered the cleft in his chin, scratched the neat mustache. "When Mr. Rio and that— that monstrous individual came in, I just didn't even think about *not* answering his questions. And I had no way of knowing what you'd said to him, anyway."

"Yeah. That's understandable. Maybe he already knew their names." I told them what had happened at the gatehouse.

Feldspen said, "They really beat you about the head?"

"Not about the head. Smack on top of it."

"You realize I knew nothing of his background."

"Yeah, Harry. But I realize something else, too. Somebody knew who and what he was—but took his dough anyway. And because of that, I've a hunch the trouble's just getting started." I paused. "Well, exactly what did you get out of Palomino, Suez, and Miss James."

They'd gotten nothing but denials. All three had been surprised and unpleasantly so, but the very idea of anybody blackmailing them was preposterous. Then Feldspen frowned slightly. "Now that I think back on it, Coral didn't really say anything. We were asking questions, Mr. Rio included, and I guess her silence went unnoticed by us all. Johnny disclaimed any difficulty. Suez said the whole idea was preposterous. But Coral just sat there looking lovely, and listened. She really didn't say a thing until you came in."

In a couple of minutes I told them I'd be on my way and would check back when I had something worth telling them. It was almost five in the afternoon, and I wanted to talk with Palomino, Suez, and Coral—alone this time. Just before I left, Ted Valentine got up from his chair and walked over to me.

He stuck out his hand and said, "I'm horribly sorry. I've bungled this in ghastly fashion I suppose."

"It'll work out."

He shook his head. "I doubt . . . well, perhaps. At any rate, I'm glad we met, Shell."

He seemed quite sincere, and again I felt that warm and pleasant feeling of liking for the man. I said, "So am I," and meant it. We shook hands and I went out.

Chapter Five

I FOUND Johnny Palomino resting between takes on the *Howdy, Stranger* set on Sound Stage Three. He had only two or three minutes until shooting would start again, but it was enough. I asked him point blank about those pinpoint pupils, adding, "I've seen eyes just like that before, Johnny. I hate to sound obnoxious, but Feldspen hired me to ask obnoxious questions."

"Oh, that's all right, Mr. Scott. I mean, Shell." He grinned widely. "My eyes are real light-sensitive, especially under these here hot lights they got to use making the picture in color. Takes a powerful lot of illuminating. My ophthalmologist prescribed some kind of drops to put in my eyes. Supposed to contract the pupils—let less light in. Okay?"

"Makes sense. You know what kind of drops they are?"

He shook his head. "Some long name like bulbar pneumonia or something, I don't recollect."

"You want to tell me who your eye doctor is?"

"I don't reckon he'd want to be bothered none," Johnny said slowly. He was still grinning, but it was bending a little. He added, "Well, Scott, I already told everybody around here three or four times that I'm in no trouble at all. Except I'm a slow study and haven't learned my lines for this next scene yet."

I took the hint and left. Well, I'd learned one thing: He'd gone back to calling me Scott.

Suez was in her dressing room on the sound stage adjacent to this one, through for the day and getting ready to go home. She answered my knock wearing a pink satin robe that looked enough like pink skin to give me quite a start, and with a start like that I was almost ready to finish it.

"The grizzly," she said with apparent pleasure. "Come on in."

I went inside the small room and she shut the door, pointed to a wooden chair for me and sat down facing me, on a small wooden bench before her dressing table, her back and long

40

black hair reflected in the big mirror behind her. As she'd turned and walked from the door to the little bench, the air had swirled around me and a sweet odor filled my nostrils.

It was different from the smell of powder and makeup in the room; I liked it. "That's nice," I said, pulling in a lungful as I sat down.

Suez crossed her legs smoothly and said, "The scent?"

"Uh-huh."

"Jasmine. All the time I wear it. Love it. You get a whiff of jasmine, Shell, you look around for Suez."

"I'll do it."

She leaned back, elbows behind her on the dressing table, legs crossed, robe pulled tight over her deep breasts and long smooth thighs. She surprised me a little by saying, "I suppose you want to ask me again about who's blackmailing me."

"That's close enough."

"Nobody. So what'll we talk about now?"

I looked at the pink robe, the way it rested without a ripple on her skin, smooth over the firm full thigh and sweeping curve of her hip. It was plain enough that either nothing was under it, or there was so little there that it would make almost no difference at all.

It must have been pretty obvious what I was looking at, because she said, "No, let's not talk about that."

I looked up, but she wasn't angry or even mildly irritated, apparently, just matter-of-fact. I said, "Well, we might talk about Lou Rio. I hear he's interested in you."

"He is. But I'm not interested in him. Okay?"

"That's great with me." I grinned at her. "I understand he put on quite a campaign to have you starred in *Sins of Messalina*. Instead of Coral James."

"He did, at that—but not a campaign. Just a few words where it counted. Didn't count enough, though. And I didn't know what a wild man he was until today. That's a fact."

"You mean you didn't know anything about his extra-legal activities?"

"Whatever that is. Anyway, I didn't know a thing about him except that he could do me good—and it wouldn't cost me anything." She paused and added with slight emphasis, "Not anything." She moved, shifting that wonderful hip, and the satin slid softly, whisperingly over the bare skin beneath. And now I knew it had to be bare skin. The robe fell open another inch at the top exposing a softly gleaming curve and a pool of shadowed darkness. I could feel a pulse ticking in my throat.

She went on slowly, "I wanted the part pretty bad. But later I got *Night Wind,* my first big part, so it worked out. But I still think I'd have made a good Messalina." She flashed the white teeth at me suddenly. "A good *bad* Messalina."

"She was bad enough. But beautiful. I think you'd have been great."

"Thanks." She paused, looking steadily at me from those big black eyes, "Listen, Grizzly. Don't you worry about Lou Rio. He goes for me, sure. But I don't go for the fat-slob type."

"That sums him up pretty well. I don't go for him either, so we have something in common. There's nothing more common than Lou."

"I go more for the big, rough husky-slob type." I was searching for something dazzling to say, but she went on before I could think of anything dazzling enough. "I've got to get dressed. And, much as you'd like it, I'm not going to do it while you're here."

"How do you know I'd like it? I would, of course."

"You plainly telegraph it, Mister. It comes in like Mayday. A lot plainer than Esperanto."

"And I'll bet we speak the same language."

"It could be, maybe. If it was time for conversation. Who knows?" She paused. "We might have a long, long talk sometime." She smiled slowly and paused again, for quite a while, then went on. "But not right now, honey."

I got up. "You almost made me forget, but I am working for Feldspen. Maybe for you."

"What does that mean?"

"Just in case any trouble should fly your way—out of all this mess today—let me know. If you want help, that is."

"Now, what kind of help could I want?"

The way she said it, a man could read almost anything into that line. She stood up then, gracefully, and as she rose from the bench that pink robe fell completely away from one leg bearing the calf and thigh and even the beginning curve of her hip as she turned away from me. Facing the big mirror, she put both hands up to her long black hair and said, " 'Bye now. You be here tomorrow? On the lot?"

"If I live. I may not live to get out the door."

It was half true. The robe had fallen back together now that she was standing, but it wasn't tied and it had not fallen completely closed. It was separated only about an inch, not any more than that, but it was an inch like a yard and a half anyplace else. It was an inch clear up and down the robe's center, and that was also the center of Suez.

Watching me in the mirror, she said, "You mentioned getting out the door, honey. So go on, now." She gathered the robe together in one hand. It helped a little. Helped the robe, that is; it didn't help me a bit. I said, "But . . . but I just thought of some dandy dialogue."

"I'll bet you did. 'Bye, honey."

"Yeah," I said. "Yeah." And with that brilliant exit line flopping loosely from my lips, I staggered about and went out the door.

I walked toward Bungalow Ten, which I figured would be my next and last stop, and my thoughts were swirling around in a very dizzying fashion. I knew my temperature must be about 102 degrees Fahrenheit, and it was pretty sure that an extra five or ten gallons of blood were being pumped around in me every minute, and I think I needed a cold bourbon-and-water right then more than anything else in the world—except one thing of course.

And then out of Bungalow Ten stepped Coral James.

I had walked past the commissary and around the corner to the row of neat, spacious bungalows there. Feldspen had told me that Miss James' bungalow was number 10, and I'd been on my way there, hoping to catch her before she left the lot. So I was prepared to see her, expecting to.

Even so, she hit me again like the first time, and the second time. Even after my five minutes with Suez, five minutes which had virtually frazzled me, the sight of Coral, that fiery hair and heart-stopping face and heart-starting body, washed all over me like thick warm air. You could breathe it in like faint perfume. You could drown in it.

She saw me and waved, walked toward me, a faint smile on her red lips. And I thought, It's too much. The afternoon had been too much. It had started with the exhilarating sight of Coral outside Feldspen's office, then I'd been clubbed and clobbered, gotten all charged up during the party with Rio and Gangrene again in Feldspen's office, and then had been charged clear up to Tilt by Suez. And now Coral again, and she was really the best and worst of it all—she was, all by herself, the most a man could expect to experience in one day.

And maybe that, I thought, is what's wrong with Hollywood. There's too much stimulation, too many assaults upon the nerve endings, all of the nerve endings. Your nerves get all giddy, as if they were made into a harp with long red fingernails plucking jazz from its delicate strings. There's too much going on at once in every direction, too many lovely women, and muscular gleaming-toothed men, too many powdered breasts and thighs—and gleaming derrieres. Too many brains pumping thoughts, too many frustrations—and opportunities. Yes, that was it. Hollywood was too much—almost.

Coral had reached me—in fact, now as well as by the other channels—and we stopped on the sidewalk facing each other. She said, "Hello, Shell. You look a little . . ."

She searched for the word and I supplied, "Dazed?"

"That will do."

"It's probably because I was hit on the skull this afternoon. From both sides. Outside, and inside."

"Were you looking for me?"

"All my life."

"Seriously."

"Yes, I was. You leaving?" She nodded and I said, "Do you drive your own car?"

"I don't drive at all. If you're offering me a ride, it will save me cab fare."

"It's saved." I offered her my arm, she took it, and we walked back to my Cad. On the way I said, "You know why Feldspen hired me. So I might as well tell you now that I've already checked with Palomino, and Suez, both of whom claim nobody ever blackmailed them because there's nothing in their past that black. I further admit that the same reason, my job, is the minor reason for my hunting you up just now. So what's your answer, and we'll have that out of the way."

"No answer."

"What does that mean?"

We'd reached the Cad. I held the door for her and she climbed inside. As I slammed the door she said, "Just that I'm not going to say yes or no, or anything. I won't say one way or another, not just yet."

"You didn't say anything in Feldspen's office, either."

"I thought nobody had noticed."

I walked around to the driver's side of the car, wondering what this conversation added up to. The next few minutes of talk didn't tell me. As we left the lot I looked very carefully around, checking the rear view mirror frequently, but I didn't see any sign of Lou Rio's Rolls, or anybody who looked like Gangrene. And nobody shot me, so it seemed probable that neither of those characters was around. Not yet, anyway.

We drove to Hollywood Boulevard, down it to Locust and then up to tree-lined, shaded Redwood. Coral pointed. "The little white house there."

"Ah, you live there alone?"

"With my mother."

"Oh." Dully.

"Who is visiting relatives in Vermont."

"Oh?" Brightly, this time.

She invited me in. I spent half an hour. We talked, and I didn't learn anything about the case. Mainly because she refused to discuss it. I wondered why. I learned a little about Coral, and she learned quite a bit about me in the conversation. She was from Vermont, had been in Hollywood for four years, and done a dozen minor parts before the big one, *Sins of Pompadour.* Now, with *Sins of Messalina,* she felt that her career was really established on a solid foundation, and life was wonderful.

I said, "You're beautiful enough to play anyone, Coral, including Messalina—if they'd ruin your hair—"

"Thank you; I wear a long wig."

"—but I'm sure you're not bad enough. She was evil, and there can't be an evil bone in your body." I grinned. "In fact, it's possible there aren't any bones at all in your body."

She laughed. "They're there."

"Well hidden then."

"Besides, how do you know I'm not bad? Maybe I'm more evil even than Messalina. Maybe I've betrayed my own Claudius, and Asiaticus, debauched dozens of lovers in my own Gardens of Lucullus." She smiled. "It wouldn't have to show."

"I don't know what you're talking about, but it sure sounds like fun. Seriously, it would show eventually." Eventually, yes, I thought; but for just a moment I wondered if this bright and lovely woman could possibly, inside, be different from the loveliness I saw. Like Rio's eyes, those gentle eyes of a brutal man. Perhaps, just as Rio's eyes would change eventually to mirror what looked out of them, Coral's face and body would change, become ugly and twisted to shape themselves around the woman inside. . . . It was an ugly, twisted thought, and I simply didn't believe it.

Especially not when Coral was smiling at me, as she was now. She said, "This conversation is what I get for playing Messalina. If you're right about me, the fact that I'm so good in the part is proof I'm an excellent actress."

"I'm right about you."

"Thank you, Shell."

After the first attempt to draw her out about Magna and the problem Feldspen had presented to me there, I let the subject drop until just as I left Coral's house. For the last ten minutes or so before leaving, though, I just sat and talked quietly to Coral, looked at her and listened to her.

It could as easily, and pleasantly, have been a day instead of ten minutes. This was a pause in the battle, surcease from saps, balm for all wounds. The voice was like the rest of her, clean and beautiful and unique. For a while I closed my eyes and listened, not looking at her. It was a voice that fell sweetly upon the ear, like the sounds of morning, like the music of spring winds in grass. Low and cool and soft, almost lazy, a voice that washed liquidly over me and caressed my ears and made me feel good just listening to it.

Finally, though, I got up and went to the door. I had to get some lines out among my informants, get on with the job. But this lovely could almost have hypnotized me out of the notion.

And the thought of the job to be done caused me once again to say to her as we stood at the door, "Coral, there's this one point I didn't mention earlier. Somebody—with or without a valid basis, I don't know for sure yet—is trying to squeeze a million clams out of Magna. The money isn't as important as the misery that might come out of this mess *if* that egg who called really has some dirt on Magna people. Right?"

"Agreed."

"O.K., if you know anything at all important that you haven't told me but *could* tell me, you'd be partly responsible for whatever happens."

She looked at me from those brown eyes for quite a while. Then she said, "Suppose I thought I had some damaging information about, oh, Mr. X, but wasn't sure it was true. I wouldn't want to say terrible things about him unless I was sure. You wouldn't want me to, would you?"

I thought about it. "Frankly, yes. I would. I'd check anything you told me. So unless it was true it wouldn't hurt—Mr. X."

"There's hurt just in the telling," she said. "If it isn't true." She paused and looked at me some more, then added, "I'll tell you this, Shell. There is something going on at Magna, but I'm not sure what it is. When I decide what to do, I'll let you know."

"O.K. But if anybody is giving you a bad time, I'll consider that my own bad time."

She smiled sweetly. "That's nice to hear. Well . . . I'll tell you this, too, Shell, because I guess you're really interested. Nobody's blackmailing me. Not anybody."

"That's a relief. Thanks, Coral."

She frowned slightly. "I . . . somebody tried . . . once. To keep it completely honest. But nobody's blackmailing me—and no one ever has."

She said goodbye, and I walked down the sidewalk to my Cad. I was puzzled. It just didn't seem that anybody was having any trouble at all—except me and my aching head. Even so, I still felt sure that where there was this much smoke there had to be some fire.

I glanced back at the little white house just before I got into the car and drove back to town. Coral stood in the open doorway. The sun was just going down. Its last red rays fell on her hair and made it look like burning blood.

I drove to Hollywood Boulevard, followed it to the freeway and then into downtown Los Angeles. The lights were on and the always surprising bustle of moving cars and people turned the streets into minor bedlam. I drove up bright and garish Broadway, past Third, and into the parking lot next to the Hamilton Building. Up a flight in the Hamilton is the one-room office of *Sheldon Scott, Investigations*. I went up.

After flipping the office-light switch I turned on the lights over the ten-gallon aquarium on top of the bookcase. I said hello to the twenty or thirty guppies, little fish much more colorful and garish than Broadway outside, fed them a helping of powdered crab, then parked behind my desk and picked up the phone.

When I hung up for the last time I had made a dozen calls, and I lit a cigarette, pushing a thought or two around in my brain. Numerous hoodlums and small-time thieves and even a couple of reasonably big-time crooks, would by now be riding the Earie, as the phrase goes in the argot, moving in the right places, trying to pick up a word about Magna, Magna people, or blackmail in large round numbers, anything that would help me. It was about all I could do this day; I'd push other angles tomorrow.

I locked up the office and drove back to Hollywood and the Spartan Apartment Hotel—home. A shower and clean sheets helped the aches, but didn't clarify my thoughts. I lay awake in bed awhile and thought about the case, then about Coral. Finally I pushed her out of my mind—gently—and, with room there to swing in, Suez came in, swinging her hips. Ah, lovely hips. She had more heat in her than a can of Sterno. In fact, it almost seemed that she *had* a can of Sterno. Especially remembering that one glimpse I'd had of it. And I wasn't about to forget it. She took some pushing, too, and there was plenty to push, but I got her out. And for just a brief moment I took another look at Johnny Palomino.

I didn't know. Maybe they were all lying to me. Except Coral; I refused to think she wasn't on the level. But wouldn't it be a laugh, I thought, if they were all telling the truth and Feldspen were lying to me instead? That proved I was really getting confused. But I was still confused when I fell asleep.

The ringing phone yanked me awake at six o'clock in the morning.

I grabbed it, half asleep. I always need about an hour and two cups of strong coffee before I wake up, and I couldn't understand why Feldspen was calling me at this time of morning.

"Feldspen?" I said. "Is that you, Harry?"

"Yes. Can you understand what I'm saying?"

"I hear you as if through a glass darkly, Harry. No, that's not what I mean—"

"Listen to me, will you?"

There was a thread of taut alarm in his voice, a shocked and perhaps even frightened note that knifed through the fog in my mind and brought me at least a little wider awake. I sat up in bed, hand involuntarily tightening around the phone. Through my bedroom window I could see the tips of trees on the grounds of the Wilshire Country Club across Rossmore. Dawn had turned the sky the cold, dull gray of lead.

"Okay, Harry," I said. "Okay. What's the matter?"

"It's Valentine."

"Valentine? Ted?" He pranced briefly before my eyes, twitching a little, digging at his finger, biting his lip, grimacing—and then grinning, suddenly tall and handsome. "What about Ted?" I asked.

"He's dead. He just killed himself."

Chapter Six

I WAS still looking through the window, but suddenly I didn't see anything out there. I was startled into silence for a moment, then I asked, "Are you sure?"

"Yes. There's no question. The police are there now—one of them phoned me."

Even in the short hour or so we'd spent together, and despite his tortured manner and the circumstances under which we'd met, Valentine had impressed me as an immensely likable guy, a man who would be a good, warm friend and amusing companion when he got over whatever was eating him. I suppose I had subconsciously been looking forward to seeing him again, and now I felt a sense of almost personal loss. "How did he do it?" I asked Harry. "Gun?"

"No. He jumped from the roof of his hotel."

"Jumped?" It started seeming a little sour then. "That's odd. I wouldn't have expected him to do it that way."

"Why not? He did it, that's the important thing. I wouldn't really have expected him to do it at all."

That was true enough. I said, "Harry, listen. Is there any chance he didn't do the job on himself. Could—"

"No, he wasn't killed or anything like that, Shell. At least not according to what the police told me on the phone. Some people saw him. Actually saw him jump. He left a note, too. I don't know what it said." He paused and sighed heavily. "You'd better get down there." He told me that Valentine had lived alone in the Madison, an expensive apartment building off San Vicente, in a quiet residential district near the studio.

I arrived at the scene probably thirty minutes or less after Valentine's death. Feldspen had been notified almost immediately, and he had phoned me within two or three minutes. So Valentine's body was still there on the sidewalk, though covered with a sheet. The police were just about through with their job

—the photos and measurements and interrogations—and soon
would be gone. The ambulance was backed up to the curb, doors
open wide, and attendants were ready to put the body inside
when I walked over to them.

The area was blocked off, but I knew most of the officers and
was passed through. A police car sat at the curb, red light flashing atop it and a call was coming in on the radio as I stopped by
the attendants. Before they put the body on the four-wheeled
stretcher, I took a look at it just to be sure.

It was Valentine, all right. The dead flesh of him, anyway.
He looked pretty bad. He was recognizable; there was no possibility that it was anybody else. The neat mustache was still
neat, and his dark blond hair was only a little disarrayed, not
bloody. But there was no longer a Cary Grant cleft in his chin.

I stood up, feeling sick. You never get used to the sight of
dead men except in war, especially crushed or twisted dead men.
The attendants put his body into the ambulance, got in and
drove away. No siren. There wasn't any hurry.

I looked around. An officer named Dennis Lavery was talking
to a man and a woman twenty feet from me, on the steps of the
Madison Hotel. I walked toward him and he left the couple,
filled me in on the situation. The couple were two of the three
people who had seen Valentine jump. The third, a middle-aged
man named Peter Fishbaum, was now sitting in a police car.
They all told the same story.

It had just barely been light. The man had appeared at the
building's edge, stood there for several seconds, then bent down
and put something at or near his feet. The couple—a man and
his wife—stated that they'd thought he was some kind of work-
man.

But after putting whatever it was at his feet, he had leaped
from the roof of the building, feet first.

I said to Lavery, "What was up top?"

"Usual suicide note," he said. "Show it to you in a minute, if
you want. And the keys and things from his pockets. Wallet,
comb, handkerchief, you know. Funny how they'll do things like
that. Don't make any difference ten seconds later. But they do it."

He let me read the note. It was on an almost square sheet of a
heavy off-white bond paper with a visible watermark of some
kind of bird, and it was short. And horrible in a way. As all
suicide notes are.

The note wasn't addressed to anybody, there was no heading.
It just started out: "By the time anyone reads this I will be dead.
I am going to take my own life. I cannot go on any longer. Liv-

ing isn't good any more. I'm sick and tired. Sick and tired of everything. God knows I tried. Sorry to cause such a fuss. Good-bye everything. May God have mercy on me . . ."

It was signed, Theodore Valentine. "I suppose it's his hand-writing," I said.

"Checks with the signature on his license, and writing on stuff we found in his room. It'll be gone over downtown, but it's his. Take my word for it."

"Good enough for me, Den."

He pointed at the note. "I've seen a dozen of these, and they're all different—and all the same. Look at it. Disjointed, rushed. He couldn't even slow down to write the note. See how the words get less legible toward the end?"

"Yeah." The lines were less firm, more wavering.

"In a hurry, rushing too fast to get it written down. I've seen the same thing, too, in notes written by suicides who took poison, or sleeping pills. They write the note on the way out and natu-rally their writing gets less steady."

We walked over to the couple. The man was about thirty, me-dium height, dark, with thinning hair. His wife was dark, too, and not bad-looking at all. About twenty-five. A little hard in appearance, perhaps, a little coarse. But maybe that was makeup and the cold gray morning light—and my mood.

They gave their names as Mr. and Mrs. Gene Gelder. It didn't take long to get their story; it was just as Lavery had given it to me. The woman said, "It was the craziest. I didn't know what he was doin' up there. Figured he was a janitor or something, you know? He puts that stuff down, then boom, off he goes. I like to passed out."

"I guess that's it. Thanks, ma'am."

"You could hear him, you know. When he lit. Never heard such an awful—"

"Yeah. Thanks for your time."

"Gene run into the hotel and called the cops right away. They was here in just two or three minutes, I'll say that for them."

"Uh-huh. Incidentally, how did it happen you were here so early in the morning?"

"We're stayin' at the Madison ourselves. Been at a party and just got home when we saw the guy up there."

Her husband let her do all the talking. He looked and acted as if he always let her do all the talking. That was the way she acted, too. I thanked them again and went to the police car, talked briefly to the third witness, Peter Fishbaum.

He told the same story. Except that he added, "Stood up there

plain as life. All alone and looking out this way. I knew he was
going to jump."

"How'd you know that, sir?"

"Just could tell. Feel it. He bent over, put something down,
straightened up and waited. Knew he was going to jump. And
off he went. I couldn't even move. Didn't want to watch, just
couldn't help it."

He explained that he lived several blocks away and had been
walking to Hollywood Boulevard to the nearest gas station.
"Guess some kids drained the tank in my old heap," he said.
"Don't mind the gas, just wish I hadn't seen this." He paused.
"The guy jumped feet first. And landed feet first." He held his
two hands in front of him about a foot apart, then slapped them
hard together. "Like that," he said. "Awfullest thing I ever saw."

I went with Lavery to the top of the building and looked over
the edge Valentine had gone over, then went back down
to my Cad and drove to Magna. I found Feldspen in his big office. He was seated behind that big desk, light gleaming on his
neatly-waved white hair, and he looked very much alone. His
red-tanned face was drawn and lined; he looked tired.

"Hello, Shell," he said. "What did you find out?"

"You know the important parts. He jumped off his hotel roof
and killed himself. And it *was* Ted Valentine. I saw his body,
talked to the police and witnesses."

"Why . . . *why* would he do a thing like that?"

"That's the big question." I sat down in the leather chair
I'd used yesterday, the one Valentine had later been sitting in
after my beef with Rio and Gangrene. "Tell me, Harry," I said.
"Did you have any idea that he might commit suicide?"

He waved both his delicate hands gracefully. "He always
acted as if he was just about to kill himself. Or die of something.
You saw him." He paused, stroked his cotton-white hair. "At
least he'd been quite disturbed for the last few months."

I frowned. "Is that all? I thought maybe he'd sort of grown up
like that."

"Perhaps five or six months. That's all. Yesterday was, I'll have
to admit, the worst I've seen him. But he's been extremely upset
for the last week. I asked him about it, but he said it was nothing, just nerves."

"Harry, do you think Valentine might have been in a bind
himself? I mean, is it possible *he* might have been one of the
three being blackmailed here—assuming there are three?"

Feldspen blinked at me. "Why, that's . . . I don't see how it
could . . ." He let it trail off, but it seemed obvious that the

thought was a new one to him, and he had to digest it a little. Finally he said, "I suppose it's possible. But I don't think it's true."

Feldspen was quiet for a minute. Then he fumbled through a drawer in his desk and finally found a sheet of letter-size paper and started silently reading it. In a moment he said to me, "I mentioned a minute ago that Theodore had been even more agitated than usual for this past week. I thought it might have had something to do with his accident."

"Accident? What kind of accident?"

"I don't know what kind. He didn't say—he wrote me about it last week end. This is the letter." He waved it in his hand. "Theodore had to take a day off from work as a consequence; he wasn't here last Monday."

That was interesting. Anything out of the unusual in Valentine's routine was interesting now that he was dead. This was Tuesday, just over a week from the time Feldspen referred to. I said, "Why did he write you? To let you know he wouldn't be able to show up?"

"Yes. He was . . . quite considerate. I assumed he'd sprained his ankle or something like that—it happened at a dude ranch near Palm Springs." He paused, then added, "Here. You can read the letter if you like."

He was so far down that desk from me that I had to get up and walk over to him to get the letter. I read it, but there was nothing very illuminating about the contents. Valentine said he'd had a slight accident and would be recuperating for a day or two, and would miss work. He was sorry, and so on.

It gave me an odd feeling to read a letter in the same sprawling handwriting as the suicide note I'd just seen. But there was something else about that letter, something which nagged at me, bothered me, made me uneasy. I didn't know what it was, but I didn't like it.

I looked at the heading printed at the top of the heavy off-white bond stationery. Across the top, in letters drawn to resemble letters formed from new yellow rope, was the name *Desert Trails Guest Ranch.* Under that was a small map showing its location, a few miles off Highway 60, and the slogan, "Enough of the old West for color, enough of the new for comfort—*Desert Trails,* where the wild West is tamed, and your cares are lassoed and hogtied. Unreasonable rates."

That didn't mean anything to me. I'd heard of the Desert Trails Dude Ranch, which was becoming quite popular with a number of Hollywood people, mainly the Palm-Springs set, but

I'd never visited the place. I looked at the stationery on which Valentine had written his letter. It was heavy, and there was a visible watermark in it that looked like some kind of bird. A scrawny eagle maybe. It just didn't register right then.

I said to Feldspen, "Letter's dated last Sunday. Nine days ago. I gather, then, that he'd been especially spooked up just about since then, right?"

"I suppose we could say that."

"And he never mentioned what this accident was, huh?"

Feldspen shook his head.

"Well, it probably isn't very . . ." I didn't finish it. Valentine's letter to Feldspen was still in my hand, and I'd suddenly realized why it had bothered me. I looked at it again, the color, weight, watermark, the works.

Except that this sheet was longer and had the Desert Trails heading, the paper seemed identical with that on which the suicide note had been written. It didn't have to mean a thing. But I got a sudden chill ripple up my spine just the same.

Feldspen told me I could keep the note if I wanted to. I asked him if I could use his phone and he dug a white job out of one drawer of his desk. I'll bet he had drawers in that thing for everything from golf clubs to potted plants. I called Homicide in downtown L.A. and talked to Lieutenant Perkins, who answered the phone.

He'd heard about the Valentine suicide, though Homicide wasn't interested, so he understood what I was talking about. "I'm pretty sure," I told him, "that the suicide note was on the same paper—only with the top cut off. I'd like your lab to check them out for me, compare the two sheets. Can do?"

"We can check them, sure. Where'd you get the stationery?"

"It's just a letter Valentine wrote from the Desert Trails Guest Ranch. The only thing I'm curious—"

"What did you say?"

"I said I'm curious to—"

"No, the name of the place."

"Desert Trails Guest Ranch. Dude Ranch near Palm Springs."

"Yeah, I know where it is. Don't you know who owns that neon rangeland, Shell?"

"No. Should I? Is it important?"

"I don't know whether it is or not. You figure it out. Papers say the owner is William Layne, but that's just the paper. Real owner is Nick Colossus."

Nick Colossus. That jarred me. Painfully.

Half a dozen angles and ideas got scrambled in my head. Lou

Rio in the case had been bad enough. But of the two evils, Rio and Nick Colossus, Rio was much the lesser.

Stacked up alongside Nick Colossus, Rio—the guy who had slugged me and kicked me in the face, who actually seemed to enjoy the company of Gangrene—was practically a softy. He was like a daisy alongside a cactus. He wasn't as big, he wasn't as tough, he wasn't as smart as Nick, not by a long shot. Of course, he was quite enough of all those things, as far as I was concerned.

"Shell? You there?"

"Yeah. That surprised me."

"Mean anything to you?"

"Just that I don't want to vacation at the Desert Trails. Nick is included among the many who fail to be overcome with gladness at the mention of my name."

"Something else you might be interested in, Shell. Monaghan over at the D.A.'s office called the Captain about it. Only reason was because he remembered Valentine's name; probably not important."

"What's not important?"

"Last Monday this Theodore Valentine called the D.A.'s office and asked if they'd gotten a letter from him. They hadn't. He seemed anxious about it—didn't want them even to open the thing if they got it. Said he thought he'd mailed it to them by mistake, but wasn't sure he'd mailed it at all."

"What kind of letter was this?"

"Four page letter, he said. Sent special delivery. That's all any of us know. He called the next day or two, then stopped."

"Any letter ever show up?"

"Nope. That's all there was to it. Only reason Monaghan called the skipper was because of the guy taking a dive this A.M. Well, file it away, Shell."

"I will. Thanks. I'll bring this letter down."

We hung up. Feldspen said, "What was all that about?"

I shrugged. "I don't know. It could be something's real screwy here. I just don't know." More than anything else I was curious to know if Nick Colossus was tangled up in this case anywhere.

And I sure hoped he wasn't. I would have much preferred Dracula.

Before heading for downtown L.A. and the police, I waited inside the gate and caught all three of Magna's allegedly blackmailed stars as they came in. I told each of them, bluntly and without warning, where Valentine was now, and why.

I got one unusual reaction.

Coral came in first, and she was shocked and sorry. It was, I thought, a normal enough reaction. She had to get to Makeup, and I spotted Johnny Palomino parking his car, so we went our separate ways. The last thing she said was a little strange. It was, "Well . . . that—that changes things."

Palomino was cool enough about it. He seemed surprised, but that was about all. As if he'd just heard that a distant cousin had robbed a bank. He asked me, "Where'd he do it?" and I said he'd jumped from his hotel. He shook his head, and went on into the lot. He seemed still to be using his "drops."

So far, so-so. But with Suez, it was different. She parked her white Thunderbird, jumped out energetically and walked toward me, green skirt swirling, dark hair bouncing against her shoulders. She wore a very well fitted, snug sweater in just about the color of green that most other gals would turn with envy when they saw it.

She spotted me and waved, smiled a flashing white smile, then stopped in front of me. "Hi. Out of hibernation for another day, hey?" she said cheerily.

"There was nobody else in the cave. I got lonely. You hear about Valentine?"

"No, what did he do?"

"Killed himself this morning."

Her face was still pleasant enough. It just froze in the expression it had had when I'd spoken. It took a little time to penetrate. She said, "Killed himself?"

"Yeah. Jumped off the roof of his hotel just about sunup."

For a moment I thought she was going to faint. She got paler and her eyes sort of went out of focus momentarily. Then she said in a tight, twisted voice, "Oh, God, no. Oh, my God. No . . . no." She put a hand out and kind of wobbled a little as she said, "I should never have—" She stopped suddenly.

I thought maybe I could get to her while she was still shocked, still not watching her tongue, and find out what she'd meant by all that, but there wasn't time for a good try. I said, "Should never have what, Suez?" She whirled around and ran to the Thunderbird, jumped in and was out of sight before I could even get my Cad started. I tried to catch up with her and find out where she was going, but she was long gone. Feldspen had given me her address, on Pepper Street, so I drove there. It was a pale brown stucco apartment building, and Suez lived in Apartment Six. But she wasn't there now. I left, hit the freeway and drove into downtown L.A., parked in the lot at the Police Building and went on inside.

I took the letter to the Criminalistics Lab and met Lieutenant Perkins, on his way out after delivering Valentine's suicide note to them. He said, "Hi, Shell. You think something smells about this suicide, huh?"

"I didn't say that, Perkins. I'm just curious about the notes."

"Yeah." He had a half-smoked cigar butt clamped between his teeth. "I'd be curious about anything that's got Colossus' name within a mile of it."

"How about this Guest Ranch you say is his? Any angles?"

"Just an investment, I guess. And a spot for his punks to hang out. Nick stays there most of the time, himself. Must have spent a fortune on his own rooms."

"Fancy, huh?"

"Not that so much. You know we've been after the bum for ten years."

I nodded. The police knew that Nick Colossus had personally committed or been accessory to the commission of virtually every crime in the book, but he'd never spent even a day in jail. He was smart, and he was careful.

Perkins said, "He must have spent a fortune to make sure he'd be safe out there. No chance of anybody getting a mike in; that place is thoroughly debugged—his rooms anyhow." He grinned. "We tried to bug it. That's probably the only place in California where he really feels safe. Nobody's going to get anything on Nick at his own place, that's for sure."

"Which also proves he's got plenty to hide."

"A fact we've known for ten years, pal. And it's not the kind of proof you take to Superior Court."

We jawed a little longer about Nick, and then I changed the subject. "By the way, Perkins, if somebody kills me today, pick up Lou Rio, will you?"

He grinned. "Sure, I'd love to. You planning to get killed?"

"No, but I think that slob's planning to kill me. It's a sure thing that Gangrene is."

"Well, it was nice knowing you, Scott. Wish we could solve all the murders this quick."

And on that happy note he went back to Homicide. Before leaving the Police Building I checked with Criminalistics. They hadn't run all the tests possible, but they'd done enough. The two sheets were identical except for the heading on the letter to Feldspen; the top of the suicide note had been cut off with a

sharp instrument, probably shears or a razor blade. It was
Valentine's handwriting on both sheets of paper; the police hand-
writing expert was positive of that.

I'd left my apartment without breakfast, and I was getting
hungry. While I have absolutely no appetite on arising, after
two or three hours I can eat a horse. So I took off and had a late
breakfast at a new and unfamiliar place which was never going
to become one of my old familiar places. I ordered planked
steak and it tasted as if they had cooked the plank. It was served
with whipped potatoes that looked like old shaving cream with
the whiskers still in it, and all that breakfast did was spoil my
breakfast. So I went to one of my old familiar places for a sirloin,
and by the time I had strength enough to reach the office, it was
eleven-thirty A.M.

The phone was ringing when I went through the door, but
I didn't reach it in time. I looked through the mail, then called
Feldspen and told him about the reactions of Palomino, Coral,
and especially Suez. He said Suez still hadn't reported for work;
he had no idea what could have been eating her.

I said, "I'll be out of touch for a few hours, Harry. I'm going
to follow up a lead at the Desert Trails. I'll check with you
later."

He wished me luck and we hung up. Almost immediately
the phone rang again. I grabbed it and a man's soft voice said,
"Is this Mr. Scott?"

"That's right."

"Sheldon Scott, the detective?"

He sounded a little worked up about something. I said, "Yes,
sir. What can I do for you?"

"I just saw the TV news. I've been watching all morning, waiting for something about the man that got killed this morning."

I sat up straight. "Valentine?"

"Yeah, that's it. It just mentioned you were there, working for
the guy's boss, something like that. So I looked up your
number."

"What about it? And what do you mean, you were waiting
for the broadcast?"

"You alone? In your office there?"

"I'm alone. Do you know something about Valentine's suicide?"

"Yeah. It wasn't no suicide. The guy was thrown off the roof.
He was murdered."

It gave me a small shock to hear the man say it, but I wasn't really surprised.

I said, keeping my voice normal, "How do you know he didn't jump? And why don't you go to the police?"

"Man, I tell you I *saw* those guys toss him off there. You think I'm nuts? I go to the cops, and maybe those same guys find out about it and drop me off a bridge. No, thanks. I'll do it this way." He paused. "I thought for a while I'd just let it ride, but I couldn't. It kept eating me—so I'll give you the whole bit. But no cops, man."

"Do you know who the men were?"

"Huh-uh. Two men, that's all. One on each side. They dragged him over the roof, put him down for a minute and did something I couldn't make out. Like they were maybe putting something there on the ledge. Then they go and give him a toss."

I asked him how he'd happened to see all that and he said he'd been up on the roof "with a babe" until a few minutes before. She'd gone down to sneak back into her room and he was having a smoke, to give her time to get in, before going down himself, and back to his own home.

"Where are you? And what's your name?"

"Hang up, man. That's all, all."

"Look, I'd like to talk to you in person. Maybe you'll remember things, if I ask you, that you think you've forgotten. Or that you don't think were important. Besides, I'd like to get a signed statement from you, if nothing else."

He wasn't for the idea, but in another half a minute he said O.K., he would at least talk to me. He wasn't promising to sign anything, though, and I had to give him my word that I wouldn't mention his name in connection with the killing without his permission. The kid wanted to help, I figured, but was still talking himself into it. I thought of him as a kid, though I didn't really know how old he was. His voice and speech didn't seem that of an old codger.

I gave him a few more reasons why he should see me, and finally he said, "O.K., Dad."

But he still wouldn't give me his name. He said that he would meet me in York Park, a small park out on Belmont Street in half an hour. He added, "I'll talk to you, but that's all. I want to cooperate, but I'm not signing anything or telling you my name. I'll give you the ball, Dad, but you got to take it over the goal line."

"That's good enough for me, friend," I said. "How'll I know you?"

"I'll have a hibiscus in my ear—hell, I'll know you. They showed your picture on that TV news show. But I am a tall and skinny cat with black hair and eyes like pools of blood—how's that?"

"I'll find you," I said, grinning slightly. I could imagine the sweet nothings this cat must have whispered to his doll there on the roof—"Baby, you *bop* me,"—or whatever such characters say at times like that. "See you in half an hour."

We hung up. My grin slowly faded. Not because of the news about Valentine's murder, but because now that the guy was off the phone a couple of things he'd said seemed a bit odd. There wasn't really anything wrong with his tale, and all he'd said might very well have been true—probably was. But I didn't much like meeting him in a wooded park. York Park was wooded, too; there were a lot of trees and brush there, as well as the cool green lawn and goldfish pond.

And what had actually occurred to me was the possibility that somebody who disliked me to the point of frenzy—like Gangrene, for example—might have pulled this just to get me out to a relatively lonely spot. I shook my head and told myself that I was reaching for trouble now, and undoubtedly that call had been exactly what it seemed to be. But I took out the .38 and checked it, felt its comforting weight in my palm for a moment, then put it in the holster and got up.

I was at the door when the phone rang again; I hesitated, then went back and lifted it to my ear.

"Shell?" It was a woman's voice. Low and cool and sweet. "Yeah. Would this be the lovely Coral?"

"It would be Coral. Thanks for the adjective. Shell, yesterday I said that when I was sure of something I'd tell you, remember."

"I remember."

"Well, now I'm more sure. I told you that once somebody tried to blackmail me. I didn't want to say who it was yesterday because if I was wrong, it might hurt him. Well, it was Valentine I had in mind. It can't hurt him now."

"Valentine? You think *he* tried to blackmail you?"

"Yes. It's a little complicated, Shell. I'm calling from Magna. I'll leave here about five, so why don't you come by my place at six and I'll tell you then, all right?"

"Fine, Coral. See you tonight then."

We hung up. For a minute I thought about what she'd said, then I dialed Magna Studios and got Feldspen on the line.

When he answered I said, "Harry, this is Shell. I've been thinking. I know you liked Valentine, so I hate to say this—but there's a chance he was behind the blackmail pitch. If so, now that he's dead there may be nothing more to worry about. Maybe the squeeze is over—"

He interrupted me. "I just had another phone call."

"Don't tell me—"

"Not half an hour ago. The same man, same voice."

"Oh." My own voice sounded rather dull, even to me. "What was it this time?"

"Essentially the same. He said that he had heard about the suicide of my assistant. And that I wasn't to assume anything was changed."

"I wonder why that was mentioned."

"I haven't the vaguest idea. He repeated the preposterous demand for one million dollars. In *cash*. And said he would phone again in six days, perhaps sooner." Feldspen paused and then added, "Shell, I'm getting rather frightened by all this."

"It's a screwy one." I glanced at my watch. I'd already spent over five minutes on the phone, and I had to get on my way. That reminded me and I asked, "Has Lou Rio been around the lot this morning? Or Death-cooled-over?"

"Who?"

"Gangrene. Little Boy Black-and-Blue. The man wearing tights-colored flesh. The chap who tried to shoot me in your office."

"Oh, no. I haven't seen either of them. Why?"

"I'd just feel better if I knew exactly where they were at this moment. Harry, I've got something important to do, but I'll see you as soon as it's done, and we'll go over all this."

He said fine, we hung up and I took off.

Automatically as I walked out of the Hamilton Building onto Broadway I looked around, and even tried to check the windows of the building across the street. There was about one chance in a hundred thousand that if anybody tried to pot me here I'd be able to see him first, but I looked anyway. Once before I'd had two rifle slugs tossed at me from a building not far down Broadway; once was enough. In fact, once was too often. But I didn't see anything except what looked like a million people, none with rifles, so I climbed into the Cadillac and dug out.

I made excellent time to York Park, but got there five minutes late. I pulled into a spot at the curb, on Belmont, got out and went down one of the sandy dirt paths into the park. The path was lined with cement-and-wood benches and curved slightly to enter the central area of the park. This was a cleared place about fifty feet across, with benches and three stone statues around its perimeter, a circular pathway before them, and a twenty-foot-wide pool in the middle, filled with fat goldfish.

Three people were in sight when I arrived. One of them, a thin guy about thirty-five, got up from one of the benches as I looked around. Except for an old lady knitting and apparently listening to the birds—on her face the distant, sort of sappy look of people who sit in parks knitting and listening to birds—the only other person was a young guy, maybe twenty-one or twenty-two years old.

He spotted me and stood up, waved a hand. He wasn't "a tall and skinny cat" as he'd described himself, but short and fat. Maybe he hadn't wanted me to know what he looked like; or maybe he'd just been horsing around conversationally, which seemed to be characteristic of him. It occurred to me as I walked toward him that this little fat guy and I were, except for the killers, the only people who knew for sure that Valentine's death was murder.

The kid grinned when I was just a couple of yards away from him. "So I ain't got a hibiscus," he said. "But I'm your boy, Da—"

I suppose he was going to say Dad, or Daddy-O, something like that. I didn't know. And I would never know. That was his last word, and he didn't even get to finish it.

I didn't hear the shot. I just saw half his chin torn suddenly from his face.

Chapter Seven

I HIT the ground before he did.

When a man is shot, it isn't like putting a hole in a paper target. It isn't a matter of just a small circle appearing in him with little or no other effect on the man. It isn't like television or movies—or anything you ever saw unless you've seen a bullet hit a man.

A .45 slug would have tossed him clear off the path, even hitting him in the chin, but whatever this was it spun him around with his fat arms flying up into the air as if they were pushed by steel springs. A squeak came out of him, not a yell or a scream, but a squeak. And then he was falling—and I saw his body jerk again, sharply, as he fell. As the second slug slapped his flesh my foot slammed hard against the path, slipping on the sand but providing enough leverage so I could hurl myself forward and hit the ground rolling, hand under my coat and out with the Special as I came up onto my knees again.

Pain gouged my knees and shoulder and there was a roaring of blood in my ears that drowned out everything else. On my knees I slapped my left hand onto the ground to steady myself, and turned back in the direction from which those two shots— or maybe more by now—had come.

Even as I'd dived forward my mind had automatically been figuring, plotting the course of the bullet which had hit the kid, deciding almost coolly, and as if separate from myself, where the man must have been standing so that a bullet would throw the chunk of chin away from the kid's face and to my left. From right to left, and away from me—so that meant he had been behind me and to my right.

That's just about where the thin guy would have been if he'd kept walking, the man about thirty-five who'd got up from his bench as I'd arrived. I didn't actually think about any of it—I just hit and rolled, slammed down my left hand and jerked my body around, gun coming up in my right fist.

I didn't see him. My sight was a little blurred, but I could
make out the path, trees. That old lady wasn't listening for birds
now. She was yelling like a young lady with strong lungs. Maybe
that's why I didn't hear the gunshot, though by now it would
have been a fairly loud sound—but the bullet hit near me.
It missed me, and probably that was why he came into view, so
he could get a clean shot at me and finish me.

He had been behind one of the park statues, a gray stone ugliness that loomed above him now as he moved away from it. He
didn't step far from it, just enough so he'd have a clean, straight
shot at me. It was enough—enough for me. I could see all of
his right side.

The sudden shock that had sent my brain into an accelerated
kind of activity and gripped it in an icy coolness, seemed to
guide my arm and hand as if it were not a part of me, almost
as if it were somebody else's arm and I was teaching him how
to fire a gun. There seemed to be plenty of time, and I got off
the first shot without haste or trouble. I saw him jerk. My slug
turned him halfway around. He pulled the trigger of his gun,
but it wasn't aimed at me; the bullet kicked up sand near his
feet. I heard the gunshot this time, but it was so faint that even
now I almost missed it. Like a twig snapping, or a man cracking
his knuckles.

I just took my time—all the time in the world, it seemed. I
could hear that blood-rushing sound like a surf in my ears, and
the hard crack of my gun, and then the crack again. He jerked
and fell, dropped his gun and tried to get up. I ran toward him.

He got onto his knees and waddled horribly forward, like an
amputee trying to walk on stumps, and fell onto the base of the
statue, clutching at it, splitting his lip on the cement, then
rolling over onto his back.

I reached him, grabbed the front of his coat and jerked him
up off the cement foundation toward me. "All right, who set
this up? Who sent you?"

Blood spilled out of his mouth.

I said, "You don't have much time, friend. Tell me fast, if
you're going to tell it."

"It . . . was . . ." He pulled his lips away from his teeth in a
grimace, straining at the words. I could see the freshly broken
tooth in front, where he'd landed on the statue's base.

He tried, he really tried. The words were there, and, as the
darkness grew behind his eyes, he struggled to get them out. It
was obvious he wanted to do that much. He just didn't have

enough time. Hanging by his coat from my hand he had raised his head up away from the cement below him, straining to speak, and when the life went out of him the muscles relaxed, his head falling with a solid, heavy jar against the cement. It made me wince, even though I knew he couldn't have felt it. It was the kind of sound you hear for a long time.

I let go of his coat and he crumpled the rest of the way to the ground, with that perfect relaxation of the newly dead. The iciness that had cloaked my brain and thoughts melted and he looked different to me. I turned my head and saw the still body of the young guy who'd phoned me. He lay with one leg under him, both arms outspread, blood spreading in a brown stain on the sandy earth beneath his head.

I felt hollow, as if something had sucked the insides from me. There was a taste of ashes in my mouth. I have been shot at before, even shot. This wasn't the first time I'd pumped bullets into a man myself, or seen men violently, brutally killed, lying ugly in their own blood. But something about this, maybe the way it had happened, the way the kid had got it, the woman's yells, or all of it together, seemed to have taken some of the life from me, too.

There wasn't any question about Valentine's death now; he'd been murdered. That meant all three of those "witnesses" had been lying. And the dead men here were proof my phone had been tapped. That last item seemed important, very important—something about it bothered me, but I couldn't pin it down.

When the police cars arrived, I was in reasonably good shape. In the first police car to arrive were Keynes, a sergeant, and another officer. They walked up to me, frowning.

"Scott," Keynes said, "what in hell are *you* doing here?"

"Come on. I'll show you." I'd met them at the sidewalk, and now I led them back to the center of the park. On the way I explained the highpoints. As the two bodies came into view I said, "My phone's tapped, and somebody heard the kid—" I pointed toward him—"tell me he'd seen Valentine tossed off the Madison's roof. That's why he was killed—whoever had the tap put on, sent that wiper out to get the kid. Get us both for that matter."

We walked to the man I'd shot.

I said, "Before you got here, I checked the punk's gun. There are marks around the base of each bullet. I think he took the bullets from all his cartridges and spilled out about half the powder, then put the pills back in—so the gun would make very little noise when one of those bullets was popped. Fairly neat job, but you can see the work was done."

Keynes blinked at me. "What put you onto that?"

"The gun's a Smith and Wesson .32 and it's got a gag on it, but there are five empty shells in the cylinder and one full round. So he fired five times—but the only shot I heard at all was the last one, and it wasn't loud. Not even a silenced .32 puts out so little noise normally, and I wondered why. So I looked. Probably there's only half a charge in that sixth cartridge."

He nodded. "Pretty good. Well, that sure makes him a pro, doesn't it?"

"Not any more."

I was getting very tired. Something was nagging at my brain, but it wouldn't come through. I tried to pull it out where I could look at it, but it stayed hidden.

Keynes said, "Who was it called us, you know?"

"There was a lady here, knitting." I remembered thinking of her listening sappily for birds. "She yelled loud enough to get you here without a phone. She was a regular wireless station all by herself."

I looked at the dead punk and the young kid he'd murdered, and for just a moment I saw again how ugly it really was. Then I pushed that thought out of my mind, and a different one took its place. It was ironic, even a little funny, and I wondered what *my* expression had been like lately.

Keynes said suspiciously, "What're you smirking at?"

"Huh? Nothing. Nothing, Sergeant." I couldn't tell him that I'd just decided the expression on the face of an old lady sitting in a park, knitting and listening to birds, couldn't really have been so sappy at that.

It was nearly one P.M. The bodies were gone, everything was wrapped up here and I'd told my story six times. I would have to tell it again downtown, to a stenographer, and then sign my statement, but I'd received permission to postpone that job temporarily.

I was about ready to leave, but in all the bustle and interrogation I still hadn't found out the name of the man I'd killed. Finally I saw Lieutenant Rawlins, an old and good friend out of Central Homicide, downtown. After we'd exchanged a few words I asked him about the hood's identity.

"Name's Dodo," Rawlins told me. "You did us a turn, Shell. We've got four of those scratched up slugs down at the office, same marks around the bases of all of "em.""

"From pulling them out to dump part of the powder, huh?"

"Yeah. These four slugs were dug out of three dead ones. More of Dodo's work, only we didn't know until now who was doing the jobs."

"He went to a lot of trouble. Well, that just about proves his business was murder. It's good riddance. But I still wish it had been Gangrene."

"Gangrene? You mean Rio's right hand?"

"Yeah. Now I've still got him to worry about. Can't figure why Lou didn't send him."

Rawlins frowned. "You mean you think this was one of Rio's boys?"

I had assumed from the beginning that Rio had tapped my phone, and thus had sent his wiper to the park. I said, "I don't have any proof, but it figures."

"Figures, hell. You mean you really don't know who Dodo worked for?"

I blinked at him. "Not for sure. Do you?"

"Yeah. As far as we know, he never worked for anybody out here except Nick Colossus."

Chapter Eight

I swung left off Highway 60 at three-fifteen in the afternoon.
I had never before visited the Desert Trails Guest Ranch because, while I am a great one for swimming pools, and shapely
dolls, and plush cocktail lounges and dining rooms—all of
which I understood the Desert Trails had in abundance—I have
never been swept off my feet by horses and chuck-wagon break-
fasts at the creak of dawn.

In fact, there is some unfortunate thing between horses and
me. It's not that I dislike them. But when I get around the animals they seem to slit their eyes and lay back their ears and
get ready to bite me. Or maybe it's all in my mind, because
they are beautiful animals with very large teeth, and I would
hate to think they might really chew on me.

Besides which, I'd had my fill of animals for one day. On the
way here I had stopped at one of those roadside hamburger-
joint-plus-zoo monstrosities which are scattered over the western
states, and while putting away a hamburger I had eyeballed the
mangy hyena, allegedly-fourteen-foot python, mangier monkeys,
and scarlet-and-blue tropical birds, among other things which
completely destroyed my appetite.

So maybe horses wouldn't look so bad to me today. In another five minutes I might be near lots of them, because by then
I would be descending upon the Desert Trails. This was not
an episode upon which I was embarking light-heartedly—in
fact, I had talked again to Lieutenant Perkins and told him to
pick up Nick Colossus first, even before Lou Rio, if I got killed
—but it had become a necessary episode.

The road turned left and slanted downward. A mile ahead
were the buildings of the Desert Trails. All of them were low
and flat except the main building, which was two stories and
had some kind of rectangular construction in the middle of its
flat roof. A number of small buildings sat to the right of the
hotel, apparently separate living quarters for guests who felt like

really roughing it. The whole thing was like a geometric oasis in the desert: there was nothing else but cactus and lizards for miles in all directions.

Around all the buildings were patches of green that stood out like jewels in this arid desert land, splotches of color where somebody had planted flowers. An oval swimming pool glittered under the hot sun, and beyond it dozens of automobiles gleamed in a rectangular parking lot at the left of the main building.

I drove on down, by a long plain building on my left and rustic-looking cabins, then past the pool to the lot. I got out and walked back to the main building. It was a lavish, low, ranch-style structure beyond a natural-wood fence and healthy green lawn. As I faced it, more cabins were on my right, and on my left was the pool, in which about a dozen people were splashing. The rim of the pool was fashioned to resemble a thick rope, a simulated running knot at one end of the pool with the "rope" extending on to become the leading edge of a wet bar, like a hundred-foot-long lariat with its loop enclosing the water. Fifteen or twenty people were guzzling highballs, while behind the bar a four-piece combo played a soft and very pleasant *Don't Fence Me In,* an oldie that built the right mood out here.

I could go for this place myself, I thought. Hadn't even seen a horse yet, and the rear view of some of those dolls at the bar, a number of them in swim suits, was a source of immense satisfaction to me. But I shrugged and turned toward the hotel; work, always work, I thought. I went through chrome-and-glass double doors into the Desert Trails lobby.

About the only concession to the Dude Ranch spirit made by the management was the trimmings outside, including some big prickly saguaro cactus planted on the well-tended lawn, and several items of Western-style furniture and decoration inside. But basically this was a rich, plush, comfortable hotel plunked down in the middle of the desert. Expensive, too. I checked at the desk and, though I didn't intend to spend the night, learned that the cheapest rooms were forty dollars a day. Then there were cabins outside if you wanted to spend more, and a few ultra-plush cabañas near the pool, presumably for people who had just discovered uranium on their oil land. There were two bars and a dining room off the main lobby, and at one end of the lobby stairs led up to rooms on the second floor.

The clerk at the desk was surprisingly accommodating. He

was a middle-aged man, not too bright in appearance, but pleasant. I expected difficulty, perhaps because I knew the place was
owned by Nick, and Nick wouldn't give me directions to the
bathroom if he could help it. However, the clerk knew nothing
of Nick's antipathy for me, and obviously didn't know who I
was, so when I asked him if I could check the registration
cards for the previous weekend he hesitated only briefly.

Twenty bucks ended his hesitation and made him even more
agreeable. He handed me a half-inch-thick pack of cards and
merely asked me not to be obvious about going through them. I
started with Saturday's registrations. The name of Theodore
Valentine was there, the card filled out in his sprawling script.
He'd been alone and had been in cabin 24. There were some
other names I recognized, movie and TV people, and one fat-cat
L.A. politician. I noted the names of two MD's who'd registered
Saturday, one of them getting Cabin 26. I was playing a hunch,
but a hunch based on logic, so I jotted down their names in my
notebook. I was almost through the pack of cards when I came
upon a name that stopped me. I picked up the card and looked
at it, wondering if it was significant or just a coincidence, of no
special interest to me.

On the card signed in large letters in bold green ink, was the
name Suez.

Back into my mind came the picture of lovely dark-haired
Suez paling when I'd told her of Valentine's death, registering
sudden shock and then taking off in a hurry. I wondered where
she'd been racing to, and why. What was it she'd said? "I
should never have—" I was going to ask her about that again.

The clerk didn't have any idea who Valentine was, so I
didn't push it. I asked him if the two doctors were still at the
ranch. He pointed at one of the two cards I'd separated and
said, "Doctor Clark's still here. I remember he signed up for
two weeks—first vacation in three years, he said." The clerk
sighed. "Them doctors, they got it hard."

Doctor Clark was the man in Cabin 26. He'd registered for
himself and his wife. That cabin was across from the one Valentine had occupied. It was worth a check.

I called his room but there was no answer. I went through
the rest of the registration cards and got some other info from
the clerk. Valentine had signed up for the weekend, then stayed
an extra day, through Monday. Suez had checked out Sunday.
There wasn't anything else of interest to me in the cards for
Sunday and I gave them all back to the clerk. He said he didn't

know where the Clarks would be, but I might try the pool or bar. Trying the bar seemed like a dandy idea—I hadn't had a drink all day—so I headed for it immediately.

By the time I reached it, I had seen several more guys dressed in outfits identical with the clerk's. I had thought it more than passing strange when I first lamped it on him, but other things had been on my mind then. Now, though, it became apparent that this was sort of an official uniform for the employees of Desert Trails Guest Ranch, the clerks and waiters and bellhops and bartenders, all of them.

They all wore white trousers and sporty off-white shoes with tasseled bows, white turtle neck sweaters and brilliant scarlet jackets. On the left breast pocket of each jacket was a gold-embroidered wagon wheel. They looked just about as much like cowboys as they did like Watusi dancing boys, but I had to admit they looked striking.

They were striking, too. If you got one step out of line they'd strike you right in the teeth. This I knew because I recognized some of them. I would estimate that I'd seen a dozen to fourteen of those resplendent cats, and so far I had recognized six of them. All six had either been in prison or were almost sure soon to make the grade. I started thinking about leaving, even though I hadn't done all I'd come here to do.

I honestly hadn't thought when I'd driven in here that there was real danger of my getting shot full of holes or otherwise given a one-way ticket to limbo; this was a very public place filled with responsible and irresponsible citizens, and even though I'd known in advance that numerous hoods would be present, I hadn't thought it likely that they would work me over, or under. But looking at the mugs on those six—and others, whom I soon spotted—I began reconsidering. None of them was at the mental level of, say, a good forger, and a couple were not even at a mental level, but rather at a decided slant. Whitey, for example.

I spotted him after I'd reached the bar. I ordered a bourbon-and-water and asked the bartender if he knew Dr. Clark. He did, but said he hadn't seen the doctor this afternoon. I turned to look over the view in and around the pool. But between the bar's end and the pool, on a rectangle of grass, were a couple of small tables and several chairs, and there at the tables were several beefy guys and two or three wispy ones. Whitey was standing at the edge of the group, his profile toward me. We had met, sort of anti-socially, a time or two and neither of us had any use for the other. I didn't know what he would do if he turned and saw me; but I knew I would prefer it if he didn't see me at all, because he just wasn't charming.

In fact he was quite a bit less than charming. Whitey was slow, vacuous, fleshy, and when he grinned it was like a giggle. His lips looked as if they had been designed only to slobber, and he had a face that looked fermented. The name he'd been tagged with didn't tell much about him, but I knew the lad. It was said that Whitey stuck pins in people and noted with mild amusement the effect on their waxen images. He pulled wings off flies and then ate the wings. He wrote letters to himself in invisible ink. He should have had his head in a splint. He was a heavy, a torpedo, a man who killed for money, a killer for hire, a wiper. He was the kind of man juvenile punks-with-knives want to grow up and be like. And they make it. He was an unsolid citizen, and I didn't enjoy being this close to him.

Or this close to some of the others, for that matter. Sitting down was another heist man named Albert something-or-other, who loved to sap people and was called, for fun, Albert Anesthesia. Standing by him were a couple of torpedoes named Jabber and Shortcake, and two others I didn't know. Jabber was a mean-looking guy now wearing one of the gay red-and-white outfits, and thus obviously employed at the ranch in some unusual capacity. Unusual for him. Any kind of non-violent employment was unusual for him.

While looking at all that menace, I had finished my drink, so I ordered another. I intended to wander down to the far end of the bar out of sight of all of those characters, but some sudden activity among them caught my eye.

Shortcake whispered into Jabber's ear, then bent down and removed one of his brown shoelaces. Jabber moved unobtrusively over to Whitey and whispered in his ear. Whitey grinned loosely and, I believe, slobbered. Jabber caught the eyes of a couple of the others and pointed to Shortcake, who now had the long narrow shoestring in his hand. They all grew facial expressions of fiendish delight.

I had to stop and watch. Something was sure going on here, and I was interested. It looked as if five of the six eggs were in on whatever was up, because the sixth, a short and fragile-appearing guy, had his attention on a sporty-looking blonde sporting at the edge of the pool and had missed all the signs, whispers, and muffled chuckles.

Then Shortcake yelled, *"Viper! Viper, look out!"*

The guy stopped watching the blonde and turned around with

his eyes bugging and mouth dropping open. "Haw?" he yelped.

Shortcake had bent over as if picking that shoestring off the grass and he yelled, "Snake! Viper, it's a *snake!*" Then he straightened up and threw the shoestring at the man called Viper.

It did look a little bit snakelike as it flew crookedly through the air, and a man with a good imagination might have thought it all wriggling and scaly, but Viper reacted as if it were nine feet long and rattling.

He let out a honk like a Greyhound bus, and his eyes bugged out unbelievably. I swear it looked as if he went straight up in the air for about six feet, like a man rapidly learning levitation, and he managed somehow to get practically turned around in the air. When he lit, he was running. That honk had turned into a piercing high keening sound and he just took off.

He ran into the pool and sank.

He just went down out of sight, and the five remaining hoods were about to kill themselves laughing. Shortcake fell clear down onto the grass and sat on his hind end, holding his knees and rocking back and forth choking with laughter. Whitey made pleased gooey sounds and Jabber slapped his thigh.

"Hey," said one of the men, "Can Viper swim?"

Shortcake strangled happily. "No!" he chortled. "Can't swim—" he choked some more—"a stroke!"

That set them all off again. Man, it was fun. A guy was really going to drown. Just big overgrown boys. They needed understanding. And I understood them.

This had caused a bit of commotion, especially since Viper had been fully clothed when he'd leaped into the pool. Some of the swimmers got out of the water, and a number of spectators gathered at the pool's edge.

Somehow Viper reached the edge of the pool himself, perhaps by crawling along the bottom; it was possible that the weight of iron undoubtedly under his arm anchored him down. He managed to clamber out and walked dripping toward the group of his pals again. And I have seldom seen a sadder specimen of homo sap. He was so sad he was almost tragic.

He had not been any Gregory Peck to start with, and now he was something for the book. The comic book. He was small, very small, one of the wispy ones. His eyes nearly met in the middle of his forehead, slightly atilt, with a mildly stunned expression in them, as if they had caught themselves peeking at each other. He had protruding and sort of upswept lips, the lower one gently nudging the upper, as if he were puckering to kiss his nostrils. And of course he dripped. His matted black hair dripped, his nose dripped, his chin dripped, water dripped from his soggy and loosely-hanging clothes.

He stood there with his arms at his sides and said sadly to the chortling hoods, "You did it again. Yep, you did it again." He shook his head. Then he lifted his arms from his sides and let them drop. They slapped soggily against his legs and he said, "Did it again."

The hoods howled and choked. I didn't get a chuckle out of it, largely because I was thinking that if this was what they did when they were almost deliriously happy, what might they do when they got irritated? I went quickly down to the far end of the bar.

The bartender there didn't know Dr. Clark. I finished my drink and went back into the hotel lobby again. Those two bourbons on my empty stomach had warmed my face quite a bit. No more for me here, not with the hoods so gay and the pool so handy. The clerk saw me and waved me over to the desk.

"Hey, I remembered something," he told me. "Dr. Clark and his wife are probably out riding. Forgot about it before. They go for a gallop practically every afternoon."

"On horses, huh?"

"We ain't got no kangaroos."

"I just didn't see any of the toothy animals when I drove in."

He smiled and nodded. "You drove right past them. The long low building on the left as you come in." He squinted out one of the big plate glass windows. "There's the doc now. Just coming in from the stables."

I followed his gaze and saw a tall gray-haired guy and a slim brown-haired woman walking diagonally from the stables toward the cabins. Both of them wore checkered shirts and blue jeans. I found another twenty and gave it to the clerk, saying, "I'd appreciate it if you forgot I asked you any questions at all."

He grinned and nodded, and the twenty disappeared magically, the way they always do. I went out of the front door and caught up with the man and woman a few feet from Cabin 26.

"Dr. Clark?" I said.

He and the woman turned. "Why, yes," he said in a pleasing baritone. Then he frowned slightly. "Have we met?"

"No, sir. Frankly I'm just playing a hunch. I thought you might know a man named Theodore Valentine."

His face stayed blank. "No. I don't think so."

So that was that. But I said, "He was here last weekend, when you checked in. Tall guy, dark blond hair, nice looking." I went on to describe Valentine as best I could.

The doctor smiled. "Oh, that must be the chap I treated here last Sunday. It always happens on vacations."

"Treated?"

He nodded. "Yes. For an overdose of sleeping pills."

Bang, there it was. Sometimes you can travel a thousand miles, spend two weeks working, and come up with nothing. I'd driven a little over a hundred miles, asked half a dozen questions, and got it all. I felt good.

I said, "You have no idea how interesting that is to me, doctor. Would you mind telling me a little more about it?"

"Not at all, Mr. . . ."

"Scott."

"Come inside, won't you?"

He introduced me to his wife and the three of us went into his cabin. In two minutes he'd told me all there was to it. "When you come right down to it," he said, "I didn't really finish treating the man—the house doctor took over."

"But the man did take sleeping pills."

"Entire bottle, apparently."

"How did it happen he was found alive?"

"A maid went in to make up the room, thinking it was empty, and found him." He pointed through the front window and said, "The fellow's cabin was 24 there, directly across from ours. So when the maid ran out of 24 she saw the rear end of my car in the garage here, facing her. She saw the caduceus on the rear bumper."

"That's the emblem with the snakes wiggling around a staff or something?" I couldn't help thinking of Viper when I said "snakes." I wondered if he was still out there flapping his arms against his sides and saying sadly, "Did it again."

Doctor Clark smiled gently. "Yes." He went on to say that, seeing the caduceus, she had known a doctor must own the car, so she banged on the door and told him a man was unconscious in the opposite cabin. He'd gone over there with his ever-present black bag, injected stimulant and done what he could. Before he'd finished, a couple of red-uniformed men and the Desert Trails' resident doctor had come in. He added, "The doctor took charge of the patient, and then a veritable giant of a man came in. He thanked me and showed me out."

Veritable giant of a man. That would have been Nick Colossus himself. I said, "Did you see any kind of note, doctor?"

"I'm afraid I was much too busy to notice anything except the condition of the patient, Mr. Scott." He paused. "What is your interest in the matter?"

I said, "I've been called in as a consultant on the case." That was true enough. But I didn't want to answer any more questions, so I got up.

Doctor Clark said, smiling. "Oh, you're a doctor?"

"Not exactly." I grinned. "Sometimes I patch up problems. But my operations are usually, well, sort of unusual. You might call me one of the unorthodocs."

That puzzled him just enough so I got out of there without having to answer any more questions. I just thanked him for the info, and took off. And I took off for the parking lot, because now I wanted to be far, far from here, and soon. I had what I'd come for, even full measure, and I wondered how long this luck was going to last.

I made it to the parking lot. When I was almost to the Cadillac I glanced at my watch. It was four-thirty P.M. Even if I hurried, I was going to be a little late for that visit with Coral. I warmed a bit inside, thinking of her. I wondered what it was she'd wanted to tell me.

And then I stopped wondering. That warmth in my middle turned to ice. I felt a chill sweep over my face and down over the skin of my body. Suddenly I knew what it was that had nagged at me there in the park where the kid and his killer had died, what it was that had nagged at me for brief moments since then.

I knew, because of the kill attempt there in the park when I'd met my caller, that my phone was tapped. Because of that tap, whoever had been listening had caused Dodo to be sent out after the kid and me—because we knew or had guessed that Valentine had been murdered.

But Coral had phoned me right after the kid had.

She had called; she'd talked about Valentine, too. I mentally squeezed my brain, trying to remember exactly what she'd said. But whatever it was she had told me on the phone—and I knew she had mentioned Valentine—it would all have been heard, probably recorded, by whoever was listening. By whoever had sent Dodo out to murder two of us. Maybe he, or somebody else, had been sent to take care of three, not just two.

Maybe right now, lovely, warm fiery-haired Coral was—I forced the ugly thoughts from my mind, turned and started to run back to the hotel. From here I could at least phone her, hope to find her alive and warn her. Coral had said for me to meet her at six P.M. She would be home by then, and was going to be at Magna until about five P.M. It wasn't yet five—I could still catch her, keep her from going to her house.

Because that's where they'd probably wait for her, if they were waiting anywhere. It would be in her house, ready as she stepped in the door. That phone call was suddenly the most important thing in my life. And, I thought, in Coral's.

I'd spun around near the Cad and had taken about two long strides toward the hotel. I was just getting a good start. And that's when they got me.

Chapter Nine

THERE WERE three of them. Whitey and Jabber, from among those who had been at the pool, were two; the third was a man who hated my guts, a man named Flint, gray-haired and thin, and just as hard as the name sounded. He was Nick Colossus' right hand man, his close friend and second-in-command.

I stopped in a hurry, my foot sliding over the surface of the ground.

The two from the pool stood behind me. I guessed that they'd stepped out from between cars near mine, where they'd been waiting. They had Army Colt automatics in their hands, held carelessly the way men very familiar with guns sometimes hold them; but Flint just held a cigarette between long fingers and looked at me with cold eyes. Those eyes looked more deadly than the .45's.

Flint was his real name, and it fit him. Hard and gray and rough and cold, he was. Under six feet, wiry, quiet. A face that looked as if it had just come out of the freezer, a face that was never going to thaw, with a heavy tight-clamped jaw that always looked like a vise screwed shut, and pale gray eyes as cold and moist as fog. I would have guessed that no matter what Nick might ask him to do, he would do it. Or die trying. And maybe except for Nick himself, they didn't come any tougher.

Flint spat on the ground. There was a short, unpleasant silence. Then he said to me, in a voice like ice breaking up on the river, "Make me happy, Scott. Try something."

"This isn't very smart, is it, Flint?" I said. "If I made a break you couldn't plug me here—not with fifty guests within earshot."

He didn't answer me—except indirectly. He looked at Jabber and Whitey and said, as calmly and flatly as if he were telling them to go buy some peaches, "If he acts itchy, shoot him. But plug him low. Nick wants some words with him."

Well, anybody who didn't believe he meant every word he

said just didn't hear him. I believed him. And I would have itched to death before I'd have scratched.

So Nick wanted to talk to me. We had talked before, on several occasions. Never socially, but never with real violence or anger, either. I had in the past gone after one or two of Nick's boys, but I'd never gotten anything on Nick himself, never really banged head-on into him—until today.

The last time I had seen him had been while testifying before that State Senate Committee, during which testimony Nick had merely sat quietly in the audience, staring at me. Maybe Nick wanted to talk to me, but, especially after the recent session at York Park, I didn't want to talk to him at all. In fact, if I could have listed the one hundred things I would least have liked to do right then, talking to Nick Colossus would have been about number three on the list, right after being eaten alive by buzzards, and dipped into a vat of boiling horse manure.

So I said, and meant it, "Okay, Flint. Tell the boys to stop squeezing so hard on those triggers. I'll go along to see Nick quietlike."

"I've got your word on that, Scott?"

"You've got it."

All the hoods who know me or know about me, including Flint, know that when and if I give them my word I'll keep it. I don't usually give them any words except swear words, but these boys, Whitey especially, might accidentally, *really* accidentally, bear down too hard on a trigger. It doesn't make any difference if you die of an accident or a plan, the important thing is that you have lost the world. Besides that, there was the thought of Coral in my mind. Maybe, just maybe, if I was agreeable, and easy-going, I could get out of here in time to make that call.

I didn't move as Jabber took the .38 from my holster and gave it to Flint. Flint pointed delicately with his cigarette toward the main hotel building. The two men put away their guns, and we walked right by the pool which Viper had entered so eagerly and left so dismally, on past the bar. The combo was playing *Red River Valley*, which was written for guitar and drawl, and it sounded weird from trumpet, clarinet, bass and piano. Or maybe anything would have sounded weird to me then.

We went right into the lobby, up the stairs to the second floor and a long hallway; at its end a curtain billowed inward. A babble of cocktail conversation poured from an open door a few feet away. Halfway down the hall, Flint produced a key and

opened an unnumbered door. Behind it was a steep flight of
stairs. And that told me, finally, where we were going.

I remembered the rectangular, or boxlike, protrusion perched
on top of the Desert Trails' main building, jutting up from the
roof. I'd seen it as I'd started down toward the ranch, and had
wondered what it was. It had been just about the right size for
a suite of rooms, I now realized—and I couldn't think of a
better spot to assure Nick of the privacy he considered essential.
Lieutenant Perkins had mentioned to me that Nick had spent a
fortune making sure he was safe here, assured of privacy, able
to talk freely and without fear of hidden microphones or people.

At the top of that steep flight of stairs Flint knocked, and a
voice said, "Come in."

I knew the voice. Imagine a cast iron throat and steel tonsils
and you'll have a rough idea. It was like a truck dumping gravel,
or an old Ford crashing into a pile of bricks. After all this time,
Nick Colossus and I were going to meet again, face to face. It
didn't seem likely that this would be a happy time for me.

The door opened, Flint gave me a shove, and I was inside
the room.

He got up from behind a big black desk. It was impressive.
Just sitting still Nick was impressive, but in motion he was magnificent. He was six and a half feet tall, an even six-feet-six,
and I would guess he weighed very close to three hundred
pounds. Not much of it was fat; he carried all that weight well,
and he merely looked like a small, well-knit giant.

Nick Colossus was dark, wide, graceful, powerful, and hairy.
On his head he had a big pile of slightly wavy black hair, gray
at the temples, and sticking up above the V of his open white
dress shirt was a gob of hair as thick and dark as steel wool.
He had a size 20 neck, fists like large beef roasts, and arms
like legs.

Nick stopped in front of me, grinning hugely. His teeth were
so big and strong and white they looked like porcelain-capped
caps, like teeth in the mouth of one of those horses, getting
ready to bite me. "Hello, Scott," he said cheerily. "Welcome to
Desert Trails."

"Well, you had the latchstring out, you yegg-head. I could
hardly resist your Western hospitality." I grinned back at him,
but without real enthusiasm.

He laughed and hauled off and hit me in the stomach. He
wasn't really trying to hurt me; it was just one of his playful
gestures. He hurt me.

He chortled and said, "What the hell you always calling me a yegg-head for, pal?"

"Because you're an intelligent crook. About the only one I know. I was always disappointed that you became a slob."

It was true. Nick was an intelligent guy, a big capable man who could have made his legitimate million. But instead he'd decided to do it the hard way. And that way included the services of hard boys like those I'd spotted outside, and the ones who'd brought me here.

I glanced around. It looked as if half the gang was here. Besides Flint and the two who'd made sure I accepted Nick's invitation, present were little Shortcake, Viper in dry clothes, Albert Anesthesia, and a couple of new ones. All told, there were ten of us, counting Nick and me, in the room.

It was a small room and we jammed the place. So this was Nick's hangout, his sanctum, the rooms in which he relaxed. It might even be the place in which I would get killed. I looked it over. On the left, through a partly open door, I could see the edge of a rumpled bed. This room, apparently, was an office. It was a room without frills, without fussiness. Besides the big black desk, on which were an ashtray made of twenty-dollar gold pieces, a small calendar and a beige phone, it contained only a padded leather chair behind the desk, and a leather couch against the left wall, plus a couple of overstuffed chairs now overstuffed with Whitey and Jabber, still in his giddy red-and-white uniform. The walls were smoothly paneled in walnut, the clean brown surface of the wood broken only by three small framed pictures on the wall behind the desk. On the floor was a thick brown carpet.

Nick said, "Don't sing any psalms for me, Shell. Every time I see you I get the reform ticket. You know I don't go for that straight-and-narrow pathology. What does it get you?"

"For one thing, it gets you much better company." I looked around at the miserable specimens here with us.

He laughed. "Hell, I'm a success. So I've surrounded myself with yeah men." He burst into laughter again. "Pretty good, huh?" That laugh of his was like a cement mixer going to pieces.

"Pretty lousy."

"Killed my boy today, didn't you, Shell?" He just threw it into the dialogue without any pause, without change of expression. He knew I'd shot Dodo, and there was no point now in trying to pretend I hadn't. At least that answered some of my own questions.

"You shouldn't have sent him out to hit me, Nick."

"I shouldn't have sent him is right. I should have sent three guys. Then one of them would have been sure to get you."

I could hardly believe it. Here we were talking about killing me as if it were somebody else. Somebody else I didn't like, at that. But as long as we were discussing such things freely, I figured I'd find out as much as I could.

So I said, "What decided you to tap my phone, Nick?"

"Now, don't try to pump me, pal. All I'm doing today is asking the questions."

"Come on, Nick. We've got no secrets between us. We're close. We even try to kill each other. So what's with Magna? You don't really think you can get a million clams out of Feldspen and those sharp-money boys who run Magna, do you?"

"Pal, I don't even know what you're talking about now." The way he said it, I couldn't tell if he really meant it or was just evading the issue once more. He grinned toothily again and said, "Besides which, I told you not to pump me."

He hauled off and threw one of those fist-boulders into my stomach again. It went in like a meal of knuckles and some breeze squirted out between my teeth. He wasn't trying to knock me down or rupture my appendix; Nick socked guys in the stomach or on the shoulder—the way kids will do in grammar school—simply as a sort of slap on the back. I had known him to knock people right on their tail, gasping horribly for breath, simply as a jolly greeting.

My blood pressure went up into the danger area, however. "Nick," I said slowly and seriously, "do that again and I'll slam you with one."

He looked at my balled fist and it seemed to make him happy. He said, "Scott, I'd really maul you if you tried anything disappointing like that. Besides which, the boys here would be all over you."

"That wouldn't help your lip."

Flint had walked past us to perch on the corner of Nick's desk. I said to him, "Flint, I told you I'd come here quietly. O.K., I've done it. But from here in, I owe you no promises."

Nick laughed heartily. "You crazy dude," he said gleefully. "You'd really bust me, wouldn't you? Right here."

"Swat me in the gut again and we'll both find out."

He guffawed. "You're really a crazy dude, for sure. But I like you. That's a fact, Scott. You're about the only guy I know —still living—who isn't afraid of me." He paused. "You're *not* afraid of me, are you, Scott?"

"No. But—" I hunted for the right words—"let's say you fill me with apprehension."

He got a charge out of that, too. When he finished chuckling he looked at me and said, "I'm going to miss you, pal. It's really going to seem a little different knowing you're not around any more."

He was looking down at me. Those eyes were four inches above mine, and they were clear blue eyes as hard and bright as stainless steel. His expression hadn't changed any; that was the way his eyes always looked.

It was kind of tragic, in a way, about Nick Colossus. He could have built corporations or bridges or cities, but he'd chosen to build a criminal organization instead. Up in one lobe of his brain, where there should have been a doodad, there was no doodad; something was missing. Nick was congenial, pleasant, clever and personable, and could be very good company—when he wanted to be. But his area was Southern California and his business was crime; and the desire to be top man in that business and area amounted to an obsession. Everything else was subordinated to that desire, and killing people was just one of the techniques he used in order to get where and what he wanted. He'd made it, too, because—except, perhaps, for Lou Rio—he was unquestionably the most powerful and prosperous hood this side of the San Francisco area.

No, he didn't mind killing people a bit. He wasn't really congenial or pleasant, that was just one of the faces he wore. And it was a false face. Underneath he was mean, cruel, and hard as a kick in the jaw. So when he said he was going to miss me, he was saying good-by.

I told him, "Nick, maybe you're not as smart as I figured. If you knocked me off, the job would have your signature—"

He interrupted me. "Relax. You're not going that quick, pal. You don't think I'd be careless enough to hit you here, do you? If I did it now, I'd be sticking my neck out—you probably told half the L.A. fuzz you were coming here. And I much dislike sticking my neck out. Oh, you'll get it; but not for a while."

"Then why'd you bring me up here?"

"I want to know how it happened that you came here and talked to the doc?"

"What doc?"

He said, "You know what doc. Clark, the one you just yacked with. Now, spill it, pal. What put you onto him?"

"It's no good, Nick."

"Don't be a chump. I'll just have the boys beat it out of you."

"You're not even sure of that. I doubt that they could get it out of me. They'd just mark me up—and you don't want me marked."

"Why not? The fuzz can't gas me if a couple of guerrillas work you over. No danger in slamming you around a little; just in putting the chill on you." He paused, thinking. "But you wouldn't enjoy it. Tell you what, Scott." He paused again, those bright, hard eyes on me. "I trust you. If you give me your word, that's good enough for me. So give me your word to tell me what got you onto the doc, and I'll let you go."

He turned and walked behind his desk, sat down in the leather chair there and leaned forward on the desk top. "You see, pal," he went on, "I know you were coming here to the ranch *before* you got that call about Valentine. You must have had the whole play figured fairly well before then."

That was true; Nick or one of his men must have heard me say something about it on my tapped phone. I thought back to those calls in my office. I'd phoned Feldspen and told him I was following up on a lead at the Desert Trails, I remembered; right *after* that, the kid had phoned and told me he'd seen Valentine pushed from the Madison roof.

Nick went on, "I want to know what put you onto the Desert Trails so soon. And why you even thought of talking to a doctor here at all. We both know, now, that he treated poor old Valentine—but how'd you figure it so fast? Or at all?" He grinned at me again. "Give me the whole thing, and your word that it *is* the whole thing, and I'll let you walk out of here—and I mean without any trouble. No beating, no lumps, nothing. I'll still put a bullet inside your head, pal. I wouldn't kid you. But you'll be out of here; you'll have a chance. Otherwise . . . we'll try beating the info out."

It sounded like the best deal I was ever going to get from Nick. And it was attractive. If these conk-crushers worked me over it would be a long time till I cracked a puffy eyelid. I glanced casually at my watch. It was twenty minutes until five P.M. If I could get out of here in ten minutes, there was still a good chance I could place a call to Coral before she left Magna.

That decided me, even though I realized there was a chance Nick didn't even know about Coral's call to me. In the flurry of activity which would have followed the kid's words about Valentine's murder, Coral's call right after that might have been missed. Consequently I was afraid even to mention her name to

Nick. No, I had to get out of here as soon as possible, out and able to navigate—telling Nick the deductions which had, even before the kid's call, decided me to come here wouldn't hurt much now.

I made up my mind. "You give me your word that if I spill it all I can walk out of here? As soon as I get it told?"

"You've got my word, Scott."

"O.K. It's a deal." I lined it up in my mind and started in. "Right after Valentine's death I went to the Madison. Three witnesses said they saw Valentine put something down by his feet then jump. As dark as it was at that hour of the morning, they might have seen him bend over, but they could hardly have seen him put anything down by his feet. Small item, but it was the first bit that didn't ring true. Hired witnesses would, of course, have their stories well prepared before the kill.

"There were a couple of odd points about the suicide note it-self. The letters at the end were less perfectly formed, straggling a bit, as if written by a man slowly losing consciousness. Besides that, it started out with the words, "By the time anybody reads this I will be dead"—a strange phrase for a man to use if he's planning to jump from a building. Those two points to-gether indicated a man waiting to die slowly, after taking drugs or poison—or sleeping pills.

Nick grunted. "That couldn't be helped, since he *did* write the note after taking the pills here. But it's no proof of anything. Keep it going, pal."

"I was starting to feel then that Valentine might have been murdered, Nick. But that was a genuine suicide note, in his hand-writing. Now, *if* it was murder, there seemed only one way there could be in existence a genuine suicide note: Valentine must have unsuccessfully tried to kill himself once before, and on *that* occasion written the note. It was written on Desert Trails stationery, I discovered, but with the heading cut off. Either Valentine had saved his original suicide note and used it again this morning, which didn't seem at all likely, or somebody *else* had saved the note—to make murder look like suicide. Moreover, either Valentine had written the note and then cut off the Desert Trails heading—not likely—or he'd written the note *on handy stationery* and then somebody *else* had cut off the top. Why? So nobody would connect the dead man, the apparent suicide, with Desert Trails. At that point, Nick, you were not smelling like a rose."

"Cut the comedy. What's the rest of it?"

"The letter I compared the suicide note with, the one on

identical stationery, was written from here on Sunday. Valentine said in it that he'd had an accident and would be at the Desert Trails for an extra day or so. I still didn't have proof he'd tried to kill himself here that weekend, but I sure had reason enough to come here and ask some questions about his 'accident.' And well before the kid's phone call—when the kid told me on the phone he'd seen Valentine tossed, and when Dodo shot his chin off, that was just final proof to add to what I already had." I paused. "So I came to Desert Trails. Clark was one of the two doctors here when Valentine tried to knock himself off. I talked to him and rang the bell."

"So now you know Valentine tried to knock himself off here at the ranch. But that's all you know, pal. It's the only thing anybody might prove, anyway."

"Maybe."

"Maybe hell. The rest is just your—wicked imagination." Nick grinned. "That's all of it, Scott?"

"Every bit."

"Well, you keep your word, all right. I'll hand you that."

"It would be even nicer if you'd hand me my gun. I'd like to take it with me."

Flint still had my gun. Nick looked at him and said, "He'd like his gun back, Flint. What do you think?" His voice had a nasty ring to it.

Flint said, "Well, we could give it to him one slug at a time first, and then the Colt."

Nick shook his big head, pretending to consider the problem. "No, not till I get a tight alibi set. We'll let Scott sweat a while instead." He looked at me. "Not a chance he'll get clear away from L.A."

"Knock it off, Nick. I've told it all, so stow the chatter and let me get out of here."

Nick ignored me and looked at Flint, "I'll bet you a dime," he said, "that you and the boys could beat the living hell out of my friend here without messing him up too much."

"Well," said Flint, "we could if he'd hold still. He probably wouldn't, though. He's the type would want to move around a lot."

"Hey—" I said.

"Yeah," Nick agreed. "You can count on that. But I wouldn't want him to wind up in a hospital. Got to have him in circulation fairly soon so you can fog him."

"I said, "Why, you lousy—"

Nick interrupted me again. He sounded almost charming.

"You have to admit the logical progression, Scott. First we take you out of circulation. Then we take the circulation out of you."

I stepped to one side, looking around. There wasn't a gun in sight. Just eight hoods and Nick. And me. There was no longer any doubt about it; the eight hoods were going to beat hell out of me, and Nick was going to watch.

He said, "Scott, I heard about the beef you and Lou Rio had yesterday. You know I can't let that crumb get ahead of me." He paused. "And anything Lou can do, I can do better."

I suppose I could have told him he could lie better, and any number of other dull things, but they would have had no effect on him, besides which I didn't want to talk to him, I wanted to hit him.

Flint came toward me and, on my left, Jabber took a step forward, grinning. For a moment the only thought in my mind was the thought of Coral James, but then there wasn't time to think of anything except arms and fists and legs and a swinging sap. I started to bring up my hands as I lunged toward Nick —I wanted to smack him just once, one good one, before the lights went out—but somebody behind me already had a grip on my arms.

He tried to pin my arms to my sides, pulling back on them, but I raised my right foot and slammed it down, felt the hard heel crunch into small, fragile bones of the man's instep. It felt as if my heels went right on down to the floor and the guy yelled horribly. Without looking around I slammed my right arm back, driving my elbow into the man's gut, then brought it forward as I took a step toward Jabber. He and Flint were almost on me, side by side. I cocked that right fist, looked at Jabber as he bobbed his head to the side—and slammed my fist into Flint's cold, frozen face.

His head snapped back, mouth coming open, lid cut and already red-smeared. Jabber jumped at me, and somebody hit me from behind. A pair of arms grabbed me. I jerked free and lunged toward Nick, Nick behind his desk looking gleeful, and there might have been murder in my heart. Something hit the side of my head, something solid and heavy, and for a moment my muscles just stopped working. I fell, seeing Nick's big, heavy, laughing face as I went down to one knee.

I scrambled forward and managed to get to my feet again. Jabber was close on my left in his red and white uniform and as I came up I came up swinging my left hand. I kept the hand open, fingers straight out, and the edge of my palm

slammed underneath his chin. I could tell from the solid satisfy-
ing thud and the ache in my hand that he was through for the
day.

Somebody was pounding on me. Fire blazed in my ear. I
tried to turn, swinging, and from there on everything got very
blurred; whatever happened just blended together. It didn't
last long, but a lot of things happened in a few seconds. All the
time I was trying to get closer to Nick, but I didn't make it.
I didn't ever really have a chance of making it. But everybody in
that room knew I tried.

I saw Flint coming up off the floor, raking the back of one
hand over his mouth and smearing a streak of blood over his
cheek. He wasn't hurrying. He just came up off the floor, cold
eyes fixed on me, and that was all I saw of him.

Somewhere in my consciousness was the thought that even
though Flint was in the fight again, at least Jabber and whoever had first grabbed me from behind were out of it. So that
was two down. Then wispy little Shortcake appeared in front of
me trying to hit me with something in his hand, and I stepped
toward him, grabbed his descending arm as I swung a hip into
him and bent over hard, flipping him across my hip and into the
middle of a flabby boy I recognized briefly as slobbering
Whitey.

I guess I'd been hit so hard by then that although I was still
on my feet I was practically out of my head, because one dizzy
thought actually flashed through my addled brain: Wouldn't
it be astounding if I cleaned up on *all* these guys?

Well, I was right. It would have been astounding.

But I had hit so many people, and it seemed there had been
so many bodies *besides* mine on the floor, that I thought maybe
I was winning. The fact was that all along I had been losing.
I'd got in a few good licks, but the real bites were on the
opposing side. For a moment, though, one glorious moment, I
felt that I was really going to half murder all eight of these
bums, throw Nick through the roof, and simply eat my way
through the walls and out.

Which goes to show what happens when you get too cocky.

I spun around and all I could see was the sap descending. I
didn't even see who was behind it. Just the sap. It seemed frozen
in air. I could see the soiled leather and the little stitches along
one side, just about like those which would probably be taken in
my head. But it wasn't really frozen; it just seemed that way. I
spun around with the light of battle in my eyes—and then the
light went out.

But I had a wonderful moment there. From the time when I thought, Wouldn't it be astounding if I cleaned up on *all* these guys? until I swung around and that sap smacked me, there was a full tenth of a second during which I felt absolutely invincible. There aren't many moments in life like that, let's face it. It was a grand tenth of a second. My real regret was that it couldn't last a couple of weeks or so.

But no, just a sudden uprush of invincibility, and then: Sponk! It got me smack in the middle of the forehead, right at the hairline. And that was all of it. The lights went out, and I could feel myself falling through darkness, with things still smacking into me from all sides.

I wasn't unconscious; I only wished I was unconscious. I could still feel guys pounding on me, smacking me—and crazily and incongruously out of a television commercial came a phrase about a facial dressing that was like "a thousand busy fingers on your skin," and that sure seemed to describe what was happening to me. This wasn't just one fist, or two, but at *least* a thousand busy fingers, and it wasn't such a great feeling after all. Besides, this was more of a facial *un*dressing. With thoughts like that in my head I knew I had lost the battle, knew that even if these slobs didn't actually kill me I would probably be left permanently addled, and the worst of it was that I could still hear Nick's cement-mixer laughter.

Then there was another blow, a good one squarely on the top of my head, but it must have been cushioned by the fat up there because it felt as if somebody had patted me with a pillow. And a pillow seemed appropriate, because right then I went to sleep.

The next thing I knew, I was dreaming. It might have been a minute later, or a day later, I couldn't tell, but I was suddenly struggling, trying to get up, and there was this dream. . . .

Chapter Ten

I SWAM through pain. It was like a sea, tangible and visible, and I learned that the color of pain was a darkness of black and gray and red and muddy blue. I swam through it, forcing one arm after the other through the dark colors that burned like acid. I reached the surface of that sea, and above me in a black sky huge birds soared. One came close and I saw that it was an angel with black wings and a face of unutterable loveliness, with pornographic eyes, deep dark brown eyes, a wonderful nude body gleaming in an unearthly light. Then I knew it was Coral, and with that knowledge something happened to the vision, as though in an instant everything inside her turned into nothingness, and suddenly then the smooth skin of face and body crumpled upon my hands as I reached for her.

I sat up. Dizziness swept over me, and my movement sent sudden throbbing pain into my head like blows inside my skull. Coral, I thought. What was it about Coral? I remembered the fight, the hoods pounding on me. I remembered, but I was still too filled with aches and dizziness to think clearly about it.

It was dark. I didn't know where I was. I cradled my head against my arms, breathing deeply and slowly until my thoughts cleared. Then I looked around. I'd pulled myself to a sitting position, and was sitting on the cold ground. Near me the grotesque shape of a saguaro cactus raised its spiny arms toward the clear sky. Beyond it I saw the outline of an automobile, undoubtedly my Cad. I looked up.

Orion wheeled slowly up there, clear and beautiful in the black sky, perhaps the most beautiful of all the constellations. Once I had looked through a friend's telescope at the nebula in Orion's sword, and its magnificence had never left my mind. Now, sitting bruised and battered in the desert, I felt suddenly out of joint, out of place on a world out of place in the universe. I must have been beaten on every inch of my body, and my head apparently banged lopsided, because for an awful instant it seemed, as I looked at the three dim stars of Orion's belt, and the dangling sword, that I must be insane to be here, beaten by Nick's men, bloodied with killing, when there were such things as the nebula in Orion.

I got to my feet—and that brought sanity back. The ripping, tearing pain of movement brought me back from wherever I'd been. A hundred yards away a car ripped the night open with its headlights. As a guess, that would be Highway 60, the car racing toward L.A.

I thought for a moment again of that black angel in my dream, then clamped my teeth against the pain and walked toward my car. You don't really have any idea how many muscles and nerves and tendons you have until a large number of them get pounded on. I figured that I must have approximately seventeen million which had been mangled, each one screaming its small, faint cry of pain, all of it blending into one symphonic *ouch*. Automatically I felt under my coat for the Colt Special. Naturally the gun was not there.

I made it to the car—it was my Cadillac, all right. The keys were already in the ignition; everything was quite convenient for me. So I guessed that Nick had been telling the truth about at least one thing—that I would be free to roam around the earth a little while longer before it was time for me to leave it. At least I was still alive. Or, rather, half alive.

I got into the car, found a mashed pack of cigarettes in my pocket and lit one. Every drag of smoke into my lungs seemed merely to join smoke from the fire already down there. I had been knocked around by Lou Rio and his punk Gangrene, and then by Nick's hoodlum crew, and now there was a hot, ugly anger deep in me. It was a suppressed violence simmering in my belly, a strange, ugly kind of heat, and I didn't like it in me.

I started the car and drove to the highway; it was 60. I swung right toward Los Angeles, and stepped on the gas. At a service station I stopped and phoned Coral James, let the phone ring and ring again until I knew there would be no answer, then hung up and went back to the car.

Coral's house was bright, lights burning inside. I rang. The front door was partly open. I rang, then went inside.

"Coral," I called. "Coral?"

There wasn't any answer. A light was on in the kitchen, and I walked to its door and inside. On the gas range sat a saucepan half filled with cold soup. A table in the kitchen had one place setting arranged on it, but there was no food on the table.

It seemed evident that Coral had been preparing something to eat when she'd been forced to stop. I felt numbed and ill at the thought of what might have happened to her.

For a moment I saw Coral, not as she'd looked the last time I'd seen her, but as she had appeared to me when she'd stepped through Feldspen's door and I had seen her for the first time, with an amused smile on those wise warm lips and laughter in her hot brown eyes. And in the next moment I thought of what Nick's man, Dodo, had done to the kid who'd phoned me just before Coral had called, saw him again in the dirt with blood spilling from his nose and mouth.

I walked through the empty house. In an ashtray I found the thick heavy ash from a cigar. In the bedroom I got a look at myself in a mirror. The corner of my mouth was swollen and there was a nasty welt on one cheekbone. At least I didn't have any black eyes. So I looked just about as beat-up as I normally do. I also looked like a man ready to commit mayhem on practically anybody who got near me.

I left the house and went directly to the Spartan Apartment Hotel. I felt exposed, uncomfortable without the gun under my coat. And I carefully checked the area around the Spartan before getting out and starting toward the entrance.

It didn't seem likely that Nick's boys would be out for my blood this evening—his reasons for letting me leave the Desert Trails in the first place still were valid ones—but there were also Rio and Gangrene roaming the night. I knew that Gangrene would toss several slugs into me if he got the chance, and it seemed likely that Rio would be right alongside him urging, "Hit him again, Ganny, shoot him in the ear this time."

I went into the Spartan and started up the stairs. Nobody shot at me, and I was just beginning to relax a little.

"Shell."

The voice came from behind me. I spun around—and there she was. Coral was getting up off one of the lobby divans, looking just as lovely as those black-winged angels of my dream, but warm and alive, smiling, that softly rippling hair bright as a flame around her head.

She stepped toward me. "Shell," she said, "where have you been?"

"Where have *I* been? What the devil do you mean, where have I been? What happened to you? I was just at your house—"

I choked it off. Relief washed over me, and the sudden pleasure at seeing her paradoxically sharpened my tongue, made me snap at her. I could have grabbed her and shaken her, and at the same time I wanted to hold her close and tell her how happy I was that she was here, now, alive.

"I'm sorry, Coral," I said finally. "I thought you were—I was afraid you'd been hurt. Badly, maybe."

She'd stopped in front of me. Looking up at me she said, "What happened to your face? Why, *you've* been hurt. You've been in a fight."

Somehow that remark impressed me as very funny. Maybe my relief at seeing Coral accentuated my reaction, but I laughed aloud. "Yeah," I said, "sort of. Eight hoodlums took turns beating on my head like a drum. I think they ruptured my mentality. Lady, you have no idea how good you look to me."

"Eight hoodlums?"

"Yeah. Come on up to my apartment and I'll show you my fish. I thought you were a black angel, bleeding."

"Are you out of your mind?"

"No, it's bruised a little. But I'm still in it. Come on up, honey, and I'll explain. We can both explain."

"Fine. Something very odd happened to me."

We went up to the second floor and down the hall to my apartment. I turned on the small lamp inside the door, then the lamps over the two fish tanks. Coral ohh-ed and ahh-ed appropriately at the gorgeously-finned *betta splendens,* the neons and other colorful tropicals, and then we were settled on the chocolate brown divan before my fake fireplace. She curled her lip at Amelia, my sensually fleshed nude with the big bazooms and the fantastic fanny, who is nearly as colorful as the tropical fish— all women curl their lip at Amelia for some reason, but I think she's wonderful.

Then I said to her, before she could tell me how disgustingly earthy Amelia was, "What happened to you? I just left your place, and something was cold on the stove—"

"Vegetable soup," she said. "That's all I'd begun fixing when they came."

"Who came?"

"Two men. It was really odd. You remember I called you and asked you to meet me at six?"

I nodded.

"Well, I was calling from Feldspen's office, and he told me I could go on home. There was a change in the shooting schedule, and I won't be needed until tomorrow. Anyway, I went straight to the house. Then I tried to call you again but couldn't reach you."

About that time, I thought, I was in York Park.

She went on, "Around four o'clock I started to fix a little snack to eat. I went into the front room and saw a car go by slowly, and the man who wasn't driving was looking at the houses—for the addresses, probably. They slowed down in front of my place, then went on. I didn't think anything about it then, but a few minutes later I saw two men coming toward the house, and one of them, the taller one, was the fellow I'd seen in that car. He was a very rough-looking man, too. There was something about them both that frightened me."

"That's understandable. They probably frighten each other."

She looked puzzled. "You know who they were?"

"No, not yet. Just what they were—go on and finish, and then I'll explain."

"In front of the house one of them said something to the other and they split up. The tall one went around toward the back. Well, I really started getting scared, Shell. I don't know how to explain it, but they just acted—well, menacing."

"That's explanation enough."

"I went to the back and the tall one came toward the door. It's all overgrown there, with trees and shrubs, so hardly anybody can see in from the neighbors' places even if they try, and he must have felt protected enough. Anyway, he took a *gun* out of his coat and did something with it, then came toward the door."

Coral looked at me wide-eyed, living the moment over again, her mouth partly open and red lips glistening. "I didn't know what they were after, but I knew there was something awful about them. He hadn't seen me, and I took off my shoes and carried them, and ran to the bedroom. There's a window there at the side of the house."

Her voice rose a little as her throat tightened, thinking of it again and telling me what had happened. "The other man was ringing the bell—at the front door. I—I felt like screaming. I suppose it's silly, but I had the most frightening conviction that they were going to kill me." She took a deep breath and managed a smile at me. "Isn't that crazy?"

I said, "No, Coral, you were probably right. I think they were going to kill you. At least that was probably one of their alternatives."

She gasped. "But they couldn't . . . kill me?"

"Either that or force you to go with them, for no telling what. Go on."

"That's about it. He rang the bell a couple of times but then he just came in. I heard the door, heard him come inside. I had the window open by then. I crawled out and went through Mrs. Watkins' back yard and Mrs.' Fellows' too, and then ran a couple of blocks to a phone booth and called a taxi. I came here, and I've been here ever since."

"I'm glad you did honey. I just wish I'd been here when you arrived." I thought about that and added with feeling, "Boy, *do* I wish I'd been here." I reached up and felt the lumps on my head. It felt as if there was one big lump with several smaller ones on it, and the big lump was my head.

Coral said, "I thought you'd know what to do, Shell. And I was scared." The way she said it, and the way she looked at me when she said it, combined to make me feel at least eight or nine feet tall.

"Ah, well . . ." I said.

"Why would those men want to kill me? And what happened to your face?"

"The whole thing started with your call, honey—or just before it. A guy named Nick Colossus had a tap on my line." I paused. "All this is making me thirsty. I have been lying out in the desert, under Orion, and I do need a drink. How about you?"

"Orion? Shell, you've said so many strange things since you got here—yes, I'll have a drink. And then you must explain about the—" she frowned delicately as she thought back—"the eight hoodlums, the black angel, and Orion. What do you have to drink?"

"All the standard items, and if I don't have your choice I'll get it, even if you drink fermented cherimoya juice with cocktail pickles."

She bent forward chuckling throatily. "Now I know what it is I like about you. You're unintelligible. Do you have Scotch? And water?"

"Coming up."

While I mixed the drinks and gave her one I explained what I'd been doing—and having done to me—this afternoon and evening. And why the two men undoubtedly had called on her. "They'd have been more careful," I added, "except that they didn't think you were there. You weren't supposed to be home till five or later."

"Then if I hadn't come home early, they'd have been there . . . waiting."

"That's the way it would have been."

She shivered and swallowed some of her highball.

"I still don't know why you called me in the first place, Coral."

"Oh, of course. It hardly seems important now." She sighed heavily and smiled at me. "It's just so good to relax, Shell. Finally. I was all keyed up until you arrived."

"Kick off your shoes. Do anything you feel like doing. I can't think of anybody in the world I'd rather relax with."

She didn't say anything, but her smile got momentarily wider, and deep in her eyes a flame flickered. Then she said, "The reason I phoned you was because of what you told me about Ted early this morning. His suicide. I wanted to think about it, but then I knew I had to tell you—I promised you I would when I was more sure, remember?"

"I remember."

"I told you, too, that somebody tried to blackmail me once. Well, I think it was Ted."

"You think? Don't you know?"

She shook her head, her hair flowing like a pale red wine under the lights. "Several months ago Ted called me to his office and talked to me about a big publicity campaign Magna was planning for me. This was just before *Sins of Pompadour,* and I didn't have any big credits. He said that while I was virtually unknown, by the time Magna completed their publicity barrage I'd be a star—and hundreds of reporters and columnists would be digging into my past. He stressed the fact that if there was anything in my past that I wouldn't want made the common knowledge of a hundred million newspaper readers, now was the time to try to bury it, to hide it some way."

"Uh-huh. And he was the boy who could help you, right?"

"Yes. He said if there was anything, anything at all, I should tell him. Then, with the Studio's resources and power and connections they could cover up almost anything. I told him there wasn't anything to cover up. He said I shouldn't be afraid to tell him, no matter what—*if* there was anything I didn't want made public. He even mentioned that the studio had been able to hide things for other employees. One who was addicted to narcotics, a girl who'd had an illegitimate child."

She paused, sipped at her drink. I said, "Did he name these others?"

"No. He might just have been making them up, so I would tell him my background—my horrible background, if I had one."

"In other words, information that *could* be used for blackmail."

"That's right. At least that's the way it appears to me now. And there's one other reason, one thing that made me suspect

Ted of being party to blackmail, although I was never sure. He was so persistent that I told him . . ." She let it trail off, eyes on me.

"Something you'd rather not tell me?"

"No, it's all right. I told you somebody tried to blackmail me, but didn't succeed. I—well, I was married before. When I was sixteen. It only lasted three weeks, just long enough so we both knew it was no good. I've never denied being married once, and I won't ever deny it—but I've never been asked." She shrugged. "I never denied the studio's version of my biography, either. I guess now I should have. Well, it wasn't just the marriage, but my husband's—record. He was several years older than I. When we split up and were divorced, he got in with a tough crowd and committed some crimes. Robberies. He got caught, went to prison, got out and did it again and got caught again. He's in prison now." She looked at me. "There it is. I wouldn't pay anybody a nickel to keep it quiet. But I told Ted about it."

"It's starting to form a pattern. Once he got all he could from you—or anybody else, things that normally would be kept in the dark—he put the squeeze on you for money. Is that about it?"

"Yes, only it wasn't Ted. A nasty little man approached me a month or so later. By then he had photostats of the marriage license, court proceedings, prison record—all of it, very thoroughly prepared. He showed it to me and tried to make me pay off."

She paused and I asked, "What did you tell him?"

"I just slapped his face. Every time he opened his mouth I slapped him. So he left. I got one more phone call from him a few days later. He said if I didn't pay he'd publish the information. I told him to go ahead. I didn't hear any more about it."

We had finished our drinks. I carried the glasses to the kitchenette and said, "It's a good thing you didn't stick a knife in somebody's gizzard, for example. That would have required more drastic action than slapping a punk's face."

"Fortunately I didn't stab a single gizzard."

I mixed two more drinks and walked back to the divan. Coral looked as lovely as anybody who has ever been on that low, long, voluptuous divan, and that includes almost as many curves as there are in geometry. I stopped a yard away and looked at her. She was relaxed against a thick cushion, hands clasped easily behind her head and legs extended in front of her, taut and heavy breasts rising gently on her slow breath.

"Coral," I said, and grinned at her to keep it light, "I would be keeping the truth from you if I failed to tell you that you are perhaps the loveliest creature ever to warm that divan, and this heart."

"How sweet you are." She smiled, teeth gleaming whitely in the soft illumination from the small lamp and the tropical fish tanks. "Are we all through with the case?"

"Not quite. But here, for the juiciest tomato I've seen in a long time, is some more tomato juice." I grinned at her and handed her the Scotch and water.

She shook her head and smiled, sipped at the highball.

We went over Valentine's technique again. It seemed that he must have told the third person about the info Coral had given him, and then the third person had performed the actual black-mail routine. Coral explained that she felt sure Valentine was the one responsible because she'd told nobody else those facts about her past. There was about one chance in a hundred that the blackmailer had stumbled on the information from another source, but it wasn't at all likely.

I said, "This guy who approached you, Coral. The one you slapped. Do you know yet who he was?"

"No. He was small. The kind of extremely close-set eyes you never expect to see. Sparse black hair." She went on to describe him as best she could.

I got it then. "And his lips look as if they're wrestling, with the top one losing."

Her eyes widened. "Yes. How did you know."

"Viper," I said. "A hood called Viper. I saw him today; he jumped into a swimming pool with his clothes on. And he works for Nick Colossus." I thought about that, then said, "Honey, we've not discussed the spot you're in." I had explained to her what that tap on my phone meant, and I told her, "You're prob-ably in extreme danger from now until half the hoodlums in town are locked up. You simply can't be wandering around."

"Oh? What will I do, then?"

"Well, uh—" I swallowed, and moistened my lips, and said casually, "you, uh, why, you, uh—you could stay here!"

She laughed. "And you'll get a room at the Hollywood Roose-velt, I suppose."

"Oh, no. No, no. I'll—I'll be here too. To protect you."

She didn't say anything. Not with her lips. Her eyes spoke volumes, volumes that would probably have been banned in many places, but certainly not in my apartment.

I said, "I'll sleep right here on this big old comfortable divan.

And you can have my bedroom. Believe me, it won't put me out at all."

"That's what I'm afraid of."

"But—no. That's—I mean to say, anywhere but here a dozen thieves and musclemen might grab you. Here you'll be safe."

"It doesn't sound very safe to me."

"You know what I mean."

"Uh-huh."

I finished my drink. And we just looked at each other. For, I suppose, a long minute or more. Finally I said, "Well, shall we have another highball?"

Slowly she shook her head. "No, Shell. I don't want to be drunk. Or even dizzy. Just in case."

"In case what."

"In case you should kiss me."

"Then stop drinking. Because I'm going to kiss you."

"I know. I stopped ten minutes ago." She smiled. "I didn't even finish my second drink."

All the light in the room seemed gathered in her eyes. They shone on my own eyes, on my lips, and her own lips curved sweetly. I looked at her glass on the low cocktail table, and it was nearly full. Odd that I hadn't noticed before.

I said, suddenly serious, "I'm glad you're here, Coral. I'm very glad."

"Me, too," she said. "Me, too." Her voice washed over me. Her breath caressed my mouth. She was only inches away, just inches and a dozen heartbeats. I looked at her for another moment, and then I leaned even closer to her.

She came into my arms as if she belonged there, as if she intended to stay, and I put my arms around her and held her to me so tightly that it must have seemed she had no choice at all about staying. But she didn't appear to mind. Her face was close to mine, her lips slightly parted, and she said, smiling, "You're crushing me, Shell. But . . . I don't want you to stop." She turned her head and the fiery hair brushed my cheek, then she looked at me with those pornographic eyes, those hot, wonderful eyes, and said softly, "I . . . don't know what to think of you. And me. And of—"

"Then don't think."

"All right—I won't." She closed her eyes and the full, rounded lids trembled slightly and she tilted her head a little more to the side, lips parting, and her arms tightened on my back, fingers of one hand curling against my neck.

She started to say something else then, but I don't know what it was. I wasn't ever going to know what it was, because my lips stopped her breath, buried the words in her soft throat, and she didn't even try to speak them again. Not for a long time, at least. And then I'm sure they were different words.

I didn't say anything else to her either then, except her name. Just "Coral" after our mouths parted and her lips touched my throat, "Coral" as her hair blinded my eyes, and again as my lips found the warm white skin of her breast. Just "Coral," and secret things.

Chapter Eleven

No MATTER how many times it's done in movies or books, or how many times it really happens, it never gets old or too "cute" or anything but delightful. I refer to the sight of a small-to-medium girl in a big man's pajamas.

The girl was Coral who, while not large, was certainly not medium anywhere, and the pajamas were pale blue covered with red and white orchids, and they were mine. Even in those tent-like pajamas, though, Coral looked as if she'd gone to Girl School and graduated at the head of the class. Where the pajamas fell against her, she seemed to lean or even thrust against the pajamas, and it was reasonably certain that they would never be the same.

It was a sure thing that I wouldn't.

She was seated at the breakfast booth in my small kitchenette, smiling lazily at me. I turned from the range and advanced toward her carrying my two bowls.

"There you are," I said, placing one bowl before her and one at my place opposite her. "How does it seem not having to cook breakfast?"

"Wonderful," she said. "I'm startled that a big rough character like you is capable . . .what *is* this."

She was looking down at the bowl before her. "Why that," I said grandly, "is breakfast."

"This is breakfast?"

"Sure. I have it every morning. When I have anything. It's lousy. Try it."

"But what is it?" She had a sort of wary look on her face as she stared at the stuff.

"Mush. It's the only thing I know how to cook."

"Mush?"

"Yeah. Oatmeal. Mush. You just boil water and pour the slop in and let it bubble. Then you eat it. Go ahead, have some."

"But there's only a bite or two there."

"How much do you want? I told you it's lousy."

Morosely she had a spoonful. I had some of mine. We weren't off to a laughing start. She looked across the table at me and said, "It is lousy."

"I told you."

"Have you got . . . well, would you mind if I—do you have any eggs, Shell?"

"I've been saving a couple for nogs. Want me to scramble them around in a pot—"

She shook her head. "No. No, I'll—scramble them around myself if you don't mind."

She went to the refrigerator and then the range, and in a minute there was the sound and smell of eggs frying. I didn't watch. Eggs just kill me in the morning. Somehow it doesn't seem civilized to eat eggs until about noon or later—and by then it's time for rare prime ribs.

Coral came back and sat down and had a great time with her fried eggs, and the conversation got livelier, more rewarding. It was a lot of fun; Coral was a lot of fun. I wished I didn't have to leave; but I had the feeling that this was going to be a big day. Not that I'd had any lack of big days lately.

Over coffee I said to Coral, "I've been thinking seriously about whether you should stay here or find a secluded hotel or motel someplace. I think it will be safer for you here."

I had some coffee and added, "My apartment might not seem like the safest spot for you, if Nick's boys are trying to grab you. But at least nobody can know you're here—you arrived while the two muggs were waiting for you at your own place."

"That's right. And I can't very well go back there, can I?"

"Nope. There's a good chance somebody's watching your house, but more important, there's just as good a chance, probably better, that somebody has an eye on the Spartan here now. Not for you; for me. But if that's true and you left then you'd be spotted for sure. No, I think you should stay here."

"Your logic overwhelms me." She smiled sweetly. "Besides, Shell, I like it here."

We finished our coffee and I went into the living room while Coral did the dishes. I smoked a cigarette and thought about a few things. It had occurred to me that, if Valentine had elicited damaging information from several Magna people—under the pretext of wanting to cover up the info—and had then used that knowledge to blackmail them, then one of those blackmailed people might have found out about it and murdered him. That would have seemed an obvious conclusion to me, except for the fat kid's story to me on the phone. I wondered about that for a while. One of the things, obviously, that I needed to do today was talk again to those three witnesses. If I could find them.

I picked up the phone and called the Madison Hotel. The desk clerk informed me that Mr. and Mrs. Gene Gelder had checked out yesterday. No forwarding address. I looked up Peter Fishbaum in the book—or tried to; there wasn't any such person listed. Information had no number for him. I considered the peculiar unavailability of all three witnesses, then phoned Feldspen.

"Harry, Shell here."

"Ah, Shell. Are you all right?"

"Yeah, to a jaundiced eye I'd look okay. Why?"

"After you phoned yesterday morning I expected to hear from you again."

Had that phone conversation been only yesterday morning? It seemed like last September. I said, "Things happened. To me. Sorry I couldn't make it, Harry. Anything new? Any more calls from our greedy friend, or trouble with Lou Rio or Gangrene?"

"No. I haven't seen those two since the altercation here in my office. Have you made any progress?"

"Yes, but I've got to pin a few people down today and get some straight answers, then I'll know exactly where I'm headed. The whole thing's shaping up pretty well, I think. I'll be out to talk with Palomino and Suez after a bit."

"That's an odd thing. Suez hasn't arrived yet. Neither has Coral James."

"Oh?" It was just a little tingle, a trickle of alarm along my spinal column. "Suez would ordinarily have arrived about eight, wouldn't she?"

"Ordinarily much earlier than that, for makeup and wardrobe. But she was expected at eight today, for publicity stills. My secretary phoned her apartment about twenty minutes ago, but there was no answer. We haven't been able to reach Miss James, either."

That tingle raced over my spine again. "I'll check it," I said. "I know where they both live. Palomino arrived O.K., then?"

"Yes. They'll finish retakes on *Howdy, Stranger* tomorrow." He sighed. "We've over three million in that one now."

I told him I'd get in when I could, and hung up. I would have liked to ease his mind about Coral, but I wasn't about to do it over the phone. Not after what had happened yesterday, and where there was a chance this phone might be tapped, too.

Coral came in and sat on the end of the divan. "What was that about Suez?"

"She hasn't arrived at Magna."

"I wonder why?"

"That's what I hope I can find out this morning. Do you know much about her? Or Palomino?"

"I don't know Johnny at all. Suez and I get along well. Lunch at the commissary often, that sort of thing. All I know about her, though, is that she's wonderful company. She seems like an awfully nice girl. I like her."

"You know," I said slowly, "Valentine named you, Suez, and Palomino as the three stars he thought must be the ones referred to by the blackmailer, the guy who called Feldspen, as the ones *being* blackmailed. Do you see what I'm getting at?"

"No, I don't." She leaned back against the arm of the divan, looking as fresh and lovely as morning, but almost lost in the folds and creases of my pajamas.

I said, "You told me last night that Valentine was undoubtedly the man digging up blackmail info from the victims—that is, from those who would then *become* his victims. If so, he would know better than anybody else who the three being blackmailed were."

"Yes, of course."

"I put Valentine in a spot where he knew he either had to name the three of you himself, or let Feldspen and me find out on our own. So he decided right then to spill the names. The true names—it's obvious on the face of it that the blackmailer knows who's being blackmailed."

She nodded slowly. "But, then, why did he name the three of us?"

"I would assume that Suez and Palomino must have been paying off. But that doesn't explain his including your name."

She frowned slightly. "I . . . it is odd. The only thing I can think of is that he knew I was *supposed* to be a victim. So maybe he just included me for that reason."

"Maybe." It sounded logical enough. I was working it over a little more when the phone rang. I grabbed it and said hello.

"Shell? Is that you, Shell?"

I felt sure I recognized the voice. Those warm, smoky tones sounded like Suez. "Yes," I said.

"This is Suez. Shell, you've got to help me."

"What's the matter? Where are you?"

"I'm at 1854 Partridge Street." She was speaking softly, almost whispering. "I came here to meet Nick Colossus, but when I got here he was—"

The line went dead.

I blinked stupidly at the phone, then jiggled the hook. The connection was broken. I didn't understand; what could Suez have started to say? I remembered the address, but she'd gone there to meet—Nick Colossus. Nothing she might have said could have sounded more like trouble. And what had she meant to say.

I got slowly to my feet, putting the phone back into its cradle. Coral said, "What's wrong?" but I didn't answer her. I was trying to think.

Suez had said quite a bit in those few words. But the most important words had been "You've got to help me." That meant she'd been in trouble; and now, with that phone suddenly dead, it seemed like bad trouble. Maybe even fatal. Nick Colossus and fatal trouble seemed to go together.

Nick—his name rang an alarm bell in my brain. But I stopped debating about it—there'd be time enough for that on the way out there. I could make up my mind on the way what I was going to do; the important thing now was to get started.

I felt for my .38 but, naturally, it wasn't in its accustomed place under my coat. Then I remembered the gun Palomino had kicked from Gangrene's hand in Feldspen's office Monday afternoon. I'd brought it home with me that night and put it in a dresser drawer in the bedroom.

I jumped to the bedroom and grabbed the .45, stuck it into my coat pocket and then said to Coral, "I've got to leave. Don't answer the phone, or even the door unless you know it's me."

"But what happened?"

"That was Suez—I'll have to explain later." I went out the door and down the stairs three at a time and was in the middle of the street before I remembered it would probably be wise not to leap into view so casually and without even a look around. But nothing happened; nobody was in sight. I started the car and took off in a hurry.

I raced to Wilshire and Hight, breaking all the laws, tramped on the accelerator for a mile and then swung onto Willow. Suez didn't live on Partridge Street. Why, I wondered, would she have been there at all? Why meet Nick?

Gangrene's big automatic was heavy in my coat pocket. I took it out and cocked it as I drove, thumbed on the safety and placed the gun on the car seat beside me. As I swung into Partridge with the tires screeching on the asphalt, I caught the number on the corner house. This was the thirteen-hundred block. That meant five blocks to go. In the eighteen-hundred block I slowed and checked the house numbers, caught the number 1854. It was a big frame house, solid, recently painted a charcoal gray. A tall TV antenna reared up from the roof.

I drove on past and took a right at the corner. There had been no cars in front of the house. None even near it. And that seemed strange. If Suez had come here to meet Nick, where was her car? She might have purposely parked it out of sight, but I was leery of this, jumpy. She'd said of Nick, ". . . but when I got here he was—" And that had been all.

I hoped she'd started to say he was dead. That would suit me just fine. But it seemed too much to hope for. I took a right at the next corner, parked at the curb and got out, .45 in my coat pocket. Looking toward Partridge Street, a block away now, I could see that tall TV antenna sticking up into the air. I headed toward it, walking alongside a brown house that needed painting. It seemed strange, unreal, to be walking through somebody's yard like this in broad daylight, hand on a loaded gun in my pocket. It was cold daylight, with thick clouds overhead.

In the backyard of the brown house a woman was hanging clothes on a line. She stared at me belligerently, her eyes asking me what right I had to go tromping around back here. At the rear of the property was a dirt alley, then the backyard of the charcoal gray house.

A little boy sat in the alley's dirt. He looked at me and said "Hi." Friendly, smiling. I wondered if the sour washerwoman was his mother. My heart was pounding and my throat was getting dry. Something was really wrong; I felt it. I made it to the gray house, paused at the back door and listened. There wasn't any sound. Just neighborhood noises, a car passing nearby on the street. The sun went behind a cloud again and it seemed colder.

I tried the door. It wouldn't open, but it was only a screen door with a small latch inside. I put my left hand against the doorframe, pulled slowly and steadily with my right hand. The screw tore out of the wood and the latch fell against the door with a light tinkling noise that sounded like a gunshot in my ears.

I pulled the door open and went inside. As I shut the door silently behind me I looked back the way I'd come. The sour woman was at the corner of her property staring at me. Her mouth was open. I waited a few seconds to let my eyes adjust to the comparative darkness, then moved into the house. This was a small, neat porch. A wooden bench with a box of detergent on it was against the right wall. I pushed open a door into a kitchen, the .45 in my right hand now, safety off. All I had to do was squeeze the trigger. There were two doors leading out of the kitchen. I walked over blue linoleum, past a gas range with a coffeepot and big frying pan on it, tried the door on the right. It opened with a soft, high squeak. I let go of it, and it swung open another twelve inches, silently.

Directly outside the door was a narrow hallway. Across the hallway was an open door. I could see something inside that room, but I couldn't yet tell what it was. There wasn't a sound except the jarring thump of my heart in my chest and the rush of blood in my arteries hissing in my ears. The room across the hall was a bedroom. I could see the foot of the bed, the bedstead; all the way across the room, against the wall, was a chest at the base of double windows with yellow shades drawn over them.

My eyes grew accustomed to the dimness in here and I could see the interior of the bedroom more clearly. Something was crumpled on the floor. Something—or someone. I waited a moment longer. Still there was no sound in the house except those I made, none at least that I could detect. I moved forward slowly, crossed the hall. Sweat from my palm made the checked butt of the Colt automatic a little slippery in my hand. I gripped it tighter, finger light on the trigger.

Then, at the door to the bedroom, a delicate scent brushed my nostrils. Jasmine. That sweet, delicately feminine odor. Suez had worn Jasmine. I remembered her saying in her dressing room, "You get a whiff of jasmine, Shell, you look around for Suez."

I almost turned my head, but I didn't. I kept looking at that form on the floor—I could tell now that it was a body—straining my ears to hear if anyone else were in this house with me. Suez was—or had been. There was another odor in the house, too; and only now, oddly enough, did I realize that it had been in my nose and mouth ever since I'd stepped into the kitchen. Gunpowder. The sharp, acrid smell that hangs in the air after a gun has been fired.

I stepped into the room. It was a man's body on the floor. I took another step forward, glancing around. Nothing moved; nobody was in sight. The door to a closet in the wall on my right was nearly closed. I glanced over my shoulder; the open doorway behind me was empty.

I took another step toward the dead man—and then alarm jangled through every nerve in my body like a sudden electric current. I don't know if I heard a sound behind me, or maybe just felt the air stir. But I bunched the muscles in my right leg and drove my body forward. Whether I heard anything or not, I saw the man's face on the floor, and that told me everything, all at once, with a shock that slammed understanding into my brain and galvanized me into motion.

The man was dead, unmistakably dead. I had been thinking of what Suez had said about Nick Colossus. So I had been prepared to see him. But the dead man wasn't Nick.

It was Lou Rio.

Chapter Twelve

I MOVED fast, but not quite fast enough.

The blow fell, but when it struck I was moving forward, leaping over the body. It missed my head and slammed into my shoulder, deadening it suddenly, and my left arm and hand went numb.

My foot landed on Lou's dead hand and my ankle turned. I fell onto my side as I tried to twist around, straining to see who was behind me.

The fall saved my life. I sprawled on my side, but squirmed around in time to see Jabber's twisted face just as he shot at me. The last time I'd seen him he'd been among those beating on me in Nick's room, and he'd been wearing one of the red-and-white uniforms; but even though he was in a dark suit now I recognized his mean, hard face the moment I saw it. A sap swung from Jabber's right hand, and the gun flamed in his left.

The bullet snapped past me, and then I had my right arm raised, the automatic tight against my palm. I had to make the first shot good; if I didn't, I was dead. Jabber wouldn't miss again, not even left-handed and hurrying the shot. The gun kicked in my hand, the heavy crack slamming against the walls of the bedroom. My slug caught Jabber somewhere in his body and jerked him violently. My second shot went right through the top of his head at the hairline. He flew backward, dead in the air, and fell hard. His head smacked the base of the bedroom wall—right next to the open closet door, where he'd been waiting for me.

I got to my feet in a hurry, and as I got up I glanced at Rio, touched him. He lay on his back, blood staining his white shirt in two places, more blood spilled down the side of his head. The stains were still spreading a little, still moist; he was warm. Rio had been killed within the last few minutes—probably, I thought, about the time I'd received Suez' phone call, or even since then. Suez—I started to wonder about her, then forced the thought from my mind; there was no time for that now.

I turned toward Jabber and saw something that puzzled me. The gun he'd fired at me lay on the floor near the wall, but another gun was stuck into the waistband of his trousers. Something about it worried me oddly, but it wasn't until I stepped to him and grabbed the gun that I understood why. It was a .38 Colt Special with a two-inch barrel, and—there was no doubt at all—it was mine. My gun, the one Nick had taken from me yesterday at the Desert Trail. It had been fired.

And that made everything clear enough. There was no gun near Rio; the little automatic with which Jabber had just tried to kill me was undoubtedly Lou's own gun. Jabber had tried to sap me first, too, instead of just shooting me in the back—and that fit the now obvious plan. If Jabber had managed to knock me out, he would then, I felt sure, have shot me with Rio's gun and put my own gun—from which the three bullets had undoubtedly just been pumped into Rio—in my right hand or next to it. Jabber would then have taken off in a hurry, leaving two dead men in a neat frame. With bullets from my gun in Rio, and a bullet or two from his gun in me, it would have been an open-and-shut double killing.

Only seconds had passed, but already I was jumping toward the kitchen again. My thoughts were racing as I tried to fit the rest of this together. There'd been no sirens yet. And that puzzled me. I was missing something. The frame had gone sour, so far, but I knew there was something I was missing.

Sudden sound banged against my ears. It came from the front of the house and as I landed in the middle of that hallway I could see the front door crash open. In a split second I saw half a dozen things—clear out in the street a car was already stopped, angled toward the curb, and another was sliding, with tires shrieking, to a stop beside it. In the doorway, at least four or five men were trying to charge inside. I recognized the guy in front as a hood named Snails Sullivan, one of Lou's men, and right behind him was a real bad one, a mean one, the man I least wanted to see now, or for quite a while.

Gangrene.

I was holding the .45 automatic in my left hand, my own gun in my right. Snails raised his arm as if pointing at me. I didn't even see his gun. But I heard the gun crack, and the bullet snatched at my left arm. I felt the hot sting as the metal ripped flesh, and the .45 clattered to the floor. I flipped up the .38 and squeezed the trigger twice, and Snails stumbled and fell.

Gangrene spotted me then, recognized me. He let out a yell and jumped forward like Death in a hurry to happen—to me. That ugly, bony, corpselike face was pierced by a hole in its middle, a hole that was Gangrene's mouth, and from his mouth the yell burst and swelled. He just let out a harsh roaring sound and charged at me.

I pulled the .38 onto his chest and squeezed the trigger—and the hammer clicked on an empty cartridge.

Behind Gangrene the other men were piling inside; a couple more shouts went up from them. But I saw them from the fringes of my vision, all my attention focused on Gangrene. As he got one step closer he flipped up his hand, a hand filled with gun, but before he could squeeze the trigger I jumped for the kitchen door, shoving my useless Colt back into its holster.

Even while pain seared my left arm and I slammed my foot against the linoleum, the realization flashed through my brain that this had really been set up, this had been a near perfect one. The sweet part of Nick's frame—because naturally this one shouted Nick Colossus, this was the way that smart, murdering louse would do it—was that he wasn't framing me with the law, not with the cops. He'd set this up to frame me with the *hoods*. To frame me with *Lou's* men. It was even possible, I now saw, that Jabber might have been going to merely sap me—leaving the killing to Lou's gang.

And it looked as if it was still going to work. Not one of these boys so close to me now would ask a single question. They'd just take turns pumping me full of slugs.

I landed in the middle of the kitchen, alongside the gas range. My eye caught that big frying pan and I grabbed it as I passed. When I skidded to a stop I turned toward the door behind me and started throwing the heavy pan before Gangrene even came in sight there.

But he wasn't about to slow down when he had me so close to dying, and I let go of the thing at almost the instant when he slid into the open doorway and tried to come in after me. The pan hit him low, about at the belt line, and it bent him over. I didn't wait to see what happened next, I was going out the door. I made the back door in two jumps, caught the wooden bench with one hand as I went out and threw it into the middle of the floor.

There were all kinds of yelling hell behind me, shouts and stamping feet and roared curses. I ran like a man possessed, like a man trying for a three-minute mile—and that's just what I was doing. The little kid was no longer in the alley's dirt.

But the woman was still in her backyard. As I spotted her a shot cracked out behind me. It didn't really mean much to me at this point. I was beyond emoting, past reacting, practically a rocketing zombie.

But it meant much to the babe. She screamed. It was a beauty. It came from both big toes and gained volume with every inch up, bursting from her mouth like an air-raid warning. And that was only the start. That was just the first one. The second one topped it by ten tortured eardrums. Windows must have cracked in nearby houses. But by the time the second scream ripped from her horrified throat I was at the Cad, and in it, and then on my way.

I heard another shot—but that was the last one. I slapped the steering wheel left at the corner, barreled three blocks and skidded around the next corner to the right. In two minutes more I knew it was over.

For now. But not for long.

There were probably forty or fifty men, I guessed, who worked for Lou Rio all of the time or part of the time. Heist men, muscle, union goons, hired gunmen—professional killers. And all of the heavy boys, all of the punks who carried guns would be carrying them. Just in case they might get a peek at me. They would all be out for my blood, out to kill the man who'd killed their boss. It didn't make any difference whether or not they'd liked Lou Rio personally—probably few of them had—but he was theirs, their kind. He was the boss.

And, too, he was not just a hood, but the big one, Lou Rio himself. No matter which little punk killed me, he would instantly be much bigger. It would be a real feather in the cap of the one who got Shell Scott.

I couldn't stay away from all of them indefinitely. Besides which, all of Nick's men would be ready, willing and able to put a bullet in me if and when a chance offered—because that would make all of Lou's boys happy. And the police would naturally assume that one of Lou's boys had got me. No, it seemed fairly certain that I wouldn't last. I just hoped that, before it happened, I could kill Nick Colossus.

I stormed into my rooms at the Spartan. Coral stepped back, saying, "I knew it was you, Shell, but I was almost afraid to open the door. You sounded so . . . so fierce."

"Come on. We're getting out of here, and fast."

"But you said it might—"

"I know what I said, but it would be worse to stay here now

than to take a chance on leaving—it's the lesser of two evils, so shake a leg." I ran into the bedroom, yanking off my coat and shirt. The bullet Snails had tossed at me had dug a nasty slice in my left forearm; it was painful, but not disabling, and I tore off a piece of my white shirt and wrapped it around the arm; that would do until I could get to the first-aid kit in the Cad. I started climbing into another shirt and a dark sports coat, and Coral said, "What happened, Shell? What's the matter with your arm?"

"I'll tell you later."

"Where are we going?"

"How in hell do I know?" I yelled at her. Then I calmed down a little and said more quietly, "I'm sorry, honey. Just take my word for it: We've got to move, and fast. A lot of guys are now so anxious to kill me that some of them are practically sure to come here. Ordinarily they wouldn't—but things have changed, believe me. So get whatever you need. Now, move."

She moved. Without another word, with no argument, she trotted out of the room. In half a minute she said, "All right. I'm ready."

"Come on." I led the way out and to the Cad. I didn't even have to stop for extra cartridges, because there are always some boxes in the luggage compartment of my car—along with a few thousand dollars worth of equipment I've used at one time or another in my job.

Coral slid into the car and I got behind the wheel, tore away from the curb. I pulled all the usual routines for shaking a possible tail, including going the wrong way up one-way streets and timing my approach to intersections so I was the last car through before the light turned red. When I was satisfied that we weren't followed I started looking for a motel. We'd left all the downtown L.A. hotels behind. When I spotted the Oasis, a sprawling, expensive-looking motel complete with coffee shop, pool, and palm trees, I pulled in and parked before the office.

"This is as good as practically any other place we might find," I said to Coral. "Believe me, honey, I'm sorry for this mess you're in. I know you were in a mess before today, but it's worse now. So, you'll simply have to stay here for a while."

She smiled and said, "Oh, shut up," but her tone and her smile made the words caress.

Ten minutes later I had paid for two of the Oasis' cabins and Coral and I were alone in number 18.

"My cabin's number thirteen—worse luck," I said.

"You're not superstitious."

"No, I just wanted eighteen."

She laughed softly. "Well, you can't have it. This one's mine, and I'm greedy."

"So is the owner. These cabins rent for no more than the cost of a small house. I asked the chap if at that price he could give me a pair labeled 'His' and 'Hers' but he only scowled at all my money."

"You are paying for these, aren't you? I feel kept. Are you going to keep me?"

"As long as I can."

She smiled. "Really?"

"Really." I looked around. "Not bad, what? Curtains on the windows and everything." I noticed that Coral had suppressed a yawn. "You're tired," I said.

She smiled. "I didn't get much sleep last night. And I could use a shower and a nap."

"I've some phoning to do. And thinking. So—off I go. Au revoir, adieu, pip-pip."

"All that? How far off do you go?"

"Just to thirteen. Call me if you see any flying saucers, or for any other reason that seems urgent."

"Why don't you call me instead, Shell? Say in a couple of hours. We can have dinner together."

"Dandy. Anything but mush, hey?"

"Anything but mush."

And with a last pip-pip I went out. This one, this Coral James, got right inside a man and stayed there, sweet and warm and comfortable. She'd started right out like a gal who'd been growing on me for quite a while, and then she'd just kept on growing. Two hours it would be; I looked forward to the dinner. Unless something new occurred, I wasn't going to be doing much else until quite a bit later this evening.

And I had a lot of thinking to do about what had happened today. I had to figure exactly how I'd gotten into this mess—and, more important, how I was going to get out.

An hour later I crushed the empty cigarette pack in my hand and lit the last smoke, lying on the double bed in the darkness of my cabin. I still didn't see a way out; in fact, the hole seemed to be getting deeper. The only possible way out seemed to be through Nick Colossus. And Nick, I knew, wouldn't cooperate at all.

But it was increasingly clear that my only hope now lay in getting to Nick. I was in so deep that unless I broke loose with a real splash, a complete unmasking of Nick and absolution of me, I wouldn't last long among the living. All of Lou's hoods now wanted to kill me; and all of Nick's hoods would have been ordered to kill me; and when the police got through checking the slugs in Lou Rio and Snails Sullivan, *they* might want to kill me. At least they would for sure greatly desire my presence for a chat. Not now, and not for a while to come, did I want my presence known to anybody—except Coral, of course.

For the most of the hour I'd been worrying the angle of how I might get to Nick, get him to hang himself with his own words and actions. I had just about decided it was hopeless. The only possible way for me to get Lou's hoods off my neck, I figured, was to have Nick personally tell them that he had killed Lou and that I was innocent as a babe. That would clear me not only with them but would explain to the police how my bullets got into the two corpses. And there was just about as much chance Nick would kindly do that for me as that he would turn into refined sugar.

There was perhaps one chance in ten that I could get into Nick's top-of-the-hotel hideaway where he spent most of his time. That was the one place where Nick would talk freely, spill anything and everything—to me, and to me alone. But there was absolutely no chance at all that I could get in there with a recorder, say, or microphone, draw Nick cleverly into confessing everything, and then get out. Not alive. And even if I could catch Nick somewhere else—he would never talk willingly in any place but that hideaway of his—and beat the truth out of him with a club, that wouldn't accomplish what I wanted. For my purpose, Nick would have to, freely and willingly, of his own accord, confess to or brag about his crimes—including the frame of Shell Scott and murder of Lou Rio.

That might do it. And if I flapped my arms, I might fly away up into the air. I gave up. There just wasn't any way to manage it.

The phone rang, but it was only the operator reporting there was still no answer at Suez' number. I thanked her and hung up. And right then it happened.

I don't know why it was then instead of another moment, but instantly, out of the blue, I knew I had it. There *was* a way to ruin Nick, to clear myself, get out from under. It was a staggering, complex, crazy idea, but at first it seemed more crazy than anything else. I got excited, rolled off the bed and stood up in the darkness, thinking. I smacked a fist into my palm. I actually thought it would work.

It was wild and complicated and dangerous—the odds were at least four or five to one that I would be killed in the first two minutes—but if it worked it would be a thing of beauty. It would be a classic, a wonderful, a near-perfect triumph of the law over the lawless, of good over evil, of me over Nick. At least that's what I told myself, and I was grinning in the darkness.

I turned on the lights, found pen and paper in a drawer, and spent five minutes playing with it. Then I used the phone and called Harry Feldspen at his home. I made him leave the house and go to a pay phone—just on the off chance his phone was tapped—then I gave it to him. He interrupted me seven times in my first run through the thing. But then he listened to it once again and when I said, "Well?" he said, "It's . . . impossible."

"You don't sound so sure this time, Harry. And what the hell do you mean, impossible? Is this the man responsible for the destruction of Atlantis, the discovery of America, and *Sins of Messalina?* Tell me again it's impossible."

He was quiet for a full minute, maybe more. And when he spoke again it sounded to me as if the president of Magna Studios was grinning. And he swore—mildly—for the first time in my hearing. "Hell no," he said, "it's *not* impossible."

I sat down on the edge of the bed, feeling good again. Feeling optimistic, hopeful, very much alive again. We settled all the details which we could settle now, and I told Harry how he might handle the rest of it. I described Nick's rooftop hideaway and added, "I'll need a helicopter so I can drop into Desert Trails and surprise dear old Nick. Do you want to charter one for me?"

"All right . . . ah, Shell. This is going to be fabulously expensive."

"Yeah. Well, you know that fabulous fee you said you'd pay me if I saved you five million or so—or even the one million?"

"Yes . . . ah, yes."

"O.K. I'll match you. Double or nothing. You pay for setting this up, which would just about double my fee. If it works, you save a million minus my fee and expenses. If it doesn't, well, Harry, you won't have to pay me."

"Well, of course I won't." He sounded indignant. "You'll be dead."

"Yeah. That's the nothing."

A little thought about that overcame his objections. While he was agreeable, I said, "And, Harry, I'll need something noisy . . .

how about one of the sound tracks in your files down there. What I'm after is something which will attract plenty of attention."

"I'll take care of it. What else do you want?"

"Let's see. A collapsible ladder. You might tape the sound track and fix me up with a good powerful recorder. Have to be battery operated."

"And portable, of course. All right."

Harry was brisk now that he'd made up his mind; he would do everything possible, I knew, and do it well. I thought a minute, then gave him the names of ten or twelve people I wanted to include in the payoff of the plan, if there were any, and he didn't even protest at the names of hoodlums and policemen.

When we'd settled everything there was little for me to do but wait. I hung up and looked at my watch, and I grinned again. It had been exactly two hours since I'd left Coral. Talk about timing—Nick Colossus had nothing on me. I phoned Coral, then went to cabin 18. She wasn't hungry; neither was I. And I understand people can go without food for days.

No wonder I was doing all that grinning. I had plenty to grin about.

Chapter Thirteen

I OVERSLEPT in the morning. But, then, I'd had very little sleep for the last two nights, and I'd been even busier in the daytime. Besides which I had been beaten up, and shot, and generally ruined. I probably wouldn't even have awakened at ten A.M. except that Coral phoned me.

"Hi, Tiger," she said.

"That's me. But my meow is worse than my bite today."

"Could you bite some breakfast?"

"Sure. How about some mush in bed—ah, that would be pretty mushy, wouldn't it? Well then, why not prime ribs? You have the primest ribs—"

"Shell! Go back to sleep."

"I'll be normal. Just don't send me back—"

"You'll never be normal. I'm dressed and hungry. If you're here in ten minutes you can take me to brunch at the coffee shop."

Despite my aches and stiff muscles and much groaning, I made it in nine.

During the morning I spent some time on the phone. I was unable to locate Suez, who, Feldspen informed me, hadn't shown up at Magna today, either. The three witnesses to Ted Valentine's "suicide" were still unavailable—quite possibly several states away by this time. After noon I called Homicide's Lieutenant Rawlins, to whom I could talk without his sending two or three squad cars after me. He took my number, and a few minutes later called back.

"Chum," he said, "I couldn't talk in the office, and I won't be able to chat with you after this—in fact, if I see you I'll have to bring you in. It could mean my job if I aided and abetted a fugitive, you fugitive. So this is more than fair warning."

"Yeah. Thanks. What's up?" I had a good idea, but asked him anyway.

"There's a call out on you because of those slugs in the two stiffs on Partridge Street. There's a lot of pressure to get you in here."

"I'll be in. Only not immediately."

"Sure. I guess you know the slugs we took out of Rio, and out of Snails Sullivan, were identical .38's."

"I had a hunch."

"I thought you would. We've released the information to the press that both Snails and Rio were killed by bullets from the same gun. We did *not* say it was Shell Scott's heater, but you know we've got a couple of slugs from that .38 of yours here in Ballistics, don't you? Dug out of other bodies long ago."

"Uh-huh, I know, Rawlins. Look, I put the pills in Snails to discourage him from killing me. I did *not* put the slugs into Lou. Somebody else did that with my gun. And that somebody was either Nick Colossus himself or one of his boys."

And right then it hit me. Lou's boys would have been reasonably sure all along that I had killed their boss, but the presence of Jabber's body there with him might well have confused the issue. Now, however, they would know that whoever had killed Snails must also have killed Rio—since the police themselves admitted the same gun had been used on both men. And Lou's boys, including Gangrene, had *seen* me use that gun to toss those bullets into Snails. There could now be no possible doubt in their weak minds that I had positively and absolutely killed Rio. I had been feeling like a man in deep water with busted water wings, but now I felt as if I were going down for the third time.

Rawlins was saying, "Nick did it, huh? We'll go right out and put the arm on him."

"Funny. But maybe I can pin it on him for you."

"Yak, yak," he said in what I considered a nasty tone. "More than four thousand of us haven't managed that in ten years. But you'll kindly do it for us."

"Stranger things have happened."

"Not this year."

"Well, you see, Rawlins, I am a man with stupendous confidence. I believe in the Magic of Believing, the Science of Mind, the Power of Positive—"

"Nuts. You do it, chum, and I'll do a coochie dance in the Police Building cafeteria at high noon wearing pink tights."

"Is that a promise?"

"It's a promise." He paused. "You might be interested to know that Lou Rio's funeral is already scheduled. Three P.M. this afternoon. They're putting him away in a hurry—and it's cremation for Lou."

"Cremation, huh? Merely anticipating the devil, I'd say."

"Yeah." He told me that the police had also been trying to find those three witnesses to Valentine's death, but without any luck. Then he added, "One other thing might interest you. There's a little hood named Arthur M. Worthington, does odd jobs for Colossus. Radio car spotted him down at McGannon's this morning, and he ran from them."

"McGannon's? What would one of Nick's men have been doing at the mortuary where *Lou* is? There's no love lost between those two gangs."

"I know. It's funny. Ordinarily Nick's boys would stay twenty miles from McGannon's. Anyhow, this Worthington ran away from the radio car, into McGannon's, then out a side door and smack into a car—new Buick driven by a young gal who got hysterical. Said her husband would never believe a pedestrian ran into her."

"Where was she driving? Up on the lawn?"

"No, where she should have been. Viper just blasted out of the building and clear into the street—"

"*Who?*"

"Viper. Arthur M. Worthington to you."

"No, Viper to me." I described the guy I'd seen at the Desert Trails and Rawlins said that was the man. It was also the man, though I didn't mention it to the Lieutenant, who had tried to collect the blackmail payoff from Coral James. I started getting a little excited. This could be the big crack in the case, the break that would save my neck.

"Rawlins, take my word for it, I've got to talk to that little mugg. Where is he now? He's not unconscious or in the can, is he?"

"No, but you won't be able to talk to him, I'm afraid."

"He's in custody?"

"No, it's not that. And he's conscious, too, but he's not talking. He can't. Hasn't moved or said a word since he banged into that Buick."

"Could he be faking?"

"I don't know. But the doc doesn't either. Paralyzed and dumb, that's the ticket. Can't move and can't talk."

I swore. Viper just might be the man who could tell me, if not all, then at least much about the frame I was in. And, of course, about the blackmail attempts against Coral—and maybe against Suez and Palomino, possibly others. If nothing else, he could tell me plenty more about Nick and Nick's habits, as well as the setup of those rooms above the Desert Trails—info of great importance to me if I went to the Desert Trails tonight. Because, unless I found out a great deal more than I'd found out so far, I meant to walk in on Nick in his own rooms this evening. Anything Viper could tell me would be as welcome as a stay of execution to a condemned man.

"I've got to see that guy, Rawlins. Where is he? And can I get to him without being picked up?"

"You can probably manage that part—he's at the Cowley Memorial Hospital on Western. But it won't do you much good if he can't talk."

"No, but if he's faking . . . well, I'm a pretty good doctor myself in treating that syndrome."

"Yeah. Watch yourself."

I told him I would, thanked him, and we hung up.

I phoned McGannon's. The services for Lou Rio were, as Rawlins had said, scheduled for three P.M. in the Chapel, after which there would be a procession to the Woodstream Cemetery for another short service, followed by cremation and inurnment. I was talking to a man named Weston, and I asked him, "Isn't that a little unusual? Procession and the second service, I mean?"

"Yes, indeed," he replied softly. "Extremely so, when there is a cremation. But the gentleman insisted. He wanted *all* the trimmings, he said."

"This gentleman, Mr. Weston. Did he look as if the vampires had just rolled him?"

"What? Vam . . . what?"

"Skip that. What was the man's name?"

"Trumbull J. Bidewell." He described Trumbull in his own way, and it was the late Lou Rio's right-hand man. Arthur M. Worthington and Trumbull J. Bidewell. I think I preferred Viper and Gangrene. I thanked Mr. Weston and hung up.

It looked as if I would have relative freedom of movement until about four P.M. That was the one thing in my favor today. Every hood who could be presumed to be or have been a friend or employee of Lou Rio's would be present at the upcoming services. That meant, at least, that they wouldn't be out hunting for me, or even roaming around town where they might lamp me.

Then I called the Cowley Memorial Hospital. I have in the past made it my business to have at least one good contact at every hospital and sanitarium in and around L.A., as well as in most offices where public records are kept and numerous other places. At Cowley I had two, a nurse and a staff doctor named Fraley. I managed to get in touch with Fraley and through him arranged to see the patient, Arthur M. Worthington in half an hour.

I got ready to go, then dropped by cabin 18. Coral opened the door. "Hi, honey," I said. "I'm taking off, and I'm probably going to be plenty busy all afternoon, and maybe into the night. Just thought I'd better let you know."

She smiled. "Don't forget where I am."

"I'll more likely forget my name." I paused and hunted for the right words. "One thing, Coral. If I don't bang on your door by tomorrow morning sometime, well, you're on your own. Call the cops and bring them up to date."

Her smile went away. "Why wouldn't you be here tomorrow? Do . . . you mean something might happen to you?"

"Dear girl, I am going to be driving in freeway traffic. Anything may happen."

"You're going to do something dangerous, aren't you?"

I grinned at her. "Not if I can help it."

"You are. I can tell." She was quiet for a sober moment, looking at me. "But I don't suppose you'd talk about it." She reached out and took my hand. "Come here."

She gently pulled me through the doorway and inside, then pushed the door shut, put her arms around my neck, pressed her wonderful body against me, and pressed her sweet lips to mine. She kissed me the way women kiss their men when they're going off to war, the way lovers have always kissed at final partings, the way we had not kissed before. It was a kiss with warmth but without passion, with a lingering and clinging tenderness.

We let each other go and she said softly, "You'll come back soon, won't you?"

I couldn't help it. She looked so woebegone and forlorn that I said, "I've changed my mind. I'm not going to leave."

"Oh—*you*—"

She started to swing a hand at me, but I warded it off, grabbed her and gave her a quick kiss, and then told her good-by and went out the door. When I looked back, she was smiling. That, I thought, was better. If I came back . . . and even if I didn't.

Dr. Fraley was in his early thirties, slim and brisk. He wore horn-rimmed glasses and his forehead was deeply creased with worry lines. We stood outside Room 28 on the second floor of the

Cowley Memorial Hospital; inside Room 28 was Arthur M. Worthington—the Viper.

Fraley said to me, "He's not my patient, but I've talked with Simondsen—the physician who looked him over. The patient might be dissembling, but we haven't proved it."

"Give me a chance and I'll prove it."

He frowned at me through the glasses. "Now, Scott, we can't have you socking the patient. I suppose that's what you mean to do."

"Socking? No, I'm not going to put the slug on him. I'll just squeeze him a little here and there, poke him a bit."

He shook his head. "But he might really be paralyzed. There's this point, too. Even if there is no true organic damage, there might be psychic trauma, a mental block."

"He's always had a mental block."

"I mean to say, Mr. Worthington may in fact be speechless and paralyzed as a result of the *shock* of the accident. Without organic damage."

"The character you call Mr. Worthington is known to crookdom as Viper. He is a hood, a punk, a parasite on the anatomy of society, biting deeply."

"Nevertheless, he is a human being."

"That's open to question, too. Well, let me see him, and I promise not to hurt him."

He nodded, opened the door, and we went inside. Viper lay unmoving on the bed at our left. In the far wall was a big closed window, and looking through it I could see two nurses in white uniforms walking across the green grass one floor below us. The doctor and I walked to the bed and looked down at the patient.

His eyes were open. They moved. At least his eyes weren't paralyzed. Those extremely close-set eyes lit on me and stuck. They were a little atilt to begin with, but they seemed to cross even more and get an even more stunned expression in them. He seemed unable to pull his eyes from me, then he closed his lids. I saw his eyes move back to center under his lids, like small moles trotting across his brain.

"Hello, Viper," I said. "You remember me."

No reaction. The lids stayed closed.

"Shell Scott," I said. "The boy Nick chose as his patsy. So he could get rid of Lou and pin the job on me. What were you doing down at McGannon's, Viper?"

No comment. I poked him a time or two, here and there, but nothing happened. Even if he wasn't paralyzed and dumb, I had to get him somehow into a mood in which he would hunger to tell me all he knew. There was so much I had to know, and so much he could tell. And I had to be sure he told me the truth, too. Just casual conversation between Viper and me wouldn't do.

I tried a while longer with notable lack of success and then Fraley and I went back into the hall. He said, "You see how it is. Without being actually inhumane, practically monstrous, it would be difficult to determine whether or not he is dissembling."

"Yeah. But, doctor, everybody has a weak spot. If you can hit it, guys open up like Chinese puzzles. If only . . ."

And there it was. Into my mind had leaped almost eagerly the picture of that hamburger stand and roadside zoo I'd passed between L.A. and the Desert Trails. And a picture of Viper, dripping wet.

"Doctor," I said, "I've got it. I know how to find out for sure if that boy is paralyzed and speechless—and I won't lay a hand on him."

"Oh? How do you propose to accomplish this?"

"If you had a guy with claustrophobia and you put him in a closet, he'd talk just to get out, right? Well, by the same token, Viper is so named because he's afraid of snakes."

"Snakes?"

"Yeah. I saw him practically faint and leap smack into a swimming pool all because of a shoestring he thought was a little bit of a serpent."

The doctor frowned. "So?"

I grinned. "So how do you think he'd react to a fourteen-foot python?"

Chapter Fourteen

IT TOOK me nearly fifteen minutes to win Doctor Fraley over to my side. And the price of two or three appendectomies. But I won—mainly because come hell or high water I wasn't going to lose this one. I knew Viper could tell me plenty, and now I knew the way to get him talking with great eagerness. If he didn't die immediately.

And, of course, if he wasn't *really* dumb and paralyzed.

Doctor Fraley looked sort of ashen as he said, "All right. I won't inform on you. But I refuse to have anything to do with it. I'm not even going to be in this wing of the hospital."

"O.K. And I'll take full responsibility."

He frowned. "But how can you possibly induce them to bring the snake here?"

"Leave that to me. Maybe I can't, but I don't think I'll have much trouble there. All I ask is ten minutes here, alone with the patient."

"All . . . right. You must *never* tell anyone that I had anything whatsoever to do with this."

"Agreed. You will admit that this should make the man spill his guts."

"He may simply spew them out his mouth." He paused. "You do realize, don't you, that the shock might kill him?"

I shrugged. "We'll have to take that chance."

He clapped his hands to his head. But despite his vow that he would be in another wing of the building, he stuck around. He seemed fascinated, as if hypnotized by the sheer horror of what might be going to happen.

I made a phone call to the Roadside Zoo. I got the owner, who also was owner of the snake. I told him I was calling from the Cowley Memorial Hospital and that the snake was needed at the hospital. I didn't tell him a thing that wasn't true. I did need that snake at the hospital. I told him that I was em- powered to pay him five hundred dollars for one minute of the

snake's time, but that mainly he would be doing a great service.
I think the five hundred dollars convinced him—people who
keep snakes and monkeys and things like anteaters in cages
usually are more concerned with the money to be made from
them than with the desires of the snakes and monkeys and
anteaters.

But still he hesitated. His name was Jarvis Beeler, and he
said, "I'd have to put him in a crate and get a coupla men to
help me bring him along. It sounds sort of goofy, don't it?"

"That's what they said about Freud, you know. And they
laughed at the Wright Brothers, didn't they?"

"Yah, I guess they did, huh? What kind of operation is it
you need Oscar for?" Oscar was the python's name.

I told him the truth again, but tried to sound like a doctor.
"There is a recalcitrant patient here at the hospital. My diag-
nosis is that he is feigning. If this is a valid assumption, and
it may be—who knows?—the situation calls for shock treatment. Time is of the essence, it is fugiting, and as this patient
has a deep-seated trauma, virtually a psychic abhorrence, with
regard to the genus *Python,* I feel that the prescription is—
Oscar."

"Yeah, well . . . I guess you know your business, Doctor."

"Of course I do!" I said sharply. "How many times must I
tell you I *need* Oscar?"

"Shock treatment, huh?"

"Yes, it should be *quite* a shock treatment."

"Won't hurt Oscar, will it?"

"There is virtually no chance that it will hurt Oscar. He,
uh . . . he won't eat the patient, will he?"

Mr. Beeler laughed gayly. "No, he don't never eat people.
Besides, he just et. He'd ruther sleep."

"Fine. You'll bring him in immediately then?"

"Five hundred bucks, huh?"

"That, certainly. And the chance to be of great service to—
well, certainly to me personally. And . . . let's say service to
more than you know."

He said slyly, after some thought. "Science, huh? To science?
This is an experiment?"

"Well, it is an experiment, all right, yes, indeed. You may
be in at the birth of . . ." I didn't finish it. I didn't have any idea
what he might be in at the birth of. The *death* of, yes.

"I'll bet you're just like Dr. Salk," he said. "Noble, dedi-
cated, sweating for humanity."

"Oh, I wouldn't say that."

"Five hundred bucks, huh."

"Yes."

"It's O.K. with everybody there?"

"Don't you worry about that, Mr. Beeler."

"O.K. I'll be there in an hour. With Oscar."

"Make it sooner if you can. Time is slipping away from us."

It was, too. It was already after one P.M.

I hung up. Doctor Fraley clapped his hands to his head again. "This can't be happening. You're *not* going to bring a fourteen-foot python into these halls, into Cowley's. It's unthinkable."

"No, it's not. I thought of it."

"But . . . what if somebody sees him—sees Oscar? Somebody of the staff?"

"Then I would give eight to five there'll be hell to pay. But relax, maybe it won't happen."

He looked as if ants were biting him. But he stuck with me, fascinated. That helped, because when staff members strolled by, it seemed to explain my presence in the corridor.

At two-fifteen all was ready. Jarvis Beeler, two of his workers —and Oscar, had arrived. I had prevailed upon Doctor Fraley to get me a white jacket and one of those concave silvered mirrors with a hole in the middle which doctors sometimes wear around their heads. With the jacket on and the mirror strapped around my forehead I looked quite professional, ready to operate. I had prevailed upon Dr. Fraley to bring a large oxygen tank to the door. Two minutes with the men outside the door of Viper's room, and all was ready. I instructed them that they were merely to introduce the snake into the room and let nature take its course. I assured them that I would be responsible for everything.

Then I stood on a chair and looked through the transom over the door. Jarvis Beeler opened a hinged panel in the end of his crate, partly opened the door to Viper's room, and I saw the big, fat, angular ugly head slide out of the crate—and around Room 28's partly opened door.

Through the transom I could see Viper, lying quietly with eyes closed. For a moment my nerve failed me. Everything had so far progressed with wonderful smoothness, but what if Viper was really paralyzed? What if he wasn't faking? What if—but it was too late.

I saw the whole long horrible length of the monstrous snake, half of it in the room and half still slithering inside. Oscar seemed to gather himself and sniff at the foot of the bed. Without taking my eyes from Viper I waved a hand at Sam and he

cracked the valve on that oxygen tank, and the escaping oxygen
hissed horribly. About the way a seventy-foot python might
hiss if it were angry and preparing to gobble you up.

From that moment on, it was perfect.

Viper's eyes opened.

He squinted slightly, obviously wondering what that hissing
sound could be. And right then Oscar started up the bedpost.
He went up it smoothly, with startling rapidity, and his head
came up over the end of Viper's bed like a slow, scaly rocket.
I waved my hand and Sam cracked the oxygen valve wide open.

Oscar paused in midair, at least four feet of him sticking up
into the air above Viper's bed. Already I felt sorry, remembering Viper and that wee shoestring. But being sorry didn't help
Viper. Nothing would help Viper now. His eyes had landed on
Oscar's head but he must still have been able to convince himself that he was merely nuts, that there couldn't possibly be
there at the foot of his bed what he saw at the foot of his bed.
That horrible hissing sound, combined with the sight of the
greatest, scaliest, hugest, thickest, hissingest snake ever about
to gobble up a poor hood was too much for Viper's immediate
comprehension.

He looked, and his eyes came out a little way, and then a little
way farther. His mouth stretched slowly, torturously open.
And right then realization hit him. Right then he knew. It *was*
a snake. Not, not a snake, but the granddaddy of *all* snakes,
the one you see in nightmares and when you go to hell for shooting people. And by now his mouth was wide open. And he
wasn't dumb, either; no, not mute; he hadn't lost his voice. Or
if he had, it had just come back. Maybe even better than new,
too. Because he let out such a shriek, such a piercing and appalling ululation, such an ear-splitting and thunderous "EEEeeeyoo-
o-oow—HaaaAAAAALLLLPPP" that it very nearly took the
leaves off the trees. I think it even scared Oscar, because Oscar
began wiggling about pretty frantically there, big head bobbing
so that it almost seemed he was smacking his chops.

Viper ran out of that breath in a hurry, he was using so much
air so fast, but he immediately sucked in more. This time he
let out a sound like a diesel locomotive honking in a tunnel.
It ran on up the scale to a kind of gobbling hoot, as if frenzied
turkeys were mating with astonished geese.

Well, he honked and gobbled and ran out his tongue like
one of those Halloween whistles and his eyes got red and
wobbly like railroad wigwags. His face got like fleshy putty,
like congealed fog, like a mass of mashed worms, and I figured

he was as good as dead right then—but there was still plenty of life left in Viper. And he sure wanted to keep it there.

Blam, he was out of the bed, either never paralyzed or instantly cured, and he landed clear out in the middle of the room and in a flash was at the window. That unbelievable combination of sounds still issued from his tortured throat, and he just ran across the floor and out through the window with a great shattering of glass, and he didn't even stop running while he was in the air.

From my transom perch I could see him almost all the way to the ground, and he didn't stop running for an instant while he was in my sight. It was a good ten or twelve feet to the ground, but his legs just kept churning like fleshy propellers. Those legs were going around so fast that it wouldn't have surprised me to see him go up like a small thin helicopter.

He hit running, smacked down on his face, but was up again in a moment and on his way. He really ran then. The running he had done in the air was as nothing compared to the running he did on the grass. At the speed he was going, in ten seconds he would be just a dwindling white dot, like one of those final scenes in Disney Cartoons where the rabbit goes over the hill. Well, this rabbit was over the hill, too.

And now that I knew he was neither speechless or paralyzed, I felt quite confident that he would tell me anything I wanted to know, and maybe even more.

I was right.

There was quite a bit of activity before I could ask the first question, however. I had to put the word out that a patient had gone overboard and escaped—they caught Viper eight blocks away, just passing a Standard oil truck—and tell Jarvis Beeler that the new shock treatment had been a new kind of shock and the experiment had been a huge success, and then explain to numerous people attracted by the wild sounds Viper had made that everything was under control. There was for a while the kind of bedlam that I seem periodically to become involved in, and then near normality was restored. Except that the superintendent of the hospital, and three other doctors in addition to a sad-looking Dr. Fraley, stood about staring at me.

I told them this was a matter of life and death, which after all was their business, so they should be interested. It was just as valid and important to save lives with snakes as with scalpels, I told them, and maybe even more important—if it was *my* life. I was so heated up by the success of the Viper experiment that I even waxed a bit eloquent, and the doctors went along with me, even agreeing to let me question Viper alone. After all, the damage was done. And even there I had them—I had cured the patient, hadn't I?

Anyway, they let me go through with it. Viper was put into another room—he absolutely refused to go back into that contaminated one. Beeler stood by with his crated Oscar, just in case Viper needed a peek at the thing again. But that wasn't necessary. Viper was completely won over to my point of view.

The first question I asked him when we were settled in a room again—with Viper in bed, claiming his legs wouldn't hold him up—was, "Viper, you can start in by telling me all there is to tell about the murder of Lou Rio, and the framing of me for that caper."

"I wasn't there. Shortcake was in on it, and all I know's what he told me. Nick and Jabber used the girl—that Suez—somehow to get Lou out there. They blasted him with your gun— Nick had it from the day before. Then Nick left and Jabber stayed behind. The idea was he'd sap you when you come in, then plug you with Rio's gun and leave your gun alongside your body. Nick said it would be so airtight nobody would even ask a second question about it."

"How was Nick able to time it so well?"

"He had Shortcake spotted in the Continental Hotel down the street from you, with a pair of glasses, and the phone already open to Nick and Jabber at the house on Partridge Street. When you took out of the Spartan, running like your pants was on fire, he seen you through the glasses and naturally knew you was heading for Partridge. Shortcake was already talking to Nick on the phone, so he just told him you were on the way. Then one of them shot Lou, and Nick beat it."

"Lou was still alive then when I ran out of the Spartan after Suez phoned me?"

"That's it. Nick wanted the body still bleedin'."

"Which one of them actually did the job on Lou?"

"Well, it was either Nick or Jabber, but you fixed it so Jabber can't tell nobody who done it. Nick's the only man alive who knows the answer to that question. And it ain't likely that Nick'll tell anybody."

That reminded me I was probably going to ask Nick that very question tonight, so I asked Viper about Nick's office, and the Desert Trails setup. Of the numerous items he willingly told me, at least one or two were interesting. Regularly after dinner every night Nick slept for an hour, from seven to eight, and especially at that time, but at other times too, one of the boys stood in the second-floor hallway to make sure Nick wasn't disturbed. Even so, it was obvious that the best time for me to try getting into Nick's office would be between seven and eight P.M.

"O.K., friend. How about Suez?" I was surprised to learn she was working with Nick. And that she'd go along with murder and a frame.

He frowned, and that lower lip nudged the upper even higher than usual. "I don't think she knew what she was doin'. The way Shortcake told it to me, she just read you something that wasn't so bad at all. Only Nick cut her off before she got to finish."

I said to Viper, "Why did she go along with Nick in the first place?"

"He had something pretty bad on her. She's been paying him off, a thousand bucks each month. I don't know what he had on her. I was just the bagman, to pick it up and take it to Nick."

"Who else did you pick up from?"

"Johnny Palomino——and just lately, June Benton, Salley Courtland. That's all. Like I said, I don't know what he had on any of 'em."

If I remembered correctly, the two names besides Palomino's were of bit players at Magna, girls who might one day reach stardom but who now were on the lower rungs of the Hollywood ladder.

"Then Nick pulled the blackmail play on Feldspen? The million-dollar bite?"

He shook his head. "I don't know about it if he did."

"You did try to put the bite on Coral James, too, didn't you?"

"Yeah. She didn't go for it."

"The way I get it, she slapped your face."

"Yeah. And how."

"Viper, listen close." He fixed his tilted eyes on me. I went on, "I'm very interested in how Suez got mixed up in that frame of me."

"I already told you all I know on what happened yesterday. Then today she called Nick herself."

"Called Nick? What for?"

"Well, Nick sort of double-crossed her yesterday, see? And somehow she'd got her hands on a letter writ by this Valentine guy. Four pages of it. The way Nick acted about it, I guess it would practically have ruined him. So she had that on Nick, and Nick had some stuff on her; what she wanted to do was make a trade."

"What was in the letter?"

"I didn't read it. Had it in my hands, but I didn't get a chance to read it—them lousy cops showed up."

"You mean at McGannon's?" He nodded and I said, "What were you doing there of all places? I'd have thought you would stay far away from Nick's boys."

"Yeah, I would have, but it was her idea—that Suez. See, she phoned Nick today and demanded that he send me to the pay phone booth at the corner of Twelfth and Fig."

"Demanded?"

"Yeah."

It seemed obvious that if Suez was demanding anything of Nick Colossus, that letter had to be dynamite.

Viper went on, "Nick really wanted to get his hands on that letter. The girl said she'd trade, but on *her* terms—so he couldn't foul her up like he done yesterday, I suppose. Anyway, Nick called me in, told me what had happened, and give me the papers Suez wanted to trade him for."

"What were they, Viper?"

"I dunno. It was in a big Manila envelope, sealed. I was just to do what she said, but get the letter from her no matter what. I never seen him so hot. Anyways, he told me to go to that phone booth, that she'd call me there and tell me what to do then, and for me to do it. She was being real careful that Nick nor nobody knew where she was. I guess she knew then that Nick would kill her sure when he got the chance—once she give up the letter. She should have hung onto it."

I heard him say it, but it didn't penetrate all the way. I said, "I still don't know what you were doing at McGannon's."

"Yeah. Well, I went to that phone booth and she called. I told her I had the stuff. She told me to bring it to McGannon's. I says, where Lou is? And she says that's it." He shook his head. "I guess she picked there because she knew me and a bunch of the boys couldn't hang around there close. On account of Lou's guys would take it unkindly and maybe blast us. But they knew he'd been hot for her, so she could trot in with no strain. Anyways, I go there. We make the trade right in the chapel—pretty smart of her, at that. If I'd tried to double-cross her even then all she had to do was yelp and some of Lou's boys would come running— and they'd of got their mitts on me *and* that letter. Which would of made Nick pretty sick. Sick enough to kill me, if I wasn't al- ready dead. Well, she takes off, and I use a phone there in Mc- Gannon's to call the boss—he'd said for me to ring him the min- ute I got the letter, so he could handle the rest of it."

The last phrase sounded odd, but Viper was continuing. "Then I strolled outside and of all the lousy luck them lousy bulls in the lousy car spotted me."

"Why'd you run from them? They didn't have a want on you."

"So what? All they had to do was give me a shake and they'd have come up with that letter—like I said, Nick would've flipped and murdered me. Besides which, them bulls stopped their heap and lit out after me. Why'd I run? With them big flat feet pounding the street behind me?"

"O.K., Viper. So what then?"

"I just spun around and took off. The idea hit me while I was runnin' back into McGannon's. I *had* to get rid of them papers, so I put them in the only place I could think of where they might be safe. Under Lou."

"What? Where?"

"Under Lou. Lou Rio. You know, the guy they're throwin' the funeral for."

"You mean under his body? In the casket?"

"Yeah. When I run back into McGannon's I run right into the room where he was on view. You know, with all the flowers and all. There he was, and inspiration hit me."

"That's what it was, all right."

He grinned. "Lou looked so peaceful. Just like he was dead. Which he was, of course. Anyways, I jammed the letter in there and flashed through the side door and out to the street. I looked back to see if them lousy cops was on my tail—and *blooie*. Something run over me. I think it was a B-52. Next thing I know I'm here. And then in come that. . . . oooohh-hh!"

Viper was remembering Oscar, and he started getting sort of green again. I said, "Did anybody see you put the letter under Lou's body?"

"Nope. I made sure of that. But I'm not sure I got it tucked away real good. Could be some of it's stickin' out. I didn't have time for an artistic job."

I looked at my watch. Two-twenty-five P.M. If I left now I might reach McGannon's before the services started. If so, there was a small chance that I could get to the casket and latch onto that letter without being spotted and killed. In the first place, it was so unlikely that I would show up at Lou's funeral, those present might find it difficult to believe I was Shell Scott even if they stared smack at me.

But there was no question about it, I *had* to try getting that letter. If it was half what it seemed, it might not only ruin Nick but save my own neck.

The whole thing now depended on my getting to McGannon's before three P.M., and the sooner the better. I would have to spend at least three or four minutes doing something to change my appearance, at least my white hair and eyebrows. Along with the rest of the stuff in the back of my Cadillac is a makeup kit, containing among other things some water-soluble hair dye. That would help; the major factor now was time. I stood up.

Viper was still talking, and then I heard the name of Suez again. I looked down at Viper. "What was that about Suez?"

"Huh? Oh, I was sayin' that I didn't get to fill Nick in on anything that happened after I called him from McGannon's so he don't know about me getting rid of the letter. I didn't have time to read it, just checked to make sure it was the goods, but I imagine it'll suit Nick if it's burned. Don't really make no difference to me; he'll kill me anyhow."

"Burned?"

"Yeah. Pretty quick now it'll be cremated. With Lou. Anyways, I was sayin' that the main thing Nick wanted, probably, was for me to get the letter from that Suez so he could take care of her. Most likely he'd of burned the letter himself."

"What do you mean, take care of her?"

"Kill her. What else?"

"*Kill* her? But why kill her? She went through with the trade, didn't she?"

"Sure. But she'd read the letter. I know it had a lot of stuff in it that was pure poison to Nick—might even put him in the can, I gathered. If she read the letter, then she knows all about it." He paused, pursing his lips.

"When was he going to kill her? How?"

"Don't know when for sure. Depends on her. But Nick's got two sets of torpedoes waiting for her. That's why I had to phone him."

"Waiting where?"

"Two droppers outside the place she works at—Magna. Couple more where she lives. She's got to go to one or the other, sooner or later. And that's it."

I swore at him, balled up my fist and leaned over the bed, almost ready to swat him in the teeth while he lay on his back. "Why in hell didn't you tell me about this sooner?"

He cringed back, pressing down against the bed, but he said, "What's all the excitement? Man, I phoned Nick from McGannon's at ten o'clock this morning. She's probably been dead for a coupla hours."

Chapter Fifteen

I JUST STARED at him for a moment. I didn't know for sure whether Suez had knowingly set me up for that frame yesterday or not. I didn't even know how deep she'd been in the dirty business with Nick and Valentine and maybe even Lou Rio—or even what it was that Nick had held over her. But there was, it now seemed, a chance she'd been pretty much on the up and up all along.

I had a choice. I could go right now to McGannon's, now while I had at least a slim chance of getting in there and out without being stopped by a dozen gunmen; or I could try to find Suez, get to her before those killers did. But I knew that as long as there was a chance Suez was still alive I didn't really have a choice. There wasn't any alternative; I had to at least try to stop her—or stop those torpedoes who were after her.

I turned and jumped to the door, went out past the assembled doctors and sprinted down the polished hallway.

As I passed the desk inside the front door I had an idea and stopped, got the nurse behind the desk to hand me her phone. I called Magna, got Feldspen.

"Harry, Shell. If it hasn't happened already, two hoods are outside Magna waiting to kill Suez if she shows up. Take my word—"

He interrupted anyway. "Kill . . . but she just spoke to me on the phone."

"When?"

"Twenty or thirty minutes ago. No longer. She said she'd been unable to report to work yesterday or today, but that everything was all right now—"

"Yeah, I know about that. But where did she call from? Where is she? Was she coming to work?"

"I don't know where she called from; but she indicated that she was tired, and wanted to go home and rest. I told her to go ahead and report for work tomorrow."

Home. There was an even chance, then, that she hadn't reached her apartment on Pepper Street yet. It depended on where she'd phoned from, but I felt the first real surge of hope that I could reach her in time. But even if I did, it would be close. At least I knew where to go.

Harry was saying, "I never got to finish talking to you on the phone, Shell. What's happening? What on earth—"

But that was all I heard because I hung up and sprinted out of the hospital.

I made it from the hospital to Pepper Street in not more than six minutes, and at least five drivers of other cars were probably still shaking their fists at me, or maybe just shaking.

The small light-brown apartment house Suez lived in was three blocks ahead. I kept the accelerator down and roared up the street—and I saw her. At least I saw that white Thunderbird parked at the curb before the stucco apartment building and a woman getting out of the T-bird—I couldn't make sure that it was Suez partly because she was too far from me, partly because another movement had caught my eye.

I was still a block away, but I saw another car pull out from the curb, maybe fifty feet from the Thunderbird. It picked up speed as it neared Suez. The woman was Suez; I could recognize that body now even from behind as she walked away from me, toward the apartments. A man's arms came out of the car's right rear window. And in his hands was a gun. It wasn't a pistol that came out of the window, not even a rifle; it was the fat, ugly barrels of a double-barreled shotgun.

The blast, when it came, would rip Suez's fine body like a bird caught in a hunter's load of buckshot. The heavy pellets would rip and tear the flesh, crack the bones. It would lift her off her feet and throw her torn and bleeding on the grass, dead before she fell. And I was still too far away to stop them. I didn't even have my gun yet in my hand. In the next moment I saw Suez take two steps more toward the building, walking swiftly, jauntily, and I saw that shotgun move toward her, center on her back.

I hit the horn with my right hand and kept it down, the hard blast blaring loud in the residential quiet. I kept the horn down, and pressed my foot against the already mashed-down accelerator. The car ahead was only fifty feet away when I hit the brakes hard, the car looming closer, twenty feet, ten . . . The Cad's tires screamed on the asphalt, the car swerved slightly, slowing. I could still see that shotgun projecting from the window—but the man holding it had turned his head toward me.

Then we hit. It was a hell of a crash, even though both cars were moving in the same direction and the driver of the Plymouth must have jammed his foot down on the gas, lessening the impact. But when we hit I was thrown forward against the steering wheel and I saw the other driver's head jerked sharply back. Whiplash—that terribly painful injury. The head thrown back hard, tearing the muscles and tendons and nerves in the neck. Automatically my mind counted him out, chalked up one of the two men as out of commission for now. But the other man wasn't hurt.

He spilled out of the car's door as the Plymouth came to rest against the curb on the left of the street, and my Cad swerved and nearly stopped, the sound of the crash still echoing in the air. The man clutched his shotgun and I saw him fall to his knees but swing those big barrels around toward me. My Cad stopped completely. Falling glass tinkled on the asphalt. Just as those twin barrels were pointed at my head I ducked, dived for the right-hand door of the car, grabbed for the handle.

The deep, throaty boom of the shotgun and the ripping blast of buckshot through the Cad's windshield seemed to blend into one crashing sound in my ears. The door came open and I leaped through, my hand finding the Colt and yanked it out of its holster. As I hit the street hard, pain ripped into my knees and flared up my hand and wrist, but I kept a tight grip on my gun. I hit the street and rolled, came up on one knee and one foot facing the man.

As I stopped moving and flipped my .38 toward him, I saw those gaping barrels swing around to aim at my middle. All his movements and my own seemed agonizingly, fearfully slow. I yanked the trigger of my .38, yanked it again, not worrying about squeezing off the shot, hardly aiming, but I saw the holes appear in his chest, saw the little puffs of dust spurt from his clothing.

My slugs jerked him, moved him, but didn't pull the shotgun barrels away from me. I kept pulling the trigger until the gun was empty. Those ugly barrels were still on me—but slowly moving away now. I couldn't move, my eyes glued to those barrels as they slowly slid aside and then hit the asphalt. The gun fell with a clatter to the street. The man fell silently, in a way the living never can fall, oddly, twisted, contorted.

Things started coming back to me. For moments there had been the blanking-out of everything except the other man and me. But now I heard Suez screaming. There was movement at the driver's side of the Plymouth, but I glanced at Suez.

She stood on the grass just off the white sidewalk leading to her apartment house. She stood crouched down, knees bent, fists pressed against her cheeks, mouth wide, screams shrieking from her stretched-open mouth.

The driver was getting out of the car. I dropped my empty gun, got to my feet, ran toward him. He turned to face me, eyes pained, mouth half open and tight gagging sounds coming from it, face contorted. I spun him around with my left hand, brought my right fist up in a hard tight arc that ended under his chin. His head whipped back, far back—and only then did I remember the whiplash injury, the muscles and tendons and nerves that must already have been torn in his neck.

He slammed into the car door, fell at my feet.

I went back and picked up my gun, put it in the holster, then walked toward Suez. I walked past the still bleeding, crumpled body in the street and toward Suez. She kept screaming as she looked at me. I didn't blame her.

I stopped in front of her.

"Easy, Suez," I said softly. "Easy."

She stopped screaming, and stood up straight again, her fists slowly opening. She pressed her open hands against her cheeks, dark eyes wide and still reflecting horror. She licked her red lips but didn't say anything. Beyond her I saw the movement of a window curtain, a white face peering at us.

That brought me back closer to normality, too. I looked at my watch. It seemed that it must have been at least an hour since I'd left the Cowley hospital, but it had taken me six minutes to drive here, and only a minute or two had gone into the crash and gunfight. It was now exactly twenty-three minutes until three P.M.

Twenty-three minutes until the services for Lou Rio began. Maybe I could still make it. But the thought moved dully through my brain. I said to Suez, "Those two men were sent here by Nick. Do you know what that means?"

Slowly she nodded, running her tongue over her lips again. "He—they must have been going to . . . kill me."

"That's right."

"I . . . Shell, I—" She broke off closing her eyes and pressing one hand to her smooth forehead, then running it back hard over her long black hair.

I said, "Snap out of it. Right now." My voice was harsh, purposely, to bring her back to normal fast if I could. I'd made up my mind. With a lot of luck, we could make it to McGannon's in fifteen minutes. That would give me maybe five minutes before the services. Without that much luck—well, I didn't even think about it.

"I—I'm all right," Suez said shakily. "It was so fast. So awful."

"Get your car started. I mean it. Quick."

I ran to my banged-up Cad, jerked the keys from the ignition and then opened the luggage compartment. I grabbed a box of .38 cartridges and the black makeup kit, then paused, trying to think. I forced myself to calm down as much as possible, looking ahead to McGannon's—and also to the possibility I wouldn't get there in time.

Then I pawed through the stuff in the trunk, grabbed a heavy, leather-covered sap, a pencil-sized flashlight, and a ring of picks and skeleton keys, dropping them into my coat pockets. That was all I could think of, and I ran toward the Thunderbird. The cars and men would have to be left as they were, in the street. Police would be all over the place in minutes, anyway. My name on the registration slip of the Cad would let the officers know where to put blame for the mess.

Suez had done as I'd told her, and was just starting the car as I climbed into it. "What's the matter?" she asked me. She sounded frightened.

"Don't worry. I just have to be at McGannon's mortuary in ten minutes."

"McGannon's—but why? It would take twenty or thirty minutes—"

"It will if you sit there yakking. Get going."

She got going. As she drove, I loaded the .38, then opened the makeup kit and started smearing black gunk on my hair and eyebrows. That would help; not enough, but it was a step in the right direction—and my face was marked up a bit anyway from the two beatings I'd had in the last three days.

As I worked on my face, I said to Suez, "Baby, you've got a lot of explaining to do. You'd better start right in."

"I suppose you mean about yesterday—when I phoned you."

"You bet I do. But . . ." I thought a moment. There were approximately eighteen things I wanted to ask Suez about, but under the circumstances that four-page "letter" Viper had told me was in Rio's coffin was far and away the most important. It was, after all, the reason I was making this wild ride—and with Suez at the wheel of her thundering Thunderbird it could hardly have been wilder. "Tell me this," I said. "Did you give some kind of letter to a little hood this morning?" She glanced quickly at me out of those wonderful black eyes, then back to the road. I went on. "Some kind of letter written by Ted Valentine?"

"Yes. How—how did you know?"

"I'll tell you if we have time. What was that letter and why was it so important? How did you get it? Why did Valentine write it? Or did he?"

"He did. It was a suicide note, Shell. And at the same time, a confession."

When she said "suicide note" the whole thing opened up in my mind like one of those Fourth of July fire-flowers. I could probably have guessed most of the rest of it then, even if Suez hadn't said another word.

"I'll just tell it the way it happened, all right?" I nodded and she said, "I lied to you when I said nobody was blackmailing me—but that's the only lie I told you. For several months I've been paying money to a little crook they call Viper. Months ago, when I was considered for that part I didn't get in *Sins of Messalina*, Ted Valentine called me into his office and said Magna was getting ready to go all out on a publicity campaign for me."

It was about the same story that Coral had told me. Ted had asked Suez if there were anything in her past which, if it became public knowledge, might hurt her; the studio could cover it up and so forth.

"Well," she said, "I told him—something. A month or so later this little creep came around and asked me for money. I, well, I paid. I just kept on paying."

"Did you know Valentine had given him the info?"

"No. I thought maybe he had, but Val was always so great it was hard to believe. I liked him. There wasn't any proof, anyway. Not until I got this letter."

I looked up from the makeup kit and said, "If I could get my hands on that letter, would it be worth risking my neck for? Would it really hurt Nick Colossus, for example?"

"It really would." She bit her lip. "But it . . . it's not available any more."

"Yes it is." I glanced at my watch. "For about fifteen more minutes it's available. But then it's gone forever. So speed up the story."

She went on, speaking rapidly. "Saturday, almost two weeks ago now, I went to the Desert Trails for the weekend—I didn't even know Nick Colossus had anything to do with it then. It was just a fun place. Val was there, too—*not* with me. He was just there. We said hello, and that was about all. Until Sunday."

Suez handled the little T-bird as if it were a four-wheeled rocket. She was a surprisingly good driver, but I had almost told her to slow down two or three times already, despite my hurry.

She was continuing. "I was coming back from the pool Sunday afternoon. My cabin was 34, down past Val's and he called to me. I stopped and went inside his cabin and talked to him, and . . . well, he looked funny. Very calm and quiet—and you know how twitchy he always was. He asked me when I was checking out, and I told him I was ready to leave. He gave me a sealed envelope and asked me to please take it off the Ranch and mail it. Personally. He stressed that I shouldn't mail it from the Ranch and I promised I wouldn't."

"Who was the letter addressed to?"

"The District Attorney of Los Angeles. It had a special delivery stamp on it, too. Val told me he was staying another day, then I went to my room. Well, I took a lot longer to get ready to leave than I'd supposed I would. For one thing, I spent a real long time in the shower."

For just a moment I almost lost the thread of the narrative there. It is, I suppose, a flaw in my character, but whenever a lovely tomato talks about being in a shower or tub or anything remotely resembling either, I almost invariably *see* the tomato in the place and state she describes—and while this may be a flaw, it is not the kind you would be especially anxious to get rid of.

Consequently, when Suez spoke of a "real long time in the shower" everything else just faded away. I have said or intimated that Suez was a truly exotic beauty, that her body was so warm and vibrant it did everything but steam, that her curves of breast and hip were sweeping and lush and sensual, a delight and provocation to behold, even from a distance.

But in that shower, with clear water pouring over those deep full breasts and streaming down that smooth velvety skin, her black hair even blacker from the moisture clinging to it, she was enough to get a man lathered without soap, and it took a near collision with a red convertible to snap me back to reality from that better place where I'd been.

I looked at Suez with bright new eyes as she said, "Because I was so long getting dressed I was still there for all the activity. Besides, Val had acted so funny I thought something must be going on. Anyway, I saw a doctor come out of Val's room carrying his bag. A little later I asked him what had happened. He told me a man had 'accidentally' taken too many sleeping pills, but I knew different. After seeing Val. Well, I checked out and drove back to Hollywood and home. But then I read the letter he'd given me to mail. Four pages of it."

She was quiet while maneuvering around a corner on two wheels and when I got my breath back I asked, "And it was a confession. That he'd been a party to blackmail, right?"

"Yes. It told the whole thing, even named names."

I said, "Was it obviously a suicide note?"

"Yes, it made that very clear." Suez paused. "For a while I didn't know what to do with the letter. You see, until I read it I didn't know that the person really blackmailing me was Nick Colossus—the only man I ever saw was that little creep. I didn't know either, until then, that others on the lot were in the same fix I was in. I couldn't mail the letter to the District Attorney, and I couldn't give it back to Val—it was my protection as long as I had it, my bargaining point. But I didn't know how to use it at first. Val naturally asked me about it when he got back on the lot, but I told him I'd mailed it." She paused. "And then he killed himself. He *really* killed himself."

I had known for so long that Valentine hadn't killed himself that it surprised me to hear Suez's words, and realize she still thought he'd committed suicide.

She went on. "It's too late now, but I guess I should have given the letter back to him. He probably would have wanted to stay alive if I had; I can't help feeling as if I . . . killed him."

"You did react like a gal going into shock when I told you about Valentine's suicide. But put your mind at rest, Suez; you had nothing to do with his death. I think he did want to live, after once being so close to dying. And naturally he would have wanted that confession back—he called the D.A. about it two or three times. But he didn't kill himself. Nick Colossus had two of his men sap Valentine and throw him off the Madison roof."

She gasped. "Are you sure?"

"As sure as I am of anything else in this case." I squinted at the mirror in the lid of the makeup kit. I'd been using the brush that came with the bottle to put on the hair dye, but it was a ticklish operation. The small towel around my shoulders was a mess, but my hair and brows were dark enough. I used the towel to blot and further dry my hair, then hunted through the kit, found some rolled cylinders of cotton and stuck one into my cheek. It helped. I looked lumpy and sick, but even less like Shell Scott.

I found another cotton roll for the other cheek and said

to Suez, "O.K. Here's your big question. Why did you phone me from Partridge Street yesterday? And very nearly get me killed?"

She took a deep breath and moistened her red lips. "I had decided to try trading Nick that letter for—for what he had that I wanted." I wondered for about the tenth time what it was in Suez's past that she so desperately had tried to hide, and was still hiding. She went on in a rush. "So I phoned Nick early yesterday morning at the Desert Trails and told him I wanted to figure out a trade for the things he had about me, that I was tired of paying and paying and worrying all the time. Well, that was as far as I got."

"What do you mean?"

"It was surprising. I never even got around to *mentioning* the letter—not then. Nick seemed to be very glad I'd phoned and said he thought sure we could work something out. He said he'd have to think about it, but he was coming into town and would call me when he arrived. He did, and asked me to come to a house on Partridge Street. I went out there, but I didn't take along the letter. That was my ace in the hole, and if I could get what I wanted from Nick without it—and it looked then as if I could—so much the better. When I reached the house, Nick said all he wanted me to do was make two phone calls, and if I did he'd give me back the—the papers and things I wanted. It seemed simple enough. Too simple."

Here it comes, I thought. "What were the two phone calls?"

She bit her lip, hesitated. Then she said, "One was to Lou Rio. The other was to—to you." She rushed on, "But I honestly didn't think I was going to get you into trouble, Shell. Honestly. Please believe me."

"Give me a chance. Tell the tale, and we'll see."

"Nick said he wanted me to phone Lou Rio and ask him out to the Partridge Street house. Nick knew that Lou liked me a lot—Lou did, he really did. I didn't pay any attention to him, but he wanted me to be— You know what I mean."

"I know."

"Nick told me that this was the only way he could get to see Lou without Gangrene setting in—that's what Nick said."

"Sounds like him—always a barrel of fun, Nick is."

"Shell, Nick was so agreeable—charming even. And so persuasive—it all seemed like a big joke. I believed him. I didn't think he was going to hurt anybody. Not then, I didn't. Now I know better."

"If you don't, think back to those two chaps in the street before your house."

She winced, then said, "I was to phone Lou—and I didn't think he'd be hurt, not really hurt. Then I was to phone you and ask you to call the police."

"Slow down," I said. "If you'd told me that, it wouldn't have been so bad, my sweet. But instead you told me to charge out to Partridge Street and help you . . ." I stopped. Actually, Suez had said no such thing. Now that I thought about it, it hadn't been her words so much as my interpretation of the little I had heard her say. "Never mind," I said. "Go on."

"I phoned Lou and he said he would come right out, alone. I saw him drive up. I'd asked him to come to the back door, and Nick's man went out back to meet him—Nick and I were in the front room at the phone. All the doors were shut, so I don't know what Nick's man said to Lou, but I didn't see Lou again."

"Probably Jabber—Nick's man—went out there and swatted poor old Lou over the head. Or maybe just stuck a gun on him." She winced again. "As soon as Lou drove up, Nick told me to call you. He'd told me what to say. I still remember it exactly. I was supposed to tell you who was calling and that I needed help, and then say, 'I'm at 1854 Partridge Street, in the bedroom. I came here to meet Nick Colossus, but when I got here he was gone. There's blood on the carpet and I'm afraid something terrible has happened. Please call the police and send them out here.'"

Suez looked at me out of those wide, deep, dark eyes and went on. "Nick said we'd break the connection then if you asked too many questions. I didn't know why he would want you to call the police, but I supposed it was something to do with having the officers catch Lou or arrest him maybe. But when I'd barely started talking to you Nick broke the phone connection. In a moment he dialed a number himself and talked to somebody. I don't know who it was."

"Shortcake," I said.

"Who?"

"A guy watching my apartment building. It's not important."

"Anyway," she said, "right then, when he broke the connection before I'd finished talking to you, I started realizing what he'd done. And I started getting scared."

She paused, and I ran over in my mind what she'd said. It could have happened just that way. Nick had probably started figuring how to frame me as soon as he took my gun at the Desert Trails, and when Suez phoned him he probably saw immediately that he might be able to use her to get Lou and me together, unsuspecting, for that neat frame. It was all logical enough, and workable enough—except for one thing. Nick just didn't let people—even people as lovely as Suez—walk around loose when they knew as much about his plans as she had known.

I said casually, "So he thanked you and you took off, huh?"

She blew air out her nose. "Hardly. I think he was going to kill me."

"Are you serious?"

"Yes. Oh, maybe it was my imagination, I was so scared. But I asked him for the—papers he'd promised me and he just laughed. A big, awful laugh."

"Yeah. I've had some experience of Nick's laughter—and promises—myself."

Suez said, "That man really scared me. He said he'd decided it wouldn't be necessary to give me back the papers, but, he added sarcastically, he did thank me greatly for the help. So, then I got mad and told him about the four-page letter I had. Val's confession involving him in blackmail. It was the first time I'd mentioned it. He didn't believe me at first, but I quoted some things in it that I couldn't have known unless I was telling the truth. He just exploded. I thought he was going to hit me, kill me right then. He was just a wild man."

I could understand now why Nick *would* have been a wild man. Suez's words would have been his first knowledge that there existed a letter or confession written by Valentine, a *second* suicide note which could put Nick right behind the eight ball. Especially since Nick was responsible for Valentine's murder —not merely blackmail, as Suez had then thought.

She said, "I told him I would still make a trade, that letter for what he had of mine. I told him the letter was safe, with a policeman—it wasn't, but he didn't ask me much about it then. He just said all right, he'd trade, and then let me go. In fact, he told me to get out in a hurry. He *really* scared me. I left as fast as I could."

That made sense. Nick would have wanted Suez to beat it fast, if he let her go at all, I thought, because by then I was well on my way to the Partridge Street address; Suez and I must barely have missed each other. He couldn't afford to kill her, not until he had that letter of Valentine's. He had undoubtedly decided right then to let Suez go, meet her terms and complete the trade, and *then* kill her. Which was just the way it had happened—except that Suez was still alive.

She was saying. "I was almost too frightened even to go through with the trade today. But I worried about it a long time and figured a way to manage it safely, I thought."

And I'd heard that story from Viper. I told Suez I had and she said to me, "Then that's all of it. It was true, too. All of it. Do you believe me?"

I looked at her. "I . . . yeah, I believe you."

She smiled. "Thanks." Then she sobered and seemed to be thinking seriously of something. Slowly she said, "I suppose you've wondered what it was that Nick was able to blackmail me with."

"The thought crossed my mind, but—"

"I'm going to tell you. I owe you at least that much. You saved my life back there—and you didn't even know then that I hadn't purposely drawn you out to that house yesterday." She paused. "I'd like for you to understand how important getting back those papers was to me, Shell. Why I lied to you about being blackmailed, and lied to Val. I . . . kind of think you should know, anyway."

She swung left on Forest Street. McGannon's was less than a mile away now. About a minute away. I looked at my watch. It was seven minutes of three. Suez said, "Everything's here in this manila folder." She tapped an envelope on the seat between us. "And I don't believe it could be duplicated now. These are photostats of the records, licenses, birth certificate and so on—but the originals aren't available now." She glanced sideways at me. "At least I managed that in these last few months. In the envelope is proof that my parents weren't married. I'm a—I'm an illegitimate child."

"You shouldn't have paid the bum a nickel, Suez."

"But that's not all. And remember, I'm very serious about my career. I'm started now and I want to keep going—this would ruin me. My career for sure." She tapped the envelope again.

We were close to McGannon's. I said, "Pull over and park."

"But we're still two blocks away."

"Two blocks is close enough for you. I'll do the rest on foot."

She pulled to the curb and parked, then said, "I told you there was more. The rest of it—" she looked squarely at me—"is about my parents themselves. My father was somebody from Georgia; I never knew him. My mother was a Negro." She paused, then added, "I'm half white, half Negro. What do you say to that, Mr. Scott?"

Her sudden statement had jarred me. But without even thinking I said, "Well . . . looking at you, Suez, I'd say it's a combination that should be tried more often." I had just said, automatically, what came into my head, but Suez didn't seem to mind.

She smiled at me and said, "Maybe we're not even yet, but I wanted to tell you."

"We're even." I grinned at her. "By the way, I'm English and Irish and Scotch and French—and I don't know *what* all. But I've no time for chitchat now. I'm off. How do I look?" This was taking time, but I did want one opinion besides my own before I walked into McGannon's. Just to pluck up my failing courage. If I looked like Dracula's father, it would help me to mingle unnoticed with Lou's boys.

Suez blinked at me. "I would hardly know it was you."

"Hardly is hardly good enough. You mean I'm still me?"

"Well, sort of. You do look a lot different."

"That will have to do, I guess." I said it sadly. Then I told Suez to go straight to the Police Building, where she'd be safe, and I got out of the car.

Suez leaned onto the doorframe. "If you live," she said lightly, "maybe you can tell me how you managed it."

I think she wanted two answers. I said, "I'll live—" I grinned at her—"to knock again on your dressing-room door."

And then I turned and walked, double-time, toward McGannon's. And though I know I had sounded very confident telling Suez I would live, I now decided I must have been kidding.

There was still six minutes to go when I walked up the steps and into McGannon's mortuary. I knew it was too late to find Lou's body on view in the adjoining room where Viper had seen it and done his work, but I'd had hope that I might be able to reach the casket before the chapel filled, while there would be at least a chance of getting a peek—and maybe a hand—into the coffin without running the gauntlet of eighty or a hundred eyes.

That wild dream vanished the moment I stepped inside the chapel door, however. The forty or fifty people present were almost all seated on long benches facing the front of the chapel. Some of them glanced casually at me, but no hoarse shouts shattered the subdued murmur of lingo. Several hoods here were undoubtedly strangers to most of the group, and probably nobody present knew all of the other names or faces. So one more oddball wouldn't cause much excitement—unless somebody who knew me took a close look.

And to avoid close looks, I had to do nothing which would

call undue attention to me. Somebody stepped up beside me and tried to show me to a seat at the end of one of the benches. I felt like removing myself, but then the tones of an organ wobbled suddenly in the air. I turned, to go, thinking there might still be time to get out—and turned almost into a particularly ugly hoodlum blocking the door two yards from me. It was Gangrene.

I swung back into the room, and suddenly realized that Gangrene and I were the only people still standing. With the sound of the organ music, the others who had been on their feet had taken their places. I ducked my head, stepped forward and took the seat previously pointed out to me.

Gangrene walked up the aisle and took a seat too close to me. Any seat would have been too close. Well, I couldn't get up now. That would, for sure, draw all eyes to me. I was here; this was the place where I'd wanted to be; and now I was stuck with it.

I don't remember any of the service. But the moment when the assembled hoods began filing past the casket for a last look at Lou was burned deep into my brain.

All of a sudden it was my turn and I was on my feet in the aisle. I stepped forward toward that coffin, and it seemed by far the craziest thing I'd done in my life.

Then I could see his face and at first my only thought was that Lou Rio looked very waxy. . . .

Chapter Sixteen

THE SOUND of another gunshot snapped me back from wherever I'd been.

When I had looked in the rear view mirror at the long line of cars barreling along behind me, I had sort of blanked out for a moment after deciding that, yes, I would be glad to do it all over again. And now I decided that I wished I *were* doing it over.

When I had emptied my gun at the car behind me, I had been able to note that it was a blue Lincoln and, more important, that the man sitting next to the driver and shooting at me, was Gangrene. He would naturally be in the number-one car behind the hearse transporting Lou.

The hearse seemed to be crawling, and the blue Lincoln had gained on me again with appalling speed. It was pulling up on my left again. And right then an awful thought struck me.

I had gone through all this misery and hell and sweat to get four sheets of paper, and I didn't even have them in my hands yet. They were still in the casket behind me, next to Lou. If nothing else, I was at least going to grab them. I held the steering wheel with the fingers of my left hand and leaned far back, stretching, running my hand along the side of the casket.

My fingers hit the papers I'd seen during the procession past the casket and I grabbed them. The hearse was weaving, and Lou's body rolled and rocked, momentarily freeing the papers. I yanked them out, jammed them into my coat pocket. I heard the gun crack again, but this time Gangrene didn't even hit the hearse.

But when I turned around and got both hands on the steering wheel again the Lincoln pulled up almost level with me, and on my left I could see Gangrene in the car's window with his gun raised. On my right was the green of the cemetery. We were there; it was a dead heat.

Fifty feet ahead was the blacktop turnoff into the cemetery. I didn't even think; I just acted. I slammed on the brakes and as

149

Gangrene's car shot ahead of me I swung the steering wheel left, slamming hard into the Lincoln's right rear fender. My foot was all the way down on the brake pedal, but at the moment of impact I slammed it onto the gas and jerked the wheel right again. The hearse skidded all the way to the turnoff, tires shrieking in protest.

The impact sent the rear end of the blue Lincoln sliding, first one way and then the other. But that was the last chance I had to look at it because I was fighting the steering wheel and straightening out the hearse on the blacktop road into the cemetery. At least Gangrene and his driver were behind me now; and it would take them a minute or so to stop, turn around, and get after me again. But as I glanced into the rear view mirror I saw the first of those other cars following me swing onto the blacktop. I had a good head start again, but that car was only the first of many; and now the hearse's left front fender was bent inward, rubbing against the tire.

Afternoon sunlight fell through closely planted eucalyptus trees bordering the road on my left. Two hundred yards ahead were the Woodstream Cemetery buildings, the mausoleum and crematorium. Headstones and monuments dotted the area all around them. Another hundred yards on past those buildings the road made its last turn to the right, continuing on around in a rough oval which marked the cemetery's limits. But straight ahead at the end of the cemetery property was part of the Dimondsen orange grove which bordered Woodstream on three sides. And where the road turned right, it was hidden for a hundred feet or more by massed banks of oleander and mock orange.

I was passing the cemetery buildings, but already I knew what I was going to do—or try to do. If the road was clear when I turned right at that last-chance turn ahead, so that the hearse wouldn't run anybody down—and even in my present jangled state, getting run over by a hearse in a cemetery seemed like perhaps the unhappiest way to get it that I could think of —then I was going to part company with the hearse and just let it roll. And hope.

I reached the last turn and skidded around it to the right. There wasn't another person in sight up here at the cemetery's end; the road ahead was clear for a hundred or more yards, all the way to the point where it swung right again—and I couldn't even see the pursuing cars now, blocked out as they were by that massed mock orange and oleander. Which meant, too, that they couldn't see me.

I slowed down enough so that I wouldn't kill myself, but the

heavy hearse was still traveling fast enough to roll a long way
if it didn't hit anything. Then I slipped the gears into neutral
and opened the car door, got ready to jump. Green rows of
orange trees flashed past thirty feet away beyond an open
wooden fence. The hearse held steady in the middle of the road
after I released the wheel, and I didn't wait any longer. I
jumped.

I hit the dirt on my feet and tried to run, but the impact was
too great. My knees buckled and I fell sprawling, the breath
whooshing out of my mouth, but I rolled over twice and came
back up on my feet. The fence danced in front of my eyes,
blurred. I hadn't sprained or broken anything, and I jumped
toward the fence, grabbed the top board and vaulted over it.
When my feet hit the earth on the other side of the fence I
took two long strides and then dived into the air and forward,
like a fullback going over the line, and landed nearly at the base
of one of the orange trees.

I rolled another yard or two, then squirmed around on my
knees and looked back. On my left the hearse was still rolling.
The door had slammed shut of its own weight. The car wasn't
moving very fast, but at least it was moving down the road,
veering slightly to its left. On my right the first of the pursuing
cars was just skidding around the curve I'd maneuvered seconds
before. I held myself motionless as the car swerved, straightened
out and picked up speed. It roared past me, thirty feet away, and
I could see five men in it. And I saw two guns held at the ready.
Undoubtedly there were more guns; I only saw two and that
was more than enough.

I spun around and ran like a fiend. After twenty strides or so
I cut over a couple of rows and then just picked them up and
laid them down, running as fast as I could through the cultivated
soil. It was soft earth, difficult to make time through; but I
made time.

There were no shots, not even sounds of pursuit. By now
either the hearse had run into something, or that first car had
caught up with it. But it would take those boys at least a minute to make sure I wasn't in the coffin, maybe hiding under Lou,
or possibly under the hood somewhere. And with the wildest ex-
hiliration I had known in a long time, I knew that if my lungs
held out I was going to make it.

My lungs held out.

I guess it was half a mile or more of slogging through that
beautiful orange grove—there would never be one more beautiful—before I reached the next road. It was a two-lane cement

highway and the second car, an old Ford, stopped for me. It was either stop or run over me because after the first driver gawked at me and ripped past, I stood squarely in the middle of the street moving my arms.

The driver who stopped had the appearance of a farmer, a man close to the soil. I figured he was close to the soil because about three pounds of it appeared still to be on him. I yanked open the door, not even waiting for an invitation under the circumstances, and jumped in. And I wanted soon to be going at least a hundred miles an hour—away from here.

"Yeah," the farmer said, "C'mon in. Where you headed?"

"Just go, man, go!" I said frantically. "Never mind where. Go, man, go!"

He looked at me disdainfully, at my hair and smeared black eyebrows, and the rest of me. "Hah," he said contemptuously, "one of them rock-and-roller."

I didn't argue with him. I knew that nothing was going to stop me now, so I just sat there soaking in my sweat while he slowly put the old Ford into gear and we chugged away.

From a pay phone booth in the service station where I had filled the farmer's gas tank and washed up—including washing the water-soluble dye out of my hair and eyebrows—I called Magna and got Feldspen. He sounded as if he'd been tearing his hair out, and he didn't calm down a bit when I started filling him in on what had been happening to me. That was understandable—it dawned on me that the last real talk I'd had with him had been last night when I'd phoned his home from the Oasis Motel. Consequently it took a while to bring him up to date.

After that I asked him, "How's the project going?"

"All right. I need some more information from you."

"I'll get what I can. There's a little crook named Arthur H. Worthington at the Cowley Memorial Hospital who can give you plenty. I found out from him that Nick takes a nap after dinner each night for an hour, with his clothes on and his gun on a night stand by the bed. That might help me if I get in there."

"Shell." He sounded weary. "Are you sure you want to go back to Desert Trails after what happened to you there?"

"I don't *want* to go back. But how else can I get to the man and do what I want to do? I've got enough to hurt him, maybe —but not enough to ruin him. And either I ruin him for sure or he'll ruin me."

"I suppose so."

"It *is* so. That confession Ted Valentine wrote would involve Nick, and might even get him a slap on the wrist, but if I know Nick Colossus—and I do—he'd wriggle out even from under this confession. But with what I hope to get from *him,* this suicide note will be the knot in the noose." I paused. "Speaking of getting info from Nick, did you charter that helicopter?"

"Yes. It's fueled and ready for takeoff at any time now, at the Curl Airport."

I glanced at my watch. It was after five P.M. "I'm on my way. About that little crook, Viper; if he tries to clam, tell him he has to either spill all or share his bed with a python."

"What? I don't understand."

"Just tell him that, and he'll cooperate. Even over the phone probably. Well, keep your fingers crossed." We hung up.

On the way out to the Curl airport in a taxi I read Ted Valentine's four-page letter again. It was written on Desert Trails stationery and the style seemed rather florid and stilted, but Valentine had, after all, worked himself into a mental state in which he could take his own life.

The message was there though, and clear enough: "In a few minutes, I, Theodore Valentine, am going to swallow enough sleeping pills so that very soon I will have no further problems or regrets. This, then, is in the nature of a confession, and—because I know that in a few minutes I will be dead—a deathbed statement. I am a blackmailer. I have been instrumental in the blackmailing of: Johnny Palomino, Suez, Coral James, Salley Courtland, and June Benton, all of Magna Studios. It is easy enough now to say that I was forced to do this by a man who knew of damning information in my background which I could not afford to have divulged; but the fact remains that I did learn, in confidence, secrets from those five people and then betrayed their confidence by divulging that information to the man blackmailing me. That man was, and is, Nick Colossus. It is ironic that I am being blackmailed by him, and as my payment must provide him, not with money, but with information he can then use for blackmailing those others."

That was the end of the first page. Valentine had then gone on to explain the mechanism by which he had discovered the "damning information" about the five whom he helped Nick to blackmail—the "publicity" angle that both Coral and Suez had told me about. He explained the mechanics of the blackmail setup, as he knew them, told of how he had originally been approached by Nick Colossus, and wrote of his growing remorse and shame which had culminated in physical illness. The last page ended, "I am unable longer to live with this burden. May God forgive me. . . ." It was signed Theodore Valentine.

The letter was a good club to have over Nick's head, and all by itself it might help to get Nick into a trial court—on an extortion charge. But that was about all it guaranteed.

And merely sticking Nick with a mild extortion rap wouldn't do me much good; I had to send him up for murder.

I reached Curl Airport, a privately owned field, before six P.M. The helicopter pilot was a stocky, pleasant-faced man of about thirty-five, named Malcolm Waters. I told him I was ready to go, and he said he'd be all set in five minutes. I decided to phone Coral before we took off. I wanted to hear her voice one more time.

There was no point in kidding myself. Even if I got into Nick's suite without being shot, there was a very good chance I wouldn't get out under my own power. I called the Oasis Motel, cabin 18. There wasn't any answer. I let the phone ring a long time, then hung up.

I didn't like it. She could very well be getting a breath of fresh air, or having a sandwich. She could be. But I still didn't like it. I phoned Magna again and got Harry Feldspen.

"Harry, Shell again."

"Are you at the airport?"

"Yes, about ready to leave. Look, Harry, Coral James is in Cabin 18 at the Oasis Motel. I just phoned but there's no answer. Would you—"

"Coral?" he interrupted. "What in the world is she doing out there?"

"Harry, I haven't time to explain. But I'd appreciate it if you'd call her again in five or ten minutes. When you get her, have her come in to Magna, O.K.?"

"Why here?"

"I'd like her there if—when I get back tonight." I thought a minute. "It might not be a bad idea to send somebody out to bring her in."

"All right."

"In fact, if you don't get her on the phone, I'd appreciate your sending somebody to check and see why she doesn't answer."

He said he would, then asked me if everything was set at the airport. "Just getting ready to fly away," I told him. I checked the stuff. "Thanks for having the recorder and ladder here. What's the sound track, by the way?"

"*Jungle Fury.* I had to decide, myself, and it seemed—"

"Say no more. I saw the movie." The helicopter pilot waved to me and trotted out to the machine. I said, "Off we go, Harry. Thanks for everything."

"Of course. Shell—just be . . . oh, good luck."

"Thanks, Harry." I hung up and ran to the helicopter. It squatted on the field like a monstrous mutant beetle, its rotors slowly turning over the half-plexiglass cabin and above the narrow tail. I climbed into the unfamiliar bug-like contraption, pulled the door shut and strapped the seat belt around my middle.

The pilot reached down and to his left, turned the throttle on the end of the control stick there, just as if he were feeding power to a motorcycle engine, and the sound increased as the twin rotors beat faster and faster over our heads. He raised the stick away from the floor and up we went, with a little lurch and sway, almost as if he were lifting the machine with his hand. Then he pushed the other stick, in his right hand, forward and for a moment it seemed that the earth, and not ourselves, was moving as it slid under and behind us, receded from us. It was a very creepy sensation for me.

The airport dwindled and I looked down through the bulging plexiglass blister to see the lights of Los Angeles spread out below us like jewels in the gathering dusk. It was a beautiful sight. I took a long look at it. There was a good chance I wouldn't see it again.

From the air, Desert Trails was the only bright spot in a world of blackness, like a liner plowing through the sea at night.

I looked at Malcolm Waters. "There it is," I said over the roar of the engine and rush of air. "I've got exactly four minutes after seven."

He checked his watch. "On the nose."

"O.K. Here's the routine for the last time. After you dump me, disappear until *exactly* seven-forty-eight. Bring this thing down a hundred yards behind the main hotel building, on the opposite side from the pool. If I'm not there, stay put until somebody shoots at you."

He grinned. "You left out the most important part. If anybody shoots at me, I get a thousand-dollar bonus."

I grinned back at him. "Yeah. But nothing extra if they hit you."

"They? That sounds like several people."

"If there's any shooting at all, it will *be* from several people. If you can call them people. But don't worry about it. They'll shoot me first—so you'll be warned by all the popping."

He grinned again, but without much tooth.

We landed in darkness, with no lights showing, more than a mile from the ranch. It was nine minutes after seven. I piled out with the recorder and ladder supplied by Feldspen in my hands, and in my pockets the smaller items I'd taken earlier from the Cad's luggage compartment: the ring of picks and keys, the sap, and pencil-sized flashlight. Malcolm Waters took off immediately.

We'd come down on the desert before the front of the ranch, so as I headed toward it, alternating walking with trotting, I could see the lights of the hotel, and pool. Several people were enjoying the heated waters of the pool this evening, and though I couldn't see the front of the bar, which faced the hotel, it was a sure thing that it was loaded, too. That was fine with me. I almost wished I was loaded.

I stopped about a hundred yards from the hotel, out past the stables, and placed the recorder on the ground. At exactly seven-thirty I started the tape unwinding, the small but powerful speaker aimed at the hotel. I had fourteen minutes before the blank tape would come to an end and the first sound—a gunshot —would come from the speaker. Exactly sixty seconds later the taped sound track would begin playing. At maximum volume.

I took off, trotting in a wide circle around the side of Desert Trails. When I was well behind it, I stopped trotting and walked, in order to catch my breath and calm my mind, to the rear of the hotel, then moved through the darkness slowly. As far as I could tell I was alone back here.

When I had been in the hotel before, and Flint with his two pals had escorted me upstairs to see Nick, I had noticed at the end of the second-floor hallway a curtain billowing inward before an open window. It was toward that window I was walking now. I found it with no difficulty; soft light spilled through it from the hallway inside. I extended four of the ladder's five sections, and the bamboo ends reached to a spot just below the window sill. It was seven-thirty-six when I started up the ladder; I had eight minutes in which to do what I'd come here for.

I paused at the top of the ladder and looked into the hall. The window was open again, sheer curtain billowing inward. In the right wall, halfway down the hallway inside, I could see the closed door through which I had gone once before to meet Nick. At first I didn't see anybody. But that was because I was looking toward the far end of the hall. Then the glow of a cigarette nearby caught my eye and I saw that a man was leaning against the wall inside on my right, not more than six or eight feet from me. He dragged on the cigarette again. It was Whitey. Slobberlips. The Un-Continental.

I tried to tell myself that I was calm, cool, and collected, by my heart was pounding as if it were the wrong size, and it would have taken at least two quarts of water to ease the dryness in my throat. I knew that in a very few minutes all sorts of noise was going to blast from that recorder I'd left in the desert; and quite a while before that happened, I had to be in Nick's room. Nick was asleep now, almost surely; but once that tape had unwound for fifteen minutes, he would be wide awake— along with every other living thing for miles around.

But I couldn't just stand here on my ladder. After all the thinking and planning, the work and expense, getting clear up to here, I couldn't let a racing heart and bunch of overactive glands ruin the whole operation. Not just because a stupid lob like Whitey was nearby. Stupid—that was, of course, the key word.

I calmed down then. I grinned, took out the sap and held it in my right hand, high overhead. Then I leaned back a little, so my face wouldn't catch the glow of light from inside, and I said softly, *"Hey, Whitey."*

He took the wet cigarette out of his mouth and looked down the length of the empty hallway away from me and I saw his jaw sag perhaps an inch. Then he squeezed his eyes shut, opened them, and stared, shaking his head just a little.

"No, stupid," I whispered. *"Over here."*

Slowly he turned his head, looking as if he really deserved the name of Old Slobberlips, which was how I now thought of him.

"Huh?" he said, looking at the wall. "What? Where . . . what . . ."

"Here, out here."

His eyes rolled toward the window.

"Yeah, here. Well, don't just stand there, stupid. Come out here."

His face got all twisted. "Who—ha—wha—" he was so bewildered that it must have ached. His expression was a complex blending of agony, astonishment, and a wild surmise. "Wha— who—" he went on wetly.

"Oh, Whitey," I said. "Don't just stand there. Come *out* here."

And finally he was able to move. And, able to move, he naturally came over and stuck his head out the window, and naturally I swatted him murderously on top of it. If you have heard old ladies thumping melons in the market, and if you can imagine the sound multiplied about five times, then you know what it sounded like when I sapped Whitey. Boy, he was a ripe one. He flopped halfway out of the window, arms dangling down the side of the building.

I couldn't leave him dangling there—at any minute somebody else was likely to wander through that hallway—and I couldn't leave him sprawled on the floor inside, either. So I pulled myself past him through the window and, standing inside, lifted his feet and pushed him out the window. He made hardly any noise when he landed on the ground below.

I headed for that door leading upstairs. The door leading to Nick's suite—and to Nick Colossus. The hallway was still empty, so I tried the knob—naturally the door was locked—then took the ring of picks out of my pocket and started working on the lock. It was a tough one. I looked at my watch. Only three minutes to go. And now I was afraid it wouldn't be nearly enough. I had to get this door open, and then open another one at the head of the stairs inside it. And then there was Nick. I had a chance just so long as I got inside Nick's room before seven-forty-five, before he woke up. I got to work on that door again.

The lock tumblers turned and I yanked the door open. Up the stairs I went, picks in my hand. I tried the same pick on the door at the top of the stairs—and it worked. My heart felt as if it were pounding inside my mouth as I eased Nick's door open and stepped into his suite of rooms—into that room where I had been severely and expertly beaten. It was dark inside here. I closed the door, leaned back against it, listening. But only for a few seconds, there couldn't be more than a minute left. I turned on my pencil flash and shot its beam briefly around the room.

It fell on the desk where Nick had sat, the long couch against the wall, the two overstuffed chairs. And then on the closed door beyond which, I knew, was Nick's bedroom—and the sleeping Nick Colossus. I reached up and felt the .38, cold under my coat, but left it in the holster. I took the sap out of my pocket again. Holding it in my right hand, flashlight burning in my left, its glow dimmed by my fingers, I walked to that closed door.

For moments I stood there, breathing deeply, filling my lungs and blood with fresh oxygen, then I took a last deep breath and held it. I turned the doorknob with the hand holding my flashlight. The door was unlocked and swung open without a sound. I stepped inside, heartbeat thudding, blood drumming in my ears. When I moved the flashlight farther into the room it dimly illumined Nick's bed—and Nick.

Silently, carefully, still holding my breath I walked to the bed, stood alongside it. Nick Colossus lay on his back, both monstrous and hairy arms outside the covers. Even in sleep, lying quietly, he looked like an avalanche that had only momentarily come to rest. The covers rose and fell over his thick body with his breathing. His jaw hung a little slack, lips slightly parted. His skin still looked bulletproof, and he needed a shave.

So we met again, Nick and I. Here was the louse who had told his boys to slug me, kick me, work me over, and dump me in the desert. The louse responsible for the cold-blooded murder of Lou Rio, and framing me for it. The slob who had caused me practically all of my hell and most of my lumps over the last lumpy days.

I grinned and slowly let out my breath, and I said softly, "O.K., Nick, now it's my turn."

Then I shifted the little flashlight in my hand so that, while I could still see Nick clearly enough, the beam of light fell full on my face—on my recently washed white hair and eyebrows, and on my cheery grin, because for this moment at least I felt cheery—and then in a loud voice, I said:

"Hey, Nick, wake up!"

Chapter Seventeen

He CAME out of sleep like a man who hadn't even closed his eyes. One moment he was lying there unconscious and the next he was coming up off the bed at me.

I'd held the light on my face so that he would be sure to recognize me, get a good look and recognize me fast, because that was important to my plan. And it worked well enough; almost too well. He recognized me immediately and came at me so quickly that I barely had time to swing the sap.

I had time, though.

I wasn't able to carefully pick a spot, but the sap landed just about an inch above the handsome gray area at the side of Nick's thick black hair. I swung the sap not hard enough to kill him, but hard enough that I wouldn't have to worry about him for quite a while. Whatever he'd started to yell came out in a whisper as he went limp and slumped back on the bed.

I threw back the blanket which had been over him. His shirt was off and his muscular chest bulged beneath a silk undershirt. Otherwise he was fully dressed, including his shoes. That was exactly as Viper had described it, as was the location of Nick's .45 on a small table next to the bed.

I dropped the sap into my pocket and shoved the .45 under my belt, then jumped into the front office and flicked on the lights. They blazed brightly in the room, shocking my eyes after the dimness.

And then there was the sound of a gunshot.

It had started. My fourteen minutes were up and the unrolling tape out there in the blackness of the desert had reached the spot where a single gunshot had been recorded. In one minute more the real noise would start—but even now everybody in and around the hotel would be looking out into the desert listening. That's what I wanted. It was too soon, but I hadn't expected this to go perfectly. Everything was working out wonderfully well so far, and I wasn't going to kick just be-

160

cause I was a few minutes behind schedule. Not yet. But that meant I had only four minutes before Malcolm Waters landed his helicopter out in back again, four minutes in which to do everything for which I'd planned to have more than twice that long.

But at least everybody was listening now, ears cocked out into the desert, wondering if they would hear any more sounds. They would. They were going to hear the sound track from *Jungle Fury,* and if that didn't jar them a bit, nothing ever would.

Well, if I had only a minute, a minute it would have to be. I swung my head around, examining the office closely. On the wall behind Nick's desk were those three framed pictures—a photo of Desert Trails itself, the photograph of a U. S. Senator, inscribed "To Nick Colossus—name it and you can have it," and an oil painting of a desert landscape. On Nick's desk were the ashtray made out of twenty-dollar gold pieces, and his small desk calendar.

I got busy. I took all three pictures off the walls and stuffed them under my shirt. They made an awkward mass an inch and a half thick, but I thought I could carry them there all right. The ashtray and desk calendar I stuffed into my coat pockets. A last quick glance around showed me the walls bare and the desk bare except for the beige phone. I jumped for the bedroom door and inside. Nick lay silently on the bed.

And then it started. I heard the rattle of sporadic gunfire, shrill screams, the thudding of drums. My minute was up and the *Jungle Fury* sound track was blasting its noises at the Desert Trails.

I felt sick. Soon slobs would be rushing up here to report to Nick Colossus that strange things indeed were afoot. And I was at this moment, according to schedule, supposed to be well away from the hotel, in the desert behind it. In three minutes Malcolm would be bringing the helicopter down—to pick me up. Cold sweat actually, literally, sprang out on my skin, from my scalp to my big feet. I think it even popped out on my toes. But I forced my mind away from possible horrible consequences and to the job at hand.

As I bent toward Nick, those sounds from the desert sands banged against my ears. It was quite faint in here—but outside it must have been a shrieking clamorousness striking amazement and maybe even curdled horror into numerous hoodlums and guests. The amount of time I had before two or three hoods burst in here depended upon the extent of their amazement and horror. Perhaps the sound track from another movie, a different Magna production, would have been better, but I had merely told Feldspen I wanted something which would provide an enormous amount of noise and snatch the attention of practically everybody within hearing distance. And he had chosen quite well. I'd seen the film itself as half of a double bill, and if I recalled the scenes, these were the sounds of the climax.

Yes, at this very moment the elephants were trumpeting out there on the black California desert. The great elephant stampede had begun. Now the savages were attacking. I could hear them screeching. They were killing everybody, all the white hunters, and soon they would be dancing around the golden-haired tomato cooking at the stake like blonde shish-kebab. It was *Jungle Fury*, all right. I would have given a thousand dollars to be at the bar right now, examining the variety of available expressions. I would have bet it all, too, that plenty of double bourbons and Scotches and martinis would be sold this night.

But all of those thoughts occupied only about four seconds in my mind, four seconds during which I grabbed one of Nick's leg-like arms and hauled him to a sitting position. I got the beefy arm around my neck and wrestled him onto my back, strained to straighten up with him. There is nothing at all weak about me, and my 206 pounds is mostly muscle and very little fat, but at first I couldn't move that flesh monster.

But then I shifted my feet, got better leverage, and strained upward. At the same moment the sound of the African "savages" screaming, *"Ogbooogi-jooweejie-bahgoa!"* or something very like it as they raced into the white man's camp squirted a little extra adrenalin into my bloodstream, and I stood erect with Nick Colossus draped limply over my back, and staggered into the brightly-lighted front room.

I made it to the door, started down the steps. I could hear footsteps pounding in the hallway below and for a moment I thought it must be somebody racing up here for Nick and I let go of his wrists with one hand, grabbed for his .45 in my belt. But the feet pounded on by the door. Probably a drunken guest fleeing from the attack. I staggered down the steps to the hallway door, and with every inch Nick got heavier.

Every rib that his thugs had banged and bent ached, and seemed about to crack. Every bruise and contusion felt as if it were getting blacker and more tender. My left arm under its bandage, seemed bathed in fire. But I made it to the door, kicked it open and stepped into the hall.

As I stepped through the door a woman in a pink dress looked at me, opened her mouth, closed it, opened it again in ghastly fashion, then silently spun around and jumped into the room behind her, slamming the door.

Now that I was out of Nick's room and in the hotel hallway, I could hear the awful noises banging eardrums in and around the hotel. That recorder Feldspen had supplied me with must surely have been one of the most powerful made, for the sounds seemed not a hundred yards and more away, but practically inside the hotel itself. The monstrous war drums boomed practically in my ears, and the shouts and battle cries and shrieks and screams blended into an absolute horror of eight-dimensional whoops and ululations.

The purpose of all this sound had originally been to draw all attention to the front of the hotel, and perhaps cause several of Nick's hoods to go out there to investigate, but also to drown out the sound of—and keep curious eyes from—the soon-to-be-descending helicopter. But hearing it now in my own ears, it seemed likely that not only would that dual purpose be accomplished, but in addition half the people here would be thrown into such confusion that I might have driven up right past the pool in a red and white sports car and taken Nick away in it.

That's what I was doing, after all. I was taking Nick away —or making a good stab at it. Yes, indeed, this was the kidnaping of Nick Colossus.

Despite my pleasure with the way this had gone so far, I knew very well that my luck couldn't possibly last much longer, not even the kind of arranged-for luck which might conceivably be expected to follow all the thinking and planning which had gone into preparing for this moment. So I moved as fast as I could, stumbling under Nick's steadily increasing weight, toward that open window.

I almost made it. Even halfway there my lungs were raw and burning, and every muscle in my body felt torn. I was making good time, though, my legs strong and reasonably steady under me. But as I reached the window and lowered Nick's body so that his feet flopped through it, and then started to shove him forward and out, I was spotted.

Nobody yelled at me this time. This time it was just a gunshot. The gun cracked and the slug snapped through the air alongside my head, crashing through the raised window with a sharp splat followed by the tinkling of glass as I spun around. I let go of Nick. He slumped limply in the window, half in and

half out of it but with his head inside, in the exact reverse of
Whitey's earlier position.

I glimpsed Nick settling into that posture as I turned grabbing the .45 and thumbing off the safety when I brought it up
from my belt. Halfway between the far end of the hall and the
open door leading up to Nick's suite stood Montana, gun raised
in his hand and aimed at me.

He hesitated, undoubtedly because of Nick behind me, hesitated for part of a second.

That gave me time. I fired twice, the slugs whistling past his
legs—and then his legs were whistling past the far end of the
hall and out of sight around it. I heard his feet thumping down
the corridor to the stairway, and he at least set a new record for
that distance. He would run just far enough, however, to spread
the word that I was stealing the boss.

I hadn't wanted to take a chance on marking Nick up, messing his clothes or bruising him anywhere except the spot on
which the sap had landed. But I couldn't be cautious now. I
grabbed his shoulders in my hands, lifted and shoved. He went
out and down—but at least he went down feet first. Not too
much damage should come from that. And then I went out
after him.

His falling body had knocked the bamboo ladder away, so I
hung by my hands and dropped to the ground. The framed pictures fell from inside my shirt, buttons tearing from the cloth. I
swore, dropped the .45 into my coat pocket and used my flash
briefly, grabbed the pictures and jammed them under my belt.

Somehow I got Nick onto my back again. Strangely, he
seemed lighter. I knew that of course he weighed exactly the
same, but I was so charged up now that for a minute or so I
would probably have been able to lug around somebody weighing
twice what Nick weighed. There must have been so many hor-
mones and gland juices in my blood that the corpuscles were
drunk on the stuff. There were screams and shouts inside the
hotel now, joining the crazy noises from the sound track—and
then, suddenly, the sound track ended. All noises from out there
in the desert stopped.

The tape would have run for another half an hour if not disturbed. Somebody among the hoods or guests or drunks had
braved the Jubongi tribe's attack and ended it all with the flick
of a wrist—or stomp of a hard heel.

And in the sudden, shocking silence, I heard the beat of the
helicopter's rotors. Malcolm Waters was coming in right on time.

In fact, he was in, he was there. I was the boy not on time. I was the late Shell Scott.

That had an awful sound: The Late Shell Scott.

I tried to run, but you don't run with a Nick Colossus on your back. And after all this trouble, all this hell, I wasn't leaving him now. Not if they shot me, stabbed me, boiled me in oil, was I leaving Nick. Either we both got out of here or neither of us left.

Blindingly, lights blazed all around me. I didn't look back but I knew what it was. There would be plenty of ordinarily unused lights, including spotlights, handy here and all of them were being used now. You just couldn't expect to kidnap Nick without stirring up a fuss. A gun cracked. Two yards to my right and ahead of me, dirt jumped; the bullet bounced invisibly from the earth and whined off over the desert with the metallic twanging sound of a ricochet.

I could see the helicopter now, in the bright flood of light. Still more than fifty yards away, it rested on the bare ground, rotor blades flashing in the light as they spun above it. I glanced back just as another gun cracked and the slug snapped past in the night air, and it looked for a moment as if those imaginary savages from the sound track were actually here, become real and attacking. Attacking—me.

At least ten, possibly as many as a score of hoods, I didn't worry about a head count, were running from the hotel building and grounds toward me. There was even one guy on a horse, galloping around the running men and charging in my direction.

I didn't look more than a fraction of a second at that miserable mass of running death. I swung my head around toward that still-too-far-away helicopter. And then even my forlorn hope of reaching it seemed to blow up in my face. Because it appeared that Malcolm Waters had seen that raging crowd behind me, too, and was getting away from it fast.

The rotors spun faster, the buglike helicopter soared up from the ground. I heard another gunshot crack loud in the night air. And behind me, like the sound of death running at my heels, swelled the drumming of hoofs.

I swung around, heavy .45 coming up toward the sound of the horse charging at me, and both horse and rider were outlined by the light behind them. I couldn't recognize the rider, but I could see the glint of light from the gun in his hand, and then the bright flash of flame as he fired. He hit me.

It wasn't bad, but he hit me. The slug slapped at my side, passing under the arm with which I still held Nick's massive wrists together and flaming through the flesh. It must have been a small handgun, because the shock didn't knock me down, or even spin me around. It jarred me, but I was still able to get off a shot. And the horseman was so close I couldn't miss.

I fired just once at him when he was three or four yards away. He was close enough so that I could pick my spot, so I aimed for his shoulder and squeezed the trigger. I heard the heavy .45 slug slap into him. He seemed to soar off the horse and through the air to thud heavily against the dirt as the horse galloped past me.

I turned the gun toward those running men and fired until the .45 was empty. The men scattered, several diving to the ground. And then I heard the roar of the helicopter's engines again— Waters hadn't been running away from those hoods, but *at* them. When I had more time, I would realize how much sheer guts that had taken.

When I turned he was just setting the machine down close to me. I stumbled toward it, wind from the rotor blades slapping at me, and somehow shoved Nick's body off my shoulders and in through the open door.

"Hurry *up,* you damn fool! Hurry up!" Waters was yelling.

Hell, I *was* hurrying. I was moving like lightning, it seemed to me. Waters twisted the throttle open even farther, making the beat of the rotors swell, the machine rock, the skids completely leave the ground. Those charging hoodlums were still charging —and close now.

Nick's .45, still in my hand, was empty; but my own .38 at my shoulder was loaded with six 158-grain bullets. I yanked the Colt Special out and it fit my hand like my palm, familiar and friendly —and deadly.

When I raised the gun and aimed at the first of the men, I had time to notice that there were eight of them running, several more behind them just getting up and starting this way. Four men, out in front of the pack, led the rest. I just swung the gun from right to left, from one man to the next, aiming at their legs, and squeezing off the spaced shots like timed fire on the police pistol range.

I saw the first man stagger and fall, the second and third kept on coming but the fourth man went down like a stone, rolled over and over yelling. The others hit the dirt then, and that stopped the men behind them. With Waters shouting loudly at my back, I squeezed off the last two shots, aiming low, and the bullets whined nastily as they ricocheted from the earth.

Then I turned and jumped into the helicopter. Waters

pulled it into the air with a jerk, swearing, shoved the right-hand stick forward and we lurched violently. I'd barely gotten onto the seat when it shoved up against me hard as Waters lifted the machine fast, spinning it around at the same time, both hands working and his mouth moving as he swore blisteringly. Below I saw three or four winking lights as somebody fired at us, but nothing hit us or the helicopter.

I looked at Waters, then at Nick, massive and inert, on the seat between the pilot and me, slumped against me. My mind seemed deadened, its resilience sapped by the tension and excitement, the sounds and violence of the last minutes, but underneath it was a pulsing exhilaration.

I'd gone into the Desert Trails and come out with Nick Colossus. I'd bearded the lion in his den and belled the big cat. Actually, now that it was over, I could see how it might have gone off without a hitch, and I could have gotten in and out without even a shot being fired. But I wasn't kicking; just to have done it, to have gone in and come out alive with the lion, was quite enough for me.

I knew, too, that I was in the deep hole now—the deepest. There was one more act coming up, the final one, but I still had to beat Nick; I hadn't won yet. And if I lost this time, I lost it all.

I became conscious of warm wetness on my side. Blood had spread on my shirt, beneath my coat, where that small slug had caused some minor damage. It hadn't bled very much, but it stung like fury. The furrow on my left arm had opened up again, too, and stained the bandage on it. There were bandages and adhesive tape in the helicopter, and I staunched the flow of blood, tightly bandaged both wounds. Neither of them would incapacitate me, but they weren't going to speed me up. I ached in just about all the places there were, and in some places I'd thought there weren't, and I felt lousy. Lousy, but exhilarated.

I took my Colt out of its holster, loaded it with fresh ammunition. My fingers were shaking. In fact, my hand and everything attached to it was shaking. As I shoved the last deadly, ugly bullet into my gun—and seen completely, in all its dimensions, a bullet is perhaps uglier than any other thing in this world—that ugliness caused a different thought to swim into my mind. I leaned forward, peering through the plexiglass blister.

Waters was still swearing under his breath, letting off steam. He growled at me, "Well, you damn fool. What are you doing? What in hell are you looking for now?"

"Just . . . Orion," I said.

We landed at Magna, in a cleared space on the sprawling lot, at a couple of minutes after nine P.M. that Thursday night. Waters set the helicopter down neatly near Sound Stage Three and we got out. Nick was still unconscious, but I'd had to tap him a second time with the sap during the flight here.

Waiting for us when we landed were Harry Feldspen and two husky men. Harry stepped forward and silently squeezed my hand. "I'll confess now," he said. "I didn't think you'd make it."

I grinned at him. "I'll confess, too. There were about a dozen times when I didn't think I'd make it, either."

"How did it go?"

"Pretty rough. But we're here. Incidentally, the Academy may have snubbed *Jungle Fury,* but I give it the Shell Scott award. It was beautiful."

"Well, I knew it would provide a great deal of noise."

"That it did. Everything ready here?"

"Yes. It was surprisingly easy once I got used to the idea except . . ." He was having trouble saying something. "Shell," he began again, and stopped.

"What's the matter?" I looked at the two men and then jerked a thumb at Nick. "Take him in," I said, then looked back at Harry.

He said, "It's Coral."

"Coral?" She had been in and out of my mind a lot during this night, but there had been too much going on for me to dwell on her for long—or on why she hadn't answered her phone earlier. But Harry's hesitation and the expression on his face sent a ripple of fright over my skin. "What's the matter with her? Isn't she here?"

"No." He shook his head.

I had been a little worried about her, when I'd been unable to reach her by phone, but I hadn't really expected anything to be seriously wrong. Fear for her was a cold weight in my stomach.

"Tell me," I said.

"Well . . . we don't know for sure, Shell. I phoned, but there was no answer, so I sent a man out there. She wasn't in her room at the motel. She hadn't checked out; she was just gone. A light was on, door open. It looked very much as if she had left suddenly. Perhaps unwillingly. And . . ."

He paused again. His phrase, "as if she had left suddenly" pushed into my mind the memory of her sudden flight from her house Tuesday night. She'd made it that time, gotten away from Nick's two men without harm, but I knew that twice would be too much. For it to have happened again, and for her to have gotten away again, would have been too unlikely a coincidence, No, if someone had caught up with her a second time, I knew in my bones that they had her still, had her now.

And then Harry said, "There was a towel on the floor. As if somebody had been hurt, and staunched the flow of blood with a handy towel."

He said "somebody" but of course he meant Coral; Harry just didn't want to say it. I told him, "There's only one way it could have happened. Nick's men got her. It must have been Nick's men." I shook my head. "How did they find her? How did they know she was in the Oasis?"

It was a rhetorical question; Harry could hardly know the answer. I said to him, "Well, I've *got* to go through with it now— more than ever, I have to go through with it. It's the only way now I might be able to help her. Show me that back door."

He showed me. At the rear of Sound Stage Three was a small seldom used door, an emergency exit. In a way, that was appropriate, because this was an emergency. Besides which, I didn't want to go in the front way; there were people in front whom I didn't want to see until later—if at all.

Harry opened the emergency door and we both went inside. Dim light filled the interior of the sound stage and as we walked toward an enclosed structure a few feet away I could see the shadowy booms and lights, cameras and overhead beams and spots. We stepped over a coil of insulated electrical cable and then were at a small door.

Harry said, "This is it."

I grinned at him, half-heartedly, in the dimness. "In more ways than one, Harry." I said, and as he turned and walked away I opened the door and stepped inside—into the Desert Trails office of Nick Colossus.

Chapter Eighteen

EVERYTHING was just the same. The walls were smoothly paneled in rich walnut. The carpet was a plain rich brown, wall to wall. Behind the big black desk was a padded leather chair. On my left was a leather couch identical with that at the Desert Trails, and two overstuffed chairs which looked to me exactly like those in which Jabber and Whitey had sat two days ago, just before helping to beat me unconscious.

Undoubtedly the lumps in the upholstery of the couch and chairs were in different places from the originals, but to me they looked identical. This was an exact-as-possible replica of Nick's office. It was possible that Nick would notice something wrong, if he had time to examine everything closely—but I didn't intend to give him time.

I was now—even though there were no guns going off, no hoods trying to slam me over the head, in fact no sounds at all —just about as excited as I had been at any other time all evening. The fright, the worry that a bullet was about to slam into me—that was gone. But I was as charged up and tense, as quiveringly on the edge of popping open with suppressed excitement as I had been at any other time today.

Because this, as Feldspen had unconsciously said, was it. This was where the men were separated from the boys. This was the end of the line, either for Nick or for me. I was clear out on the end of my limb now, and I could either saw it off or get back to firm ground somehow. The next few minutes would tell.

The two husky men who had carried Nick here now stood in a doorway on my left, a doorway which led into another small— and, I knew, incomplete—room containing a bed. And now containing also, I presumed, Nick Colossus.

The taller of the two men asked me, "In here where you wanted him?"

"Yeah. He make any noises yet?"

"Nope. Still cold."

I walked to the door. Nick was lying on top of the bed. I said, "Give me a hand," and had them lift him up while I pulled the blanket down. Then they lowered him to the bed and I pulled the blanket up over him, under his arms as I'd seen him, a hundred miles away, over an hour ago.

"Thanks," I said to the men. "That's all."

They left. As they went out of the room it looked, even to me, as if they must be going out and then down the stairs to the Desert Trails hallway, instead of into a dim sound stage. I added the final touches. With a last look at Nick I walked back into the "office." I had carried in the stuff I'd brought from Nick's real office—the three pictures, the ashtray and desk calendar. Hooks were already in the walnut paneling behind the desk, in the location which I had remembered from my first visit to the Desert Trails, and as I'd thus described their location to Feldspen when I'd first broached this idea to him yesterday.

I hung the three pictures on the hooks, in the same order as they'd been at the Desert Trails. They seemed spaced well enough, at least as far as I could tell. I put the gold-coin ashtray and small calendar on the desk in approximately the same positions they'd occupied on Nick's real desk, shoved the beige phone to its far side. That beige phone was a dummy, not connected, but I had to take the chance Nick wouldn't have time to try using it. If he tried . . . well, I'd worry about that when it happened. I placed Nick's empty gun and my leather-covered sap on the desk top and stepped back. Everything looked okay to me. That was all I could do until Nick woke up.

I went into the next room and stood over him. Minutes later he stirred and a soft sound pressed through his lips. I walked back into the next room, leaving the door open a foot so Nick couldn't miss the light streaming through into his darkened "bedroom," and started slamming the desk doors open and closed as if searching for something.

My only worry at this point was that Nick might decide to look around his bedroom first, before charging in here. But I had a hunch that his last memory—of my gleeful face in the beam of my own flash just before the lights had gone out for him—would be the first thing in his mind when he came to, and thus he would charge in here right off the bat.

And that's just about the way it happened.

While pretending to be much occupied with the desk, I heard the faint creak of bed springs, the soft sound as Nick stepped to the door and looked in at me. I could see him from the corner of my eye as he pulled the door slowly wider, getting ready to send his huge bulk through it. I tensed my muscles, pulled a drawer open and then slammed it shut, turned my back partly to Nick as I reached for another drawer.

For just a moment I ran over some details in my mind, trying to find any flaw. But I found nothing wrong, not yet anyway. Nick's last memory would have been of going to bed at the Desert Trails and then waking suddenly to see me—and be sapped by me. He was now awake. But there was no way in the world that he could know it had been more than, say, a few minutes since he'd been sapped.

His head would be hurting, but after a sapping it would naturally hurt. For all Nick knew, his thick hair and skull had kept him from being out very long and consequently he would assume he was going to catch me by surprise as I went through his desk.

And that's just what he did. He eased the door wide, took two long strides as silently as he could toward me, and then jumped at me. I let him get almost to me before I swung around with a startled shout.

It just about ended right then. His big beef of a fist was roaring through the air at me, and I almost swung around squarely into it. That would have been all, the end. That would have meant Nick, in about ten seconds after I became unconscious, would have learned of the trick played on him. And, if that happened, there would be absolutely nothing to prevent Nick from walking right out of here and going—a bit bewildered maybe, but free and vengeful—back to the Desert Trails.

But the blow didn't land squarely. That rock-hard fist caught me a glancing blow on the side of the jaw and bounced me away from him. The room went a little out of focus—but that was all right. It was fine, in fact, because I had to make this part look good too. I couldn't afford one single thing from now on that might make Nick suspicious. Nick had to beat me, to lick me, in a fair or foul fight. And he had a good start. Maybe that blow almost made us even, because Nick couldn't be feeling too chipper after being sapped twice on the head.

He came at me like a bull who ate matadors, head lowered, arms out like horns and reaching for me. I let him come, stepped in between the reaching arms and slammed my right into his gut and poked my left against his jaw. About all I did was ruin the knuckles of both hands. The jarring movement tore at both bandaged spots, on my side and arm.

He roared with rage, not pain, and swung a paw at me. It hit me and caved in my chest. At least it felt as if it had caved in. I sailed backward and landed on my fanny, flopped flat on my back—then rolled to the side just in time as Nick leaped at me and tried to stomp me. He actually went up into the air and came down toward my face with his heels driving, as lumberjacks used to do occasionally, when they wanted to rip a man's face off with the spiked soles of their boots.

And that got to me, that really bored into my brain and lit a hot fire there. All the fun went out of this, all the kicks. I just couldn't find a kind thought or feeling anywhere in me for Nick Colossus. I rolled over and got to my feet and waited for Nick, and this time I was going to mess him up a bit if I got the chance. For a little while there I forgot exactly where we were, and it was just Nick Colossus and me facing each other with a lot of hot blood between us.

He came at me more slowly this time, eyes flicking around. He saw the .45 and the sap on his desk, then his eyes came back to me again, those blue eyes as hard and bright as stainless steel, eyes with murder in them now. And he grinned a little this time. Grinned and stepped toward me. He feinted with his left and then started his right at me, but I was expecting it, moved just enough to let the launched fist plummet past my chin, and then I stepped in close to him with my own right fist driving.

It caught him squarely on the mouth and his head snapped back. He threw one arm out and staggered, caught his balance. His lips were mashed, bleeding. He put his arms out and rushed me again. He was big, but he was slow. I got out of his way without trouble and as he went by close on my right I thought for a moment of Coral, of his hired hands slugging me, of his hard laughter—and I caught his cheek with a jolting left hand.

He went down, sprawling on hands and knees. Partly it was from being knocked off balance; he wasn't out or even close to it. And those two taps on the head earlier had taken a lot out of big Nick Colossus. But even so, that moment was a good moment for me, because even banged up and half-mutilated as I was I knew I had him, knew I could take him then. Even at his best, I could take him. And that made it easy for me to lose to him.

When he came at me this time, I purposely moved slowly, too slowly. He swung his left hard and I managed to turn, catching the blow on my shoulder, but then the next fist landed high on my head and I went down. I also went about halfway out, something roaring in my head and the light dimming and slowly surging up again, as if regulated by a rheostat.

But I had enough control to fall toward the desk and grab for its edge, straining a hand forward as if trying to reach the gun there. And that was another ticklish moment. If Nick had decided to slam me a couple more times, I would have had to get up off the floor—or try to—and go around some more with him. But the suggestion inherent in my reaching for the gun was enough; it did the trick.

Nick reacted in the normal, logical fashion. Before my fingers could touch the .45 he stepped forward and grabbed it. Then he slapped the slide back with one fast motion of his left hand and aimed the gun at me.

"Nick—wait!" I shouted it, as I jumped to my feet, and there was a kind of panic in my voice that must have gotten to Nick. But the reason it was there was because I knew the gun was empty, and if Nick pulled the trigger he would know it too—when I just sat there shouting instead of getting filled with heavy slugs. That would blow the whole thing up in my face, too, and I yelled again, *"Hold it, Nick. Don't—"*

Ah, he liked that. He liked it a lot. Shell Scott was panicked, was crawling, pleading. Nick was big again; maybe he could even convince himself soon that I hadn't knocked him down, hadn't been ready to ruin him. He stepped away from me, holding the gun casually now. Big Nick, at ease once more, in control.

And that, of course, was perfect. That was exactly the way I wanted Nick Colossus. On top, in control, the situation well in hand, safe and secure in his familiar suite atop the Desert Trails hideaway.

He said softly, "Scott, you crazy slob. You jerk. What in hell made you think you could come in here and get away with this?" He paused. "How'd you get in, anyway?"

"I came in through the window at the end of the hallway, sapped Whitey and picked the locks."

He nodded slowly. "I got to hand it to you, Scott. But what did you expect to get? You can't bug this place, clear out in the desert and set up like we are."

"I haven't tried to bug the joint."

"Even if you tried, you couldn't get out. You're dead this time, Scott. This time you go all the way." He glanced at the desk I'd been going through when he'd come out of the next room. "There's nothing in the desk," he said. And he spoke more truth than he knew. There was absolutely nothing in the desk. He went on, "What in hell possessed you to come here again?"

"I had a wild idea that I might get enough on you to send you to Q."

Nick got a boot out of that. His hard face cracked in a grin; it was a little like a block of granite splitting open and chuckling. "You always were good for a laugh, Scott," he said.

"I thought maybe I could even get you to tell me the few things I don't know. Why not, Nick? You've got a sense of humor. And you must admit I've worked hard for the answers."

He slapped his thigh—but not with the gun hand. "Why not?" he said. "I don't really hate you, pal—it's O.K. with me if you die happy." He chuckled some more, through bloody lips. "You sure made a mistake coming back here again, Scott. I really figured you for more sense."

"You had me in the kind of spot where almost anything I might get on you would help. I wasn't going to live long anyway."

"That's true enough. I suppose you mean the spot I fixed for you with Lou's boys."

"That's part of it." There were other things I was more anxious to know about, but I had to ease Nick along and let him think he was guiding the conversation. So I followed his lead and said, "I talked to Suez, so I know how you set that party up. But why did you kill Lou Rio at all, Nick?"

He said casually, "The area never was big enough for both of us, so Lou had to go. The only question was when. I'd have killed that bum a long time ago, Scott, only everybody knew we hated each other's guts and I'd have stood out unless it was handled just right."

"An alibi, you mean."

"I could fix an alibi for the law easy enough, but the main thing was to keep Lou's boys from knowing I burned their boss down. That's a tougher court." He grinned, those great white teeth flashing at me. "After the way Lou and Gangrene worked you over, chump, it was a perfect time for it—you had all the motive I needed." He paused. "Besides, I persuaded Valentine to tell me that when Lou and Gangrene worked you over you'd just told Lou somebody was putting the bite on Magna for a million."

"Yeah. I told him, and he seemed surprised. No wonder. He *was* surprised."

Nick chuckled again. "Uh-huh. But besides being surprised,

he could have found out fast who was behind it, and that would
have caused me a lot more trouble than Feldspen—or you. I
didn't even know Lou had money in the studio until last
Monday. No, Lou's time was up; it was the perfect time for him
to go."

"Jabber didn't blast Lou then? You did it yourself, Nick?"

"The pleasure was mine. Jabber just met him at the back door
with a heater and showed him inside." He grinned again.
"Lou nearly died of fright before I shot him. He knew what
was coming, and he begged me not to do it. Last thing he said
was 'Oh, God, save me' and then I let him have three pills.
Three of *your* pills."

"The medicine cured him of living, Nick." I didn't move. I
just continued to stand still facing him, but Nick seemed to be
quite at ease now, completely unsuspecting, so I asked the
question uppermost in my mind. "Another reason I took a chance
on coming here was because of Coral James."

"What about her?"

"Somebody snatched her from the motel she was in. At least
that's the way it looks. Right, Nick?"

"The boys got her, huh?"

"What boys?"

"Flint and Shortcake," he said conversationally. "I sent
them to the Oasis for her—and you, pal, especially for you—as
soon as we found out where you two had holed up."

"That still puzzles me, Nick. How did you find us?"

"Easy. I had a man planted in the Continental Hotel. He saw
you leave in a hurry for Partridge Street after I had that dame
call you." I remembered Viper had told me about that man with
field glasses in the Continental Hotel down the street from the
Spartan. Nick went on, "He also saw you come *back* to the Spartan after you shot up Jabber." Nick shook his head. "I still don't
know how you managed to get away from Jabber *and* Lou's
boys. I put in a call to Gangrene right after I banged Lou and
said you'd killed him. They must've been there in three or four
minutes after I left."

"They were, but I outran their bullets."

Nick laughed, and it sounded like nuts and bolts rattling
around in a washtub. "Scott, I hate to kill you. I never saw a guy
about to die so calm."

I kept him talking. "So you had a man in the Continental
Hotel and he saw me come back. So what?"

"Figure it out, pal. A minute later you took off with the
dame, with Coral, and lit out. I didn't know where to, but it

was a fairly sure thing you'd check into a hotel or motel. I
knew the approximate time you'd be registering. So I just had
the boys start phoning to check hotel and motel registrations—
motel managers nearly always copy down license numbers; and
a friend supplied me with the plate number on your Cad. It was
just a matter of time and a little trouble." He looked at his
watch. "Flint was supposed to phone me at eight." As he looked
at his watch, a puzzled expression grew on his face. "What in
hell time is it?"

There must have been a new expression on my face, too.
A sick expression. Not only about Coral; that was bad enough.
But also because I had forgotten to set Nick's watch back. Mistake number one. I looked at my own watch—it was nearly
nine-thirty P.M. Nick would know something was screwy, know
that I couldn't have been rummaging around in his office for an
hour or more without being spotted by his men.

So I pretended to wind my watch, but instead pulled out the
stem and changed the time by several hours in case Nick looked
at it. "This thing's haywire," I said.

That puzzled look stayed on Nick's face. I said quickly, "What
will Flint and Shortcake do to her?"

He shrugged. "I just told them to pick you both up, but if
you weren't there to bring her here. I want to ask her some
questions, find out what she knows about Valentine, among
other things. As close to you as she *obviously* is, Scott, she
must know it all. So I'll probably have to kill her." Nick grinned
through his puffed red lips. "Maybe the two of you can share
the same hole in the ground. How would you like to share a
grave with Coral James, pal?"

Then his grin went away. He looked at the beige phone on
his desk. But the phone he thought he was looking at was a
hundred miles away. "They should have called me by now," he
said, then shook his head in exasperation. "What time have you
got?"

I looked at my watch. "This one's way off. I've got four-thirty
last Saturday. Tell me, Nick, how about Valentine? Did you
do that yourself too or just have it done?"

"Hold it up, pal." I thought for a moment I'd said something
wrong, but Nick was just changing the setup a little. He said,
"You always carry a rod, so out with it. I don't have to tell
you . . ." He let it trail off, but he didn't have to tell me not to
get fancy. With great care I took out the .38. "On the floor
easy, and kick it," he said casually.

Nick was enjoying this. And only now did I realize what a

good thing it was that I'd decided Nick and I should have a small battle before he took charge of the situation. Because it was my slugging him around a time or two, and knocking him sprawling, which made him now enjoy lording it over me for a while. He picked up my gun—flipped the cylinder out and checked the loads, then shoved the .45 into his waistband, and held the .38 on me.

My jaw sagged. Mistake number two. I hadn't planned this at all. Nick was supposed to stand there holding an empty .45 on me, not my gun with live cartridges in it. Not this one—this one could kill me.

Chapter Nineteen

I SAID unhappily, "That's the second time you've had my gun, Nick."

"Yeah," he grunted. "In fact, pal, it was having your gun that gave me the whole idea for the Rio job. Back up about two steps." I stepped back and he walked around behind his desk to the leather chair there. He sat down and looked at me, then looked all around the room as if everything had gone just a little out of focus.

He knew then that something was wrong. Something—but he didn't know what it could be. And I didn't want him thinking about it. I said, "You started to tell me about Valentine."

"Not much to it. I had Jabber and Shortcake pick him up and sap him, then give him the toss, and beat it. The witnesses were all set; they're in Mexico now, living it up at the Del Prado on my money." He reached out and picked up the phone.

I got a weak feeling at the back of my legs behind the knees, and unconsciously I held my breath for a moment, then said, "Why kill him at all when he was your source for the blackmail info?"

"Val had served his purpose, Scott." Nick put the dead phone to his ear and went on. "Besides, even before he took the pills here at the ranch, he'd been getting more and more upset about the jobs he'd done for me. He wasn't any more good to me, and I was afraid he might crack up. Well, he sure did. Cracked wide open." Nick was frowning, listening to the phone against his ear and frowning.

I was sweating again. It seemed as if I must have sweat forty gallons tonight. Nick went on. "The minute I saw the suicide note he wrote here, I knew how I was going to kill him. But I had to wait a few days after the doc pulled him out of it. So it would look like he'd tried it again and made the grade the second time. Maybe the smartest thing I did was using that old suicide note to cover up the kill there at the Madison."

"Then you didn't kill him because I'd come into the picture."

Nick shook his head. "No, but your being in it helped me decide the time had come. His time. Besides, I'd already made the big pitch to his boss, so Val was just in the way."

Nick frowned at the phone in his hand, then reached over and banged the cradle up and down a few times, put the phone to his ear once more.

"You mean the million dollar bite," I said.

"Yeah. I'll still get it from Feldspen's moneybags; might take a little longer, thanks to you, Scott. But there'll still be a pay-off." He banged the phone receiver with his hand again and swore, then glared at me. "You didn't cut the line here, did you, pal?"

"No, I didn't. Something puzzles me, Nick. You had Flint tell Feldspen on the phone that there was thirteen million tied up in unreleased films. The only way it comes out that way is including Coral James' two pictures—but she wasn't paying off."

"No, she wasn't. But I still had some dirt on her; she wouldn't pay to hush it, but maybe H. J. would.—Besides, thirteen million sounds a lot better than five million especially when I was asking for a cool million." He chuckled. "I mean, a hot million."

Then he stopped chuckling, looked at the phone in his hand and slammed it violently back in the cradle, anger suddenly darkening his thick face. "What in the hell's with that dame? She off the switchboard again? Can't get a thing. Phone's dead or something."

I swallowed. "What did you have on Valentine, Nick?"

He kept on scowling, but he said, "Not such a hell of a big thing. Just enough to get him started—"but *after* that, of course he was a blackmailer. And I had *that* on him. I planned this around Valentine, Scott. First I learned from one of Flint's friends that Johnny Palomino was on M." I remembered Palomino's pinpoint pupils. "That gave me the idea. I figured out that Valentine would probably be the best bet to dig up dirt on other stars. So I really did a complete check on Valentine. The only thing I came up with was that he'd done a year and a day for clouting a car when he was twenty-one. But it scared him." He shrugged. "Besides which I scared him another way; said I'd kill him if he didn't do the job for me. Or Flint told him for me. Flint did all the contact work—even phoning H. J. Feldspen—except Viper picked up the cash." Nick paused, brow furrowed in thought for a moment. "Valentine almost broke it off in me at that," he said.

"Yeah, he set it up pretty well," I said, "considering the fact that he decided to kill himself sort of on the spur of the moment, and thought he'd be dead in a few minutes. Actually, Nick, he made only one mistake."

"What was that?" Nick looked puzzled.

"He didn't die. If he *had* died when he took those pills, his confession would have been mailed to the D.A., you'd have been named as the would-be blackmailer of Magna—none of this would have happened."

"Yeah. But it did happen." He was silent for a moment, thinking. "Too bad about Val in a way. I made him pull some tricks, but he wasn't such a bad head." He grinned. "On the other hand, he was not Prince Val."

"No. But, then, you're not Saint Nick, either."

He shook his head. "Man, you're a cool one. And you're going to get a lot cooler." Nick stood up suddenly, those hard bright eyes boring into mine. He transferred my gun to his left hand and picked up my sap from the desk top. "Too bad about you, too, in a way, Scott."

It looked to me as if the talk was over. That was all right. It was fine, now. The rest of it could come out later—and I had a hunch that in just a minute Nick wouldn't care much what he said. Right now I wanted out of here and on my way to Coral.

Nick said, still glaring at me, "You should never have tapped me with this, pal." He wiggled the sap. It looked shrunken in his big fist. "Maybe you better turn your back. You won't want to watch this."

He walked around his desk and started toward me. Probably he meant to beat my skull in, or brains out, and then yell out the door for one or more of his boys, since something was wrong with his phone.

I let him get just around the desk and then I said, "Hold it there, Nick."

He looked at me, startled. There was a new sound in my voice, and it got through to him. "What?" he said.

"Just stand there, friend. I'm going to tell you the facts of life."

His face flushed. He didn't like my attitude a bit, or my tone, obviously. He started to take another step.

"*Hold* it, Nick," I told him. He stopped. I said, "Think back to what we've just said, friend. Do you think maybe you spilled enough to wrap you up in Quentin? I mean, if some cops and numerous other people were listening, could that maybe get you a one-way trip to Q?"

It really puzzled him. "What the hell—"

"Answer me, Nick. I'm serious. Pretty soon you'll know how serious."

He actually appeared to think back over what he might have said. Then he grinned. "Maybe if I'd said it all in one of the 'I' rooms at the Police Building in L.A., I'd have a twinge of worry. But I don't get you. Nobody's listening."

"That might mean something *if* you were in your office, Nick."

"In my office?" He looked around. "Where do you think we are. You out of your skull, Scott?"

"We're both in Hollywood, Nick. On a sound stage at Magna Studios." I grinned at him. "These walls are just thin plywood, paneled. You could push them over yourself. In fact, there's a big boom outside right now, with a hook on cables that will lift all four walls twenty feet in the air if I give a yell."

"What?" He thought I'd gone crazy. "Boom?"

"You know, a winch pulling a cable attached to these walls. This whole place is practically portable. It's just a set. I'll bet there's twenty or thirty people right outside, including a few police officers, listening to everything we say."

Suddenly Nick laughed. "I've got to admire you, Scott. Really I do. I've heard that you could talk yourself out of eight dungeons in a row, but not this time, pal. And not even you can expect me to believe anything as silly as that."

"Take a good look friend. Take a *good* look at this office of yours."

He turned those hard blue eyes on me. The muscles in his jaw were starting to work. He looked at the walls, the pictures on them, then he stepped to his desk. Something about it was wrong. When he looked back at me there was an expression I had never seen in those stainless-steel eyes before. It was fear. Just a trace, and just beginning, but it was there, in the eyes of Nick Colossus.

I said, "I told you how I got into your suite of rooms at the Desert Trails. What I didn't tell you was that after I sapped you, I carried you out back and to a helicopter there, and flew you to Hollywood. We're in Sound Stage Three at Magna right now. Nick, it's simple—you went to sleep at the Desert Trails and woke up at Magna."

It was beginning to get to him that maybe I wasn't kidding.

At least not about all of it. And he was starting to look like a man shot full of novocain.

I said, "This is just a duplicate of your office. Don't you suppose an expert movie-production crew could build something like this in twenty-four hours? I can understand your doubt, Nick. Even Feldspen himself thought I was a little crazy until I reminded him that he had destroyed Atlantis and recreated ancient Rome, among other things. So take your time, Nick. It'll get to you."

He stared at me for about a minute. After that he stepped behind his desk and jerked open its middle drawer. Then, frantically, he slammed the rest of the drawers open and shut.

When he looked up at me again his face was ashen. "But . . . but . . ." He was sputtering. Nick had never, so far as I knew, sputtered before. Calm always-in-command Nick wasn't in command any more. "But . . . it's impossible."

"Not impossible, killer. Not even difficult. In fact, the only difficult thing was thinking of it in the first place. Only the idea was tough, Nick—after that, it was just a matter of careful planning, and spending a lot of money. Fortunately the money was available—from the man you tried to tap for a million dollars. From the President of Magna—and here we are *at* Magna. Nice, huh, Nick? Almost poetic?"

He was shaking his head. "You couldn't have. . . . How . . . you're lying, you lousy—"

"Let me lay it out for you fast, Nick. The dimensions of the room, structure, all that part of it we got from the original architect, the man who designed Desert Trails for you—Andrew T. Jameson of Las Vegas. He was glad to cooperate with Harry Feldspen, boss of Magna Studios. As was Dee Mintino—she's the interior decorator who did the hotel for you, including your office, the couch and desk and chairs. Feldspen simply got duplicates of the items and 'aged' them a bit. The pictures on the wall? And the gold-coin ashtray and desk calendar? I took them from your office after I sapped you. I brought them along when I brought you. *Get it through your head, we're in Hollywood.* You're on a Magna sound stage right now."

He still didn't, or wouldn't, believe me. Somehow, some way, I was trying to trick him. I leaned forward, "Nick, old pal," I said softly, "when this really hits you, it's going to very nearly kill you. You've just confessed to half the crimes in your history, including murder and murder again—complete with details only the killer himself could have known

about—to members of the Los Angeles and Hollywood police departments. I don't know how many are outside in the
sound stage there, right outside that door now, but I know
there'll be more than one or two."

He was still shaking his head. He was finally starting to
believe it all. So I broke off the last of it in him then, at what
really did seem the psychological moment. "And one more
thing, friend. I so admired the beautiful way you framed me
for *your* murder of Lou Rio, that perfect frame which got
—not the police so much—but all of Rio's men hot after me,
that I made sure at least a couple of the late Lou Rio's boys
would be present outside tonight." I paused and grinned at
him while he actually got a little paler under that bulletproof skin, then I went on, "I wanted *them* to hear you tell
me just why and how you killed Lou."

It was quiet then. Nick knew I'd told him the truth. The
real proof was just coming up, but now he believed me without it. He looked like a man being hit on the head with a
giant invisible hammer, like a man whose pants had fallen
down on the boulevard, like a man whose brain had just rolled
out of his ear.

I raised my voice and yelled, "Lift it up, Harry."

I had been telling Nick the truth about the winch ready to
lift the "office" walls up into the air above us, but there wasn't
any sudden whisking away of the walls and miraculous
transformation of this room into no more cluttered floor
space. There wasn't even anything especially dramatic about
it. The walls slowly started rising; I could hear the powered
winch turn, and slowly the walls were raised up into the air
a foot, then two.

The really dramatic thing wasn't the movement, but a complete *absence* of movement—Nick's absence of movement.
He stood frozen, rigid, staring, looking as if he were going
to go right out through his eyesockets. He didn't move as the
walls went up high above us and lights flooded the entire
interior of the sound stage around us now.

I got a pretty good shock myself. I had expected to see
perhaps twenty people out in the room. There must have
been two hundred or more. I didn't have any idea where
they'd all come from. There were many more uniforms than
I'd expected to see, too. Some of the uniformed men were
only a few feet from us, on the other side of where the walls
had been. But they didn't move forward just yet. Obviously
Nick was in no shape to resist them.

My gun still dangled from his fingers. I stepped to his side and took it from him, put it into my holster. He didn't resist. Nick looked pretty bad. His jowls actually sagged, as if some of the vital force had already gone out of him. And probably it had, because finally, maybe for the first time in his life, he knew he was licked, really licked. This one was the big entry in the books; this one was the big X after his name, the red ink, the line drawn through Nick Colossus.

He moved then, reaching out as if grasping for something on which to steady himself, but nothing was there. His hand pawed aimlessly, almost comically, at the air—but there wasn't really anything comic about it. Not even Nick, blackmailer, thief, murderer, not even Nick was comic while he died a little.

He seemed to shrink, to shrivel, to become less bulky, less of a man. But there was still a little of the old Nick Colossus left, the tough, grinning, gravel-voiced Nick. Just a little. He turned and looked at me and put on half a grin and said to me, "You sure put the blocks to me, pal." He paused, swallowing, and said, "I—got to hand it to you."

Then policemen were all around us. I saw Rawlins from Homicide downtown. He said to Nick, "You shot Lou Rio yourself, huh?"

Nick nodded. There wasn't much point in holding back anything now, and obviously he didn't mean to. "Yeah." He straightened himself slightly and squared his shoulders. "Yeah, but he was no loss. No talent anyway, not Rio. A bum with lots of know-who, that's all. Sure, I burned him. Next question."

He was trying to carry it off with a flair, do it big and he almost made it. He did fairly well, considering the fact that he must have been thinking of the gas chamber up at San Quentin.

Well, it was over. This part of it, anyway. I found Rawlins, and gave him the four-page confession Valentine had written; I'd left it in the helicopter during the night's flying about. Rawlins told me that the whole session just ended had been recorded, besides which a police reporter had written down the salient bits of Nick's unwitting confession in Nick's own words, and Nick had already signed it. Nick had, as the phrase goes, had it.

Several reporters and newscasters and some photographers were present, a number of whom I knew, and all of them

were trying to talk to me at once—it was just beginning to
dawn upon me what a big thing this really was, with Nick
Colossus involved, and Harry Feldspen, and Magna studios,
and blackmail of budding starlets and budded stars, and this
windup here at Magna—and it seemed that half of the news-
men and newsgals were congratulating me and the other half
were trying to get me to say something for the record.

But I had to tell them all that I would talk to them later,
then Rawlins and I got Nick to a phone. A real, usable phone
this time, and I had him use it—to call the Desert Trails.

I said to him, "Ask for Flint, Nick. Tell him and Shortcake
that I'll be there in an hour or so—for Coral."

He nodded, dumbly.

I went on, "Tell Flint to pass the word around. She'd better be all right, unharmed in any way—and all your boys
are to stay out of my way and my hair. Will they do it?"

He filled his enormous chest with air. "They'll do whatever
I tell them to do." Nick was getting over much of his shock;
but he wouldn't beat this rap and he knew it. "I'll tell them,"
he said, and managed another grin. "What have I got to lose?"

He spoke to Flint. Apparently Flint argued—naturally
enough, considering the fact that I had just been at Desert
Trails causing great pandemonium, and that Nick was or-
dering him to let me walk around living—but Nick said,
"Shut up. Do what I tell you, Flint. And knock off the questions." He listened, said "Okay," and slammed the phone
down into the cradle.

He looked at me. "Flint said you shot hell out of the
place already. And he wanted to know where I was. I'm
damned if I was going to tell him. But he'll go along with
everything the way you want it."

"She's there then? She's all right."

"Yeah."

"They haven't hurt her?"

"No, they haven't hurt her."

I left him with half a dozen officers.

There was a small hitch—from Lieutenant Rawlins. At first
he felt that I shouldn't leave, that I couldn't just walk out in
the middle of the act so to speak. There were a lot of people down at the Police Building who wanted to talk to me.
Just routine, now, but it had to be done.

I said, "And it can be done *later,* friend. Say tomorrow at
noon in the Police Building cafeteria. I'll bring the pink
tights."

"Pink . . ." He looked absolutely stricken, remembering. ". . . tights."

"Yeah. For your coochie dance. Isn't that what you said, Rawlins? Coochie?"

And then I was on my way—immediately after I promised Rawlins that between here and the Desert Trails I would forget any promise he might *ever* have made to me.

Harry Feldspen stood by the helicopter as I prepared to get into it for the third time tonight. I had thanked him profusely, and he had returned my thanks for saving him a million dollars, among other things, and said there would be a grossly fat check for me in the mail tomorrow.

I said to him, "Harry, tell me. Where did all those people come from?"

"Everybody who worked on the 'Colossus' set wanted to see the results of their work." He hesitated, then smiled. "In fact, I insisted. You see, Shell, if word had gotten out about what we were doing, and had reached Mr. Colossus . . ."

That would have blown up the party before it started. I hadn't even thought of it. I thanked Harry again and he said, "Besides those people, after the first officers arrived several more officers came. Just to witness the proceedings, I believe. Some of them were off duty, I know. And you asked me to get two or three of Mr. Rio's men here, but at least a dozen showed up." He smiled again, and then got off the closest thing to a gag I'd ever heard him say. "If I had just known how popular this show was going to be, I could have sold tickets."

And on that line, I left him. Malcolm Waters looked at me with a kind of weary tolerance, and lifted the helicopter into the air. This time I enjoyed the smooth soaring toward the sky, the dwindling of the buildings and streets and lot, the emergence of the brilliance and sparkling beauty of the city below us as we got farther and farther from it.

That is, I enjoyed it until I remembered one question I hadn't asked Nick. About that towel found in the Oasis, and the stain on it. The bloodstain.

Nobody had yet explained the blood.

Chapter Twenty

THIS TIME we landed right in front of the hotel, near the end of the bar and smack before the Desert Trails entrance. There were quite a number of people near the bar and pool, and they ogled us strenuously as we landed. But I didn't see a single one of the red and white uniforms, nor any faces recognizable as employees of Nick's.

I hadn't thought about it before, but once I'd managed to get away with their boss, the remaining hoodlums would quite naturally have begun feeling somewhat ill at ease. If that could happen to the boss, no telling what might happen to the underlings. Maybe this was a new kind of raid; maybe a jet-propelled jail would drop out of the sky and surround them all. The law was already interested in most of them, anyway; and with what Nick could spill, if ever he began spilling, their continued freedom must have seemed increasingly unlikely.

At any rate, none of the boys was in sight. Just numerous rather subdued guests, most of them clutching highballs and staring glassily at me as I trotted to the entrance.

I ran into the lobby—and there she was.

She looked tired, mussed a little, but still warm and electric and wonderful. She was standing, looking toward the front doors, and when I burst through them she broke into a run toward me, arms going out and reaching for me while she was yards away.

I didn't let her run that whole distance by herself; I met her halfway. I would always meet this one halfway. She said, "Oh, Shell, I thought I was . . . gone. I thought—I didn't think you'd find me, or . . ."

"Hey, hold it. Relax. Are you all right, honey?"

"Yes. Yes. Scared—oh, I was scared. But they didn't hurt me."

"There was blood on a towel in the motel room—"

"Oh, that. I fought them." She smiled slightly. "They scared me, and I fought them. I gave the one called Flint a bloody nose. It really bled a lot."

I laughed, feeling good, feeling almost as if I could float up into the air at least a little way even without a helicopter. I owed Flint a bust in the snoot myself, but it could wait; I'd had quite enough violence and nerve-unraveling and snoot-busting for one evening—and, anyway, Coral had apparently taken care of that item well enough for now, all by herself.

Then I noticed that the lobby was empty. Not another soul was in sight "Where is everybody?" I asked Coral.

"Most of the men, including that horrible one called Flint, left right after he got a phone call here. An hour or more ago. There are still a few of them around somewhere, I think, but a lot of them left in a big hurry."

After my previous visit here, Flint would have known Nick wasn't calling of his own free will. So the ones left, I thought, were probably the few with no records or worries. Well, the others—the ones we wanted, including Flint and Shortcake—would be rounded up soon enough.

I said to Coral, "You're *sure* you're all right?"

"Absolutely." She looked up at me, and I knew she wasn't intentionally turning on the heat, but those hot brown eyes lit my fuse anyway. This gal didn't have to turn it on; she just couldn't turn it off.

I said to her, "Come on, we can finish this conversation in the helicopter."

"Is that what all the noise was out front?"

"Yeah." I grinned at her. "It's my version of a white charger. Come. Join me in a mad race over the desert sands to my secret tent. I have dates and camel milk and Zaffir wine."

She smiled. Hotly. She couldn't help it. She always smiled hotly. "All right. What's Zaffir wine?"

"Why, it's bee-stung honey fermented with lotus blossoms. It puts moonbeams on a woman's lips, and night winds in her eyes. Whatever that means. Sounds good, what?"

"I'll have a pint of it."

"A pint? This is madness."

"Good. I feel like some madness." She laughed, then put her hand up slowly and touched my cheek. "Shell, I wouldn't have believed it."

"Believed what?"

"Not more than ten minutes ago I was—Oh, everything was awful. But now, well, it's as if it didn't really happen at all.

Those terrible men bursting into the room, and grabbing me, and bringing me here—but it didn't really happen, did it?"

"Of course not. Well, here we are at Happy Ranch, kiddies. It's Game Time. Come on." I grabbed her hand and pulled her outside. Some of the people stared at us, others were still at the bar. A dignified-looking fellow in a dark suit was mixing drinks. Not a hood was yet in sight.

I pulled Coral after me to the helicopter, helped her in and then climbed in myself. When we got settled, I was in the seat and she was on my lap, and the helicopter seemed much nicer than it had ever seemed before. I saluted Malcolm, who was eyeballing Coral as if he were seeing his first woman, and then I introduced them—briefly—and said to Malcolm, "Shall we go?"

"Go?" He was dazed. "Go . . . where?"

"Well, you might try up."

He blinked, sighed, and we went up.

Desert Trails dwindled and soon was just a bright dot in the blackness below us. It seemed almost like a symbolic dot, though, because I was sure there was soon going to be a lot more brightness. Nick's men were scattered, the hoodlum monster was headless. Lou's men knew now that I hadn't chilled their boss, and with that knowledge—and the fact that I'd turned up the real killer—they would cease thirsting for my blood. Feldspen was happy, his big problems solved. I was rich, until tax time. The police had in a cell the man they'd wanted most, and the other big local mobster was no longer among the living.

And on my lap was Coral James.

With her sweet, warm mouth close to my shot-up ear—the one I occasionally refer to as my "Shell-like" ear, Coral said, "Where *are* we going. Besides up."

"Why, to my tent. And the Zaffir—"

"Be serious for a minute. Really, Shell, where are we going? And what are we going to do?"

I looked around. The rotors spun above us, and now they had a pleasant sound; it seemed almost a happy sound. We raced through the night, through blackness, but all the hell and pain and trouble was for sure behind us. There were still several things to do, threads to wind up—I had to talk some more to Suez, with Palomino and some Magna bit players, and to the police and a few other people—but the big things, the urgent things were done, and the view really did look very good ahead now.

I looked back at Coral, at the wonderful face so close to mine, the brown eyes and blinding hair and sweet lips, and I tightened my arms around her waist, just a little.

"I honestly don't know yet, Coral, not for sure." I grinned at her. "But . . . I'll think of something."

THE END
of an Original Gold Medal Novel by
Richard S. Prather